John Byrom

Miscellaneous Poems by John Byrom

John Byrom

Miscellaneous Poems by John Byrom

ISBN/EAN: 9783744707848

Printed in Europe, USA, Canada, Australia, Japan

Cover: Foto ©Andreas Hilbeck / pixelio.de

More available books at **www.hansebooks.com**

MISCELLANEOUS POEMS,

BY

JOHN BYROM, M. A. F. R. S.

SOMETIME

Fellow of TRINITY COLLEGE, CAMBRIDGE,

And Inventor of

The Univerſal ENGLISH SHORT-HAND.

In TWO VOLUMES.

MANCHESTER:

Printed by J. HARROP.

M DCC LXXIII.

CONTENTS

Of the SECOND VOLUME.

A Di-

(iii)

The

Familiar

AN EPIS-

EPISTLE

TO

A Gentleman of the TEMPLE.

Occasioned by

TWO TREATISES,

WHEREIN

The FALL of MAN

Is differently Reprefented; viz.

I. Mr. LAW's SPIRIT of PRAYER.

II. The Bifhop of LONDON's APPENDIX.

SHEWING

That, according to the plaineft Senfe of SCRIPTURE,

THE

Nature of the FALL is greatly miftaken in the latter.

AN
EPISTLE
TO A
Gentleman of the TEMPLE.

SIR, upon casting an attentive Look
　　Over your Friend the learned SHERLOCK's
　　　　Book,
　　One Thing occurs about the FALL of MAN,
That does not suit with the *Mosaic* Plan;
Nor give us fairly, in its full Extent,
The Scripture Doctrine of that dire Event.

When tempted ADAM, yielding to Deceit,
Presum'd of the forbidden Tree to eat,

B 2

The

The Bishop tells us, *That he did not die:*
Pray will you ask him, Sir, the Reason why?
Why he would contradict the sacred Text,
Where Death to Sin so *surely* is annext?
*The Day thou eatest——*are the Words, you know;
And yet, by his Account, it was not so:
Death did not follow, tho' it surely wou'd:
How will he make this hardy Comment good?

Sentence, says he, *was respited——*But, pray,
Where does the Scripture such a Saying say?
What Word that means to *respite* or revoke
Appears in all that GOD or *Moses* spoke?

It will be said, perhaps, that it appears,
That *Adam* liv'd above Nine hundred Years
After his Fall——True——But what *Life* was *that?*
The very *Death*, Sir, which his *Fall* begat.
The Life, that *Adam* was created in,
Was lost the *Day*, the *Instant*, of his Sin.
Just as the rebel Angels, when they fell,
Were *dead* to Heav'n, altho' *alive* to Hell:
So Man, no longer breathing heav'nly Breath,
Fell to this Life, and dy'd the *Scripture Death.*

While in the State of Innocence he stood,
He was all living, beautiful, and good:
But when he fed on the forbidden Fruit,
Whereof Corruption was the latent Root,

He

He *dy'd* to Paradife, and, by a Birth
That fhould not have been rais'd, he *liv'd* to Earth;
Fell into beftial **Flefh, and** Blood, and Bones,
Amongft the **Thorns and** Briars, **Rocks** and Stones.
That which **had** cloath'd him, when a Child of Light,
With all its Luftre, was extinguifh'd quite;
Naked, afham'd, confounded, and amaz'd,
With *other* Eyes, on *other* Scenes he gaz'd.
All Senfibility of heav'nly Blifs
Departing from him——what a *Death* was This!

    His Soul, indeed, as an immortal Fire,
Could **never die, could never not defire**:
But, Sir, he had what glorious Angels claim,
An *heav'nly* Spirit, and an *heav'nly* Frame;
Form'd **in the Likenefs of the facred Three,**
He ftood immortal, powerful, and free;
Image of *Father, Son,* and *Holy Ghoft,*
The deftin'd Sire of a new heav'nly Hoft;
Partner **of their** communicated Breath,
A *living* Soul, unfubjected to Death.
Since **then** he fell from this fublime Eftate,
Could lefs than Death have been his real Fate?
No; as in Life he chofe not to abide,
It muft be faid, that *Adam furely dy'd.*

    Say, that he dy'd not, as it was foretold,
But when Nine hundred Years and Thirty old,
And then, **if** Death be Sentence for a *Fall,*
How proves the Bifhop that **he dy'd** *at all?*

For

For if the Death he **talks of be** this laſt,
How does *that* **anſwer to the** *Sentence* paſt?
Was his Departure from *this World* the Time
That our Firſt Father ſuffer'd for his Crime?
One rather ſhould believe, or hope at **leaſt,**
That (ſo be it!) his Sufferings then ceas'd;
And that the Life, which had been loſt at firſt,
Was then regain'd, and he no longer curſt.

If on the Biſhop's 'Scutcheon, when he dies,
(Long be the Time deferr'd) **the** mourning Eyes
Should read MORS VITÆ JANUA, in Paint,
What muſt they **think** him, Sinner, *then*, or Saint?
Muſt not theſe Words direct them to ſuppoſe
An End of all **a Chriſtian** Biſhop's Woes?
Who, like to *Adam*, Father of Mankind,
Had paſs'd his Time of Penitence **injoin'd;**
Who, like to CHRIST, the Second *Adam* too,
Had always had *Redemption* in his View;
Had taught himſelf and others to **revive**
From *dead in Adam* **to** *in Chriſt alive;*
Had been **as** true a Shepherd to his Flock,
As the poor Hind that really wears a Frock;
So trod this earthly Paſſage, that, in Sum,
Death **was to** him *the Gate of Life* become.

'Gate of *what* **Life?** Undoubtedly the ſame
That *Adam* **fell** from, when he firſt became
A Creature **of** this World; when firſt he fell,
Thanks to Divine Foregoodneſs! not to **Hell,**

But

But to *this Earth*——this **State** of Time and Place,
Where, dead by ***Nature*,** **Man** revives by *Grace*;
Where, tho' his *outward* **Syſtem** muſt decay,
His *inward* ripens to eternal Day;
Puts off th' *old Adam*, and puts on the *New*;
 And having found the *Firſt* ſad Sentence true,
Now finds the Truth of what the *Second* ſaid,
The Woman's Seed ſhall bruiſe the Serpent's Head.

 Again —— to urge **the Inſtance** that I gave,
Attend we this good **Biſhop to his Grave:**
The Prieſt comes **forth to meet the ſable Hearſe,**
And then repeats the well-appointed **Verſe;**
——Verſe, one would think, **that might decide** the
        Strife:——
I AM THE RESURRECTION AND THE LIFE——

 What Life is that which JESUS is, and gives,
In and by which the true Believer lives?
That of *this World?* Then were it moſt abſurd
To a dead **Biſhop to** apply the Word.
'Tis that which **human** Nature had before;
Which, being *Chriſt's*, Chriſt *only* can reſtore.
What *Meaning* is there, touching the Deceas'd,
Now from the *Burden of **the** Fleſh* releas'd,
But that his Soul is **going to be clad**
With *heav'nly* **Fleſh** and Blood; **which** *Adam* had,
Before he enter'd into *that* which *Paul*
Beſy of Death **might very juſtly** call?

A

A Flesh and Blood, that, as he hints elsewhere,
Not born from Heav'n, can never enter there:
Mass of this World, whose Kingdom *Christ* disclaim'd,
The Life whereof is but a Life so nam'd;
A Life of *Animal* and *Insect* Breath,
That, in a *Man*, is rightly stil'd a *Death*.

 Thus, Sir, throughout the *Burial Office* run,
You'll find that it proceeds as it begun.
Read any Office-----*Baptism* if you will-----
From first to last, you'll find the Reason still,
Why *any*, or why *all of them* are read;
Reason of all that's either sung, or said,
Is by this one great solemn Truth explain'd,
Of Life *in* Adam *lost, in* CHRIST *regain'd*:
Lost at the *Fall*·····not at the End of Years
That *Adam* labour'd in this Vale of Tears,
When Death thro' Christ was *happy*, 'tis presum'd,
And vanquish'd *that* to which he first was doom'd.

 Doom'd-----not by any *Act of Wrath* in God;
(A Point wherein the Bishop seems to nod)
No Death of *pure*, of *tainted* Life no Pain,
Did his severe inflicting Will ordain:
He is all Glory, Goodness, Light, and Love,
LIFE that from *Him* no Creature can remove;
But from *itself* it may, as *Adam* did,
If it will choose what Light and Love forbid:
Truly forewarn'd of what would *truly* be,
His Life was poison'd by the *mortal* Tree:

He

He *eat*----he *fell*----**he dy'd**----'Tis all the fame;
One Lofs of Life under a triple Name.

    No Teft was made by *pofitive Command*,
Merely to try if he would fall or ftand,
Like *that*, the ferpentine Satanic Snare,
Of which the Man was bidden to beware.
Eat not thereof, **or thou wilt** *furely die*,
Was fpoken to *prevent*, and not to *try*;
To guard the Man againft his fubtle Foe,
Who fought to teach him *what 'twas* **Death to know.**

    Death to his priftin, *Spirit-life* divine,
And *Separation* **from its facred** *Shrine;*
The pure, unmix'd, incorruptible Throne,
Wherein God's Image firft embody'd **fhone:**
Tho' form'd to rule the new created **Scene,**
Built from the *Chaos* of a former Reign;
To bring the Wonders of this World to View,
And ancient Glories to **an Orb** renew;
He alfo had, as being to command,
See, **and be feen, in** this new-formed **Land,**
This **intermediate** temporary Life,
Where, only, Good and Evil are at Strife,
Outward **corporeal Form,** whereby he faw,
And **heard,** and fpoke, and gave to all Things Law;
They none to him——His far fuperior Mind
Was, as he pleas'd, united or disjoin'd:
So far united, that all *Good* was gain'd;
So far disjoin'd, that *Evil* was reftrain'd:

C

It

It could not reach him——for, before his Fall,
Nothing could *hurt* this human Lord of All,
No more than **Satan,** or the Serpent, cou'd,
If in his Firſt Creation he **had ſtood.**

Such **was his bleſt** Eſtate——wherein is **found**
Of *Adam*'s happy Ignorance the Ground.
His *outward* Body, and each *outward* Thing,
From whence alone both Good and Ill could ſpring,
Could not affect, while he was free from Sin,
The **Life** of the celeſtial Man *within.*
Glorious Condition! which, **howe'er,** imply'd,
That Man, at firſt plac'd in it, muſt be try'd:
Not from God's Will, or arbitrary Voice;
His Trial follow'd from his *Pow'r of Choice :*
God will'd him That, *Himſelf* was to *re-will,*
And the divine Intentions to fulfil;
To uſe his outward Body as a Means,
Whereby to raiſe in Time and Place the Scenes
That ſhould reſtore the *once* angelic Orb,
And all its Evil introduc'd abſorb.

Evil, that, prior to the Fall of Man,
From him, whoſe *Name in Heav'n* is loſt, began.
Moſes has plainly *hinted* at the Fiend;
Whoſe Malice in **a** borrow'd Shape was ſcreen'd:
Who, under Reaſon's plauſible Diſguiſe,
Taught our Firſt Parents to be worldly wiſe:
Succeeding Lights have riſen up to ſhow
Of God and Man, more *openly,* the Foe.

Hc,

He, *once* a thron'd *Archangel*, had the Sway
Far as this Orb **of our** created Day;
Where, then, no Sun was wanted to give **Light,**
No Moon to chear yet undiscover'd Night;
Immensely luminous his total Sphere,
All Glory, Beauty, Brightnefs, ev'ry-where:
Ocean of Blifs, a limpid *cryftal Sea*,
Whofe Height and Depth its Angels might furvey;
Call forth its Wonders, and enjoy the Trance
Of Joys perpetual thro' its whole Expanfe:
Ravifhing Forms arifing without End
Would, in Obedience to their **Wills, afcend;**
Change, and unfold frefh Glories to their View,
And tune the *Hallelujah* Song anew.

If, when we caft a thoughtful, thankful **Eye**
Towards the Beauties **of** an Ev'ning Sky,
Calm we admire, thro' the ethereal Field,
The various Scenes that even *Glouds* can **yield;**
What huge Delight muft *Nature's Fund* afford,
Where all the rich *Realities* are ftor'd,
Which **God** produces from its vaft **Abyfs,**
To **his own** Glory, and his Creatures Blifs?

His Glory, firft, *all Nature* muft difplay,
Elfe **how to** Blifs could Creatures know the Way?
Order, thro' all Eternity, requires,
That to his Will they fubject their Defires;
That, with all Meeknefs, the created Mind
Be to the Fountain of its Life refign'd;

Think,

Think, fpeak, and act, in all things for his Sake:
This is the *true Perfection* of its Make.

    Both Men and Angels muſt have *Wills* their *own*,
Or God, and Nature, **were to them unknown**:
'Tis their *Capacity* of **Life and** Joy,
Which **none but** *they* can ruin or deſtroy.
God, in Himſelf, was, is, and will be, good,
And all around pour forth th' enriching Flood.
From Him——('tis ***Nature's*** and *Religion*'s Creed)
Nothing *but* Good **can poſſibly proceed.**
That *Creature* only, whoſe recipient **Will**
Shuts itſelf up within *itſelf*, is ill:
Good cannot dwell in ſuch an harden'd Clay,
But ſtagnates, **and** evaporates away.

    Thus when **the Regent** of th' angelic Hoſt,
That *fell*, **began** within himſelf **to boaſt**;
Began, endow'd with his *Creator*'s **Pow'rs**,
That nothing could reſiſt, **to** call them *Ours*;
To ſpread thro' his wide Ranks the *impious Term*,
And they their Leader's Doctrine **to** confirm;
Then *Self*, then *Evil*, **then** apoſtate *War*
Rag'd thro' *their Hierarchy* wide **and far**;
Kindled to burn, **what** they eſteem'd a Rod,
The Meekneſs **and** Subjection to a God.
Reſolv'd **to pay no** hymning Homage more,
Nor, in an Orbit of *their own*, adore:
All Right **of** Heav'n's eternal King abjur'd,
They thought *One Region* to themſelves ſecur'd;

                                            One

One **out** of *Three*, where Majesty **divine**
Shone in its glorious *Outbirth unitrine*;
Shone, **and will shine eternally, altho'**
Angels or Men the shining Blifs forego.

Strait, with this proud Imagination fir'd,
To *Self-Dominion* strongly they afpir'd;
Bent all **their** Wills, *irrevocably* bent,
To bring about their devilifh Intent.
How ought *we Mortals* to beware of *Pride*,
That fuch great Angels could **fo** far mifguide!
No fooner was this horrible Attempt,
From all Obedience to remain **exempt,**
Put forth to Act, but inftantly **thereon**
Heav'n, in the Swiftnefs **of a** Thought, **was gone:**
From *Love's beatifying* **Pow'r** eftrang'd,
They found their Life, their Blifs, their Glory, chang'd.
That State, wherein they were *refolv'd* **to** dwell,
Sprung from *their Lufting,* **and** became **their** Hell.

Thinking to rife above **the God of All**
The Wretches fell, with **an eternal Fall;**
In Depths of Slavery, without a Shelf:
There is no Stop in felf-tormenting *Self.*
Juft as a Wheel, that's running down a Hill
Which has no Bottom, muft keep running ftill:
So down their own Proclivity to wrong,
Urg'd by impetuous Pride, they whirl along
Their own dark, **fiery, working** Spirits tend
Farther from God, **and farther** to defcend.

HE made no *Hell* to place his Angels in;
They ftirr'd the Fire that burnt them, by their Sin:
The Bounds of Nature, and of Order, broke,
And all the Wrath that follow'd them awoke:
Their own diforder'd Raging was their Pain;
Their own unbending harden'd *Strength* their Chain:
Renouncing **God** with their eternal Might,
They funk **their** Legions into endlefs Night.

Mean while **the** glorious Kingdom, where they dwelt,
Th' Effect of their rebellious Workings felt:
Its clear *Materiality*, and pure,
Could not the Force of raging Fiends endure:
Its *Elements*, all heav'nly in their Kind,
In *one* harmonious Syftem when combin'd,
Were now difclos'd, divided, and opake:
Their *glaffy Sea* became a *ftormy Lake:*
The Height and Depth of their angelic World
Was nought but Ruins upon Ruins hurl'd:
Chaos arofe, and, with its gloomy Sweep
Of *dark'ning* Horrors, overfpread the Deep:
All was Confufion, Order all defac'd,
Tohu, and *Bohu*, the *deformed Wafte*.

Till **the** Almighty's gracious *Fiat* came,
And ftop'd the Spreading of the hellifh Flame;
Put **to each** fighting Principle the Bar;
And calm'd, by juft Degrees, th' inteftine War.
· *Light*, at his Word, th' abating Tempeft chear'd;
Earth, Sea, and Land, Sun, Moon, and Stars, appear'd;

Creatures

Creatures of ev'ry Kind, and Food **for** each;
And various Beauties clos'd the various Breach:
Nature's **Six** *Properties* had each their Day,
Loſt Heav'n, as far as might be, to diſplay;
And in the *Sev'nth,* or *Body* of them all,
To reſt from, what they yet muſt prove, **a** *Fall.*

For had not this diſorder'd Chaos been;
Had not theſe Angels caus'd it by their Sin;
Nor had compacted Earth, nor Rock, nor Stone,
Nor *groſs Materiality,* been known:
All that in Fire, **or** Water, Earth, **or Air,**
May now their *noxious* Qualities declare,
Is as unknown in Heav'n **as** Sin or **Crime,**
And **only laſts for** purifying Time:
Till **the great End,** for which we all came here,
Till God's *reſtoring Goodneſs,* ſhall appear:
Then, as the rebel Creatures falſe Deſire
Awak'd in Nature the *chaotic Fire;*
So when *redeeming Love* has found a **Race**
Of Creatures worthy of the heav'nly Place,
Then ſhall *another* Fire enkindled riſe,
And purge from Ill theſe *temporary* Skies;
Purge **from the** World its Deadneſs, and its Droſs,
And of *loſt* Heav'n recover *all the Loſs.*

Why look we then with ſuch **a** longing **Eye**
On what this World can *give us,* or *deny;*
Of Man and Angel fall'n, the ſad Remains?
It *has* its *Pleaſures*——but it *has* its *Pains.*

It

It has, what ſpeaks it, would we but attend,
Not our deſign'd Felicity ——an *End.*
Sons of Eternity, tho' born on Earth,
There is within us a *celeſtial Birth*;
A Life that waits the *Efforts of our Mind,*
To raiſe itſelf within this *outward Rind.*
This *Huſk of ours,* this ſtately *ſtalking Clod,*
Is not **the Body that we** have **from** *God :*
Of Good and Evil 'tis the *mortal Cruſt;*
Fruit of *Adamical* and *Eval* Luſt;
By which the Man, when heav'nly Life was ceas'd,
Became an helpleſs, naked, biped Beaſt :
Forc'd, on a *curſed Earth,* to ſweat and toil;
To *Brutes* a native, *Him* a foreign Soil :
And, after all **his** Years **employ'd to know**
The Satisfactions of **a Life ſo low,**
Nine hundred, **or Nine hundred** thouſand, paſt,
Another **Death** to come, and *Hell,* at laſt——
——But **for** that **new** myſterious *Birth of Life;*
That *promis'd* **Seed** to *Adam* and his *Wife;*
That *quick'ning* **Spirit** to a poor *dead Soul;*
Not *Part* of Scripture Doctrine, but *the Whole;*
Which Writers, *figuring* away, have left
A mere **dead Letter,** of all Senſe bereft;
But for that *only* Help of Man forlorn,
The *Incarnation* of the Virgin-born.

This *Serpent-Bruiſer,* Son **of God** and *Man,*
Who, from the firſt, his ſaving Work began,

Revers'd,

Revers'd, in full Maturity of Time,
In his own SACRED PERSON, *Adam*'s Crime;
Brought human Nature from its deadly Fall,
And made Salvation poffible for *All.*

Without acknowledging that *Adam dy'd,*
Scripture throughout is, in Effect, deny'd:
All the whole Procefs of *Redeeming Love,*
Of *Life,* of *Light,* and *Spirit from above,*
Lofes, by Learning's *piteous* Pretence
Of *Modes,* and *Metaphors,* its real Senfe:
All the glad Tidings, in the Gofpel found,
Are funk in empty and unmeaning Sound.

If, by the Firft Man's Sin, we underftand
Only fome Breach of abfolute Command
Half-punifh'd, half-remitted, by a Grace
Like that which takes in human Acts a Place;
The more we write, the more we ftill expofe
The Chriftian Doctrine to its reas'ning Foes:
But, once convinc'd, that *Adam,* by his Crime,
Fell from *eternal Life* to that of *Time;*
Stood on the Brink of *Death eternal* too,
Unlefs created unto Life *anew;*
Then ev'ry Reafon teaches us to fee
How all the Truths of facred Writ agree;
How *Life reflor'd* arifes from the *Grave;*
How Man *could* perifh, and how CHRIST *could* fave.

Man perifh'd by the deadly Food he took,
And needs muft *lofe* the Life that he *forfook,*

D

Not

Not unadvis'd—— the Moment he inclin'd
To this inferior Life his nobler Mind,
God kindly warn'd him to continue fed
With *Food* of *Paradife*, with Angels Bread;
To fhun the **Tree**, the **Knowledge**, whofe fad Leav'n
Would quench in him the **Light and Life** of Heav'n;
Strip him of that angelical Array,
Which **thro'** his *outward Body* fpread the Day;
Kept it from ev'ry Curfe **of** Sin and Shame,
From all thofe Evils that had yet no Name:
That prov'd alas! when **he would not** refrain,
The Lofs of *Adam's proper Life* too plain.
Who can fuppofe that God would e'er forbid
To eat what would not *hurt him,* **if** he *did?*
Fright his lov'd Creature by a falfe Alarm;
Or make what, *in itfelf,* was harmlefs, *Harm?*

O **how** much **better he from whom** I draw,
Tho' deep, yet clear the Syftem, Mafter LAW!
Mafter, I call him; not that I incline
To pin my Faith on any One **Divine;**
But, Man or Woman, whofoe'er it **be,**
That fpeaks true Doctrine, is a *Pope* **to** me.
Where Truth alone is *Intereft,* and *Aim,*
Who would regard a *Perfon,* or a *Name?*
Or, **in the Search of** it *impartial,* fcoff,
Or fcorn **the meaneft** Inftrument thereof?

Pardon me, **Sir,** for having dar'd **to** dwell
Upon a Truth already told fo well;

Since

Since diff'rent Ways of telling may excite,
In diff'rent Minds, Attention to what's right;
And **Men** (**I** measure by Myself) sometimes,
Averse to Reas'ning, may be taught by Rhimes;
If where One fails, they will not take Offence,
Nor quarrel with the *Words*, but seek **the** *Sense*.

Life, Death, and such-like Words, in Scripture found,
Have certainly an higher, deeper Ground,
Than **that** of **this** poor perishable Ball,
Whereon Men doat, **as if it** were their All;
As if they were like *Warburtonian Jews*,
Or, *Christians* nam'd, had still **no** *higher* Views;
As **if their** Years had never taught them Sense
Beyond——*It is all one a Hundred hence.*

'Twas of such Worldlings that our Saviour said
To one of his Disciples, *Let the Dead*
Bury their *Dead: But do thou follow me.*
He makes no more Distinction, **Sir,** you see,
But that, with Ref'rence to a Life *so brute,*
The *speaking Carcases* interr'd **the** *mute.*

Life, to conclude, was lost in *Adam's Fall,*
Which **Christ,** our *Resurrection,* will recall:
And, as *Death* came into the World by *Sin,*
Where *One* begun, the *Other* must begin.
Why will the learned Sages use their Art,
From *Scripture Truth,* so widely, to depart?
But above all, a *Bishop,* grave, and wise,
Why **will he** shut, against *plain Text,* his Eyes?

D 2

Not

Not fee that Heav'ns Prediction never ly'd;
That *Adam* fell by eating, finn'd, and dy'd,
A *real* Death, as much as *Lofs of Sight*
Is Death to ev'ry Circumftance of *Light;*
Tho' a blind Man may feel his Way, and grope,
Or for *recover'd Eyes* be made to *hope;*
We might as well fet Glaffes on his Nofe,
And Sight, from common Helps of Sight, fuppofe,
As fay, when *Adam*'s heav'nly Life was kill'd,
That Sentence was not *inftantly* fulfill'd.

Perfuade your Mitred Friend, then, if you can,
To *re-confider*, Sir, the *Fall of Man;*
To fee, and own the *Depth* of it; becaufe,
'Till *that* is done, we may as well pick Straws,
As talk of *what*, and *who*, the Serpent was
That brought the Fall, *not underftood*, to pafs.

One Thing he *was*, Sir, be what elfe he will:
A *Critic*, that employ'd his fatal Skill
To cavil upon *Words*, and take away
The Senfe of *that* which was as *plain as Day.*
And thus the World, at prefent, by his Wiles,
Tho' not in *outward Shape*, he ftill beguiles;
Seeking to turn, by Comments low and lax,
The Word of God into a Nofe of Wax;
To take away the *Marrow*, and the *Pith*,
Of all that Scripture can prefent us with.
May Heav'n deliver from his winding Tours,
The *Bifhop*, and *us all!* I am, Sir,

       Yours.

ENTHUSIASM;

A

POETICAL ESSAY.

IN A

LETTER

TO A

FRIEND in TOWN.

Dear Friend,

I HAVE here sent you the Verses which you desired a Copy of. The Book * that gave Occasion to them has treated the Subject whereon they are made in such a brief, sensible, and lively manner, as might well excite one to an Attempt of this Nature. Just and improving Sentiments deserve to be placed in any Light that may either engage the Attention of a Reader, or assist his Memory; and Verse, as I have found by experience, does both: For which Reason, when I first met with an Account of *Enthusiasm* so quite satisfactory, I chose to give it the Dress wherein it now appears before you.

Enthusiasm is grown into a fashionable Term of Reproach, that usually comes uppermost, when any thing of a deep and serious Nature is mentioned. We apply it, through an indolent Custom, to sober and considerate Assertors of important Truths, as readily as to wild and extravagant Contenders about them. This indiscriminate Use of the Word has evidently a bad Effect: It pushes the general Indifferency to Matters of the highest Concern into downright Aversion. The best Writers upon the best Subjects are unattended to; and the Benefit accruing from their Love, and their Labours, is not perceived by us; because we are hurried on, by the idlest of

all

---

* Mr. Law's *Appeal to all that doubt, &c.* p. 305.

all Prejudices, to condemn them without a Reading, or to pronounce them to be unintelligible, upon such a slight one, as can hardly be called an Endeavour to understand them. We have heard it said, and have seen it printed, that they are Enthusiasts; and, to avoid the Imputation of that Character, we run into it at second Hand, and adopt the Rashness and Injustice of impetuous Originals: We take the stalest Exclamations for the freshest Proofs; and the affected Retailing of *Madness, Mysticism, Behmen-ism,* and the like decisive Outcries, contents us as if there were something of Sense, Wit, or Demonstration, in it.

When this low Kind of *Enthusiasm* is alert enough to gain its Point, the Writer of a good Book may possibly lose the Applause, which it is highly probable that he never sought for. But what does a Reader get the while, by his tame Resignation of the Right of judging for himself to such incompetent Authority? Men of superior Fluency in expressing their own Conceptions are not always sedate enough to examine, or judicious enough to discover, the Principles which might undeceive them. The first Obstruction to their Hypothesis may pass, with them, for an immediate Confutation of any Book whatsoever: They may shew their Learning, their Zeal, or their Contempt, and speak of an *Enthusiasm* different from their own, as quickly as they please; but where the Question is momentous, and the Celebration of their Fame quite foreign to it, what should induce any one, who is really desirous of Information, to remit the Freedom of Enquiry after it for their Dicacity?

How

How many pathetic Accounts of living Piety, how many excellent Treatifes compofed for the Advancement of it, are neglected, or unknown, becaufe we are fo eafily prepoffeffed by popular Hearfay, and wretched Compilers? How many has the Sournefs of Controverfy, the Bitternefs of Party, and the Rotation of Amufement, in a manner fuppreffed? The *Enthufiafm* which is hence enkindled reigns and rages unfufpected, while that of a jufter Kind, the genuine Effect of a true Life and Spirit, arifing from what is lovely, harmonious, and fubftantial, is in danger of being extinguifhed by it; and, whenever it is fo, the Variety of Delufion with which a different Spirit may then poffefs its Votaries, will centre, properly fpeaking, in *Endemoniafm*.

In fhort, there is a right *Enthufiafm*, as well as a wrong one; and a Man is free to admit which he pleafes: But one he muft have, as fure as he has a Head; as fure as he has a Heart that fondly purfues the Object of its Defire, whatever it be. If that be pointed right; if it reach after that Godlike State and Condition, to which all Mankind were originally created; if it long to be freed from the Diforders of its prefent State, to be reftored again to that enduring Reft, Light, and Liberty, which alone can accomplifh and beautify it; how can it be too conftant, or too vigorous?

If the Defire be otherwife inclined, how little does it fignify to the main Purpofe what Ingenuity, Parts, or Learning, what natural, or what acquired Talents, Men

may

may be poffefs'd of? So long as they have only Light enough to hate Light, they may, upon the firft Glimpfe of it, retire into their Earthlinefs, and pufh out their Works as thick as Mole-hills: But, in Reality, a fingle Page, proceeding from a right Spirit, whofe *Enthufiafm* they all defpife, is worth a Library of fuch a Produce.

In fuch a fpirit I take the *Appeal*, to which the following Lines are owing, to be written; and am perfuaded, that if any fober-minded Deift, who is prejudiced againft Chriftianity, becaufe he does not really know what it is; that if any Chriftian fo called, who has been led into Miftakes about it, becaufe he does not really know what it is not; in fine, that if any one, whofe Heart is fo far converted as to defire Converfion, fhould be difpofed to read it through, he would find his Account in it; he would be ftruck with, he would be edified by it.

There is, apparently, fomething fo folid, and fo animated, thro' the Whole of it; fuch an impartial Regard to Truth, where-ever it may be found; and fuch happy Illuftration of it, where it really has been found; that I had fome Thoughts of tranflating it for the Ufe of Foreigners, believing that fuch a Service would be acceptable to the more fearching and unbiafs'd Difpofitions amongft them, and alfo help to fix many awakening and comfortable Truths upon my own Mind; which is the Intereft that I would propofe to obtain by it. If I fhall find myfelf capable of executing this Defign with Juftice to the Original, you fhall hear further from me. In the

E

mean

mean time I have tranfcribed for you thefe Verfes upon the incidental Subject of *Enthufiafm*, as they were firft compofed for private Recollection; and, as I can rely upon your Judgment concerning them better than I can upon my own, they **are wholly** fubmitted to **your** Correction and Difpofal.   I am,

Yours, &c.

Manchefter, Sept. 3, 1751.

J. B.

ENTHU-

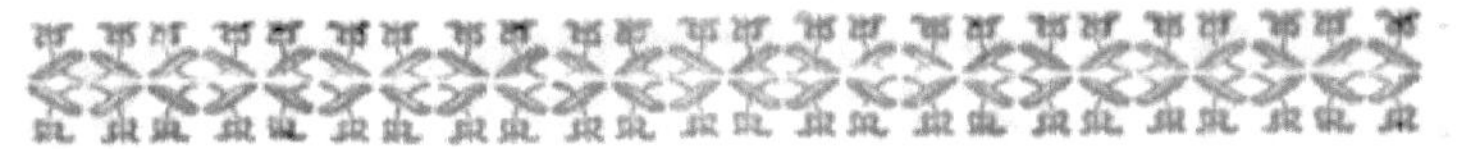

ENTHUSIASM.

A

POETICAL ESSAY.

F LY from **Enthufiafm——** *It is the Peft,*
    Bane, Poifon, Frenfy, Fury——and the reft.
This is the Cry that oft, when Truth appears,
Forbids Attention to our lift'ning Ears;
Checks our firft Entrance on the main Concern,
And, ftunn'd with Clamour, we forbear to learn;
Mechanically catch the common Cant,
And fly from what we almoft know we want;
A deeper Senfe of *fomething* that fhould fet
The Heart at Reft, that never has done yet;
Some *fimpler Secret*, that, yet unreveal'd,
Amidft contending Syftems lies conceal'd.

  A Book, perhaps, beyond the vulgar Page,
Removes at once the Lumber of an Age:
Truth is prefented; ftrikes upon our Eyes;
We feel Conviction, and we fear Surprize:
We gaze, admire, difpute, and then the Bawl——
Fly from Enthufiafm——That anfwers all.

E 2

Now

Now, if my Friend has Patience to enquire,
Let us a while from noify Scenes retire;
Let us examine Senfe, as well as Sound,
And fearch **the** Truth, **the** Nature, and the Ground.

'Tis *Will*, *Imagination*, and *Defire*
Of thinking Life, that conftitute **the Fire**,
The Force, by which the ftrong **Volitions drive,**
And form the Scenes to which we are alive.
What? tho', **unfprouted** into outward Shape,
The Points of Thought our groffer Sight efcape?
Nor bulky Forms in prominent Array
Their fecret cogitative Caufe betray?
Once fix the Will, and Nature muft begin
T' unfold its active Rudiments within;
Mind governs *Matter*, and it muft **obey:**
To all its **opening** Forms Defire **is Key:**
Nor Mind nor **Matter's** Properties are loft,
As that fhall mold, **this muft appear** emboft.
Imagination, trifling **as it feems,**
Big with Effects, its own Creation teems.
We think our Wifhes and Defires a Play,
And fport important Faculties **away:**
Edg'd are the Tools with which we trifle thus,
And carve out deep Realities for us.
Intention, roving into Nature's Field,
Dwells in that Syftem which it means to build,
Itfelf the Centre **of** its wifh'd-for Plan;
For where the Heart of Man is——there is Man.

Ev'ry

Ev'ry created, underſtanding Mind
Moves as its own Self-bias is inclin'd:
From God's free Spirit breathed forth to be,
It muſt of all Neceſſity be free;
Muſt have the Pow'r to kindle and inflame
The Subject-matter of its mental Aim:
Whither it bend the voluntary View
Realities, or *Fictions*, to purſue:
Whether it raiſe its Nature, or degrade,
To Truth ſubſtantial, or to phantom Shade,
Falſhood or Truth accordingly obtains;
That only which it wills to gain——it gains:
Good——if the Good be vigorouſly ſought,
And *ill*——if that be firſt reſolv'd in Thought.
All is one Good, that nothing can remove,
While held in Union, Harmony, and Love.
But when a ſelfiſh ſeparating Pride
Will break all Bounds, and Good from Good divide,
'Tis then extinguiſh'd, like a diſtant Spark,
And Pride ſelf-doom'd into its joyleſs Dark.
The miſcreant *Deſire* turns **Good** to Ill,
In its own Origin, the *evil Will*:
A Fact, that fills all Hiſtories of old,
That glares in Proof, while conſcious we behold
The Bliſs, beſpoken by our Maker's Voice,
Fixt, or perverted by a Man's own Choice.

Now when the Mind determines thus its Force,
The Man becomes Enthuſiaſt of courſe.
What is Enthuſiaſm? What can it be,
But Thought enkindled to an high Degree?

That

That may, whatever be its ruling Turn,
Right, or not right, with equal Ardour burn.
It muſt be therefore various in its Kind,
As Objects vary, **that** engage the Mind:
When to Religion we **confine the Word,**
What Uſe of Language can be more abſurd ?
'Tis juſt as true, that many **Words beſide,**
As Love, **or Zeal,** are only thus apply'd :
To ev'ry Kind **of** Life they all belong;
Men may be eager, tho' their Views be wrong:
And **hence the** Reaſon, **why** the greateſt Foes
To true religious Earneſtneſs are thoſe,
Who **fire their** Wits upon a diff'rent Theme,
Deep in ſome falſe *enthuſiaſtic* Scheme.

One Man politely, ſeiz'd with claſſic Rage,
Dotes on old *Rome,* **and** its *Auguſtan* Age ;
On thoſe great Souls who then, or then abouts,
Made in their State ſuch Riots **and ſuch Routs.**
He fancies all magnificent and **grand,**
Under this Miſtreſs of the World's Command :
Scarce **can his** Breaſt the ſad Reverſe abide,
The Dame deſpoil'd of all her glorious Pride :
Time, an old *Goth,* advancing **to conſume**
Immortal Gods, and once eternal *Rome* ;
When **the** plain Goſpel ſpread its artleſs Ray,
And **rude unſculptur'd** Fiſhermen had Sway ;
Who ſpar'd no Idol, tho' divinely carv'd,
Tho' **Art,** and Muſe, and Shrine-Engraver, ſtarv'd :

Who

Who fav'd *poor Wretches*, and deftroy'd, *alas!*
The vital Marble, and the breathing Brafs.
Where does **all** Senfe to him, and Reafon, fhine ?
Behold —— in *Tully's* Rhetoric divine !
Tully! Enough —— High o'er the *Alps* he's **gone**,
To tread the Ground that *Tully* trod upon ;
Haply **to** find his Statue, or his Buft,
Or Medal green'd with *Ciceronian* Ruft :
Perchance the *Roftrum*—— yea, the very Wood,
Whereon this elevated Genius ftood ;
When forth on *Cataline*, as erft he fpoke,
The Thunder of *Quoufque tandem* broke.

   Well may this *Grand Enthufiaft* **deride**
The Dulnefs of a *Pilgrim's* **humbler Pride,**
Who paces to behold that Part of Earth,
Which to the Saviour of the World gave Birth ;
To fee the Sepulchre from whence he rofe ;
Or view the Rocks that rented at his Woes ;
Whom Pagan Reliques have no **Force to charm,**
Yet ev'n a modern Crucifix can warm :
The facred Signal who intent **upon,**
Thinks on the Sacrifice that hung thereon.

   Another's *heated Brain* is painted o'er
With ancient *Hieroglyphic* Marks of yore :
He old *Egyptian Mummies* can explain,
And raife 'em **up** almoft to **Life again ;**
Can into deep antique Receffes pry,
And tell, of all, the *Wherefore* and the *Why* ;

How this *Philofopher*, and that, has thought,
Believ'd one Thing, and quite another taught;
Can Rules, **of** *Grecian* Sages long forgot,
Clear up, as if they liv'd upon the Spot.

What Bounds to *Noftrum? Mofes,* and the ***Jews,***
Obferv'd this learned *Legiflator*'s Views,
While *Ifrael*'s Leader purpofely conceal'd
Truths, which his whole Oeconomy reveal'd;
No **Heav'n** difclos'd, but *Canaan*'s fertile Stage,
And no *For·ever* —— but a good *old Age*;
Whilft **the** well untaught People, kept in Awe
By meanlefs Types, and unexplained Law,
Pray'd **to their** *local God* to grant a while
The *Future State*, **of** Corn, and Wine, and Oil;
Till, **by** a late Captivity fet free,
Their deftin'd Error they began **to** fee;
Dropt the *Mofaic* Scheme, **to** teach their Youth
Dramatic **J** o **b,** and *Babylonifh* Truth.

To foar aloft on Obelifkal Clouds;
To dig down deep into the Dark —— for Shrouds;
To vex old Matters, chronicled in *Greek,*
While thofe of **his own** Parifh are to feek;
What can come forth from fuch an *antic* Tafte,
But a *Clariffimus Enthufiaft?*
Fraught **with** Difcoveries fo quaint, **fo new,**
So deep, fo fmart, fo *Ipfe-dixit* true,
See Arts, and Empires, Ages, Books, and Men,
Rifing, and falling, as he points the **Pen:**

See

See Frauds and Forgeries, **if** ought furpafs,
Of nobler Stretch, the Limits of his Clafs,
Not found within that Summary of Laws,
Conjecture, tinfel'd with its own Applaufe.

Where Erudition fo *unbleft* prevails,
Saints, and their Lives, are *legendary Tales*;
Chriftians, a brainfick, vifionary Crew,
That read the *Bible* with **a** *Bible View,*
And **thro' the** *Letter* humbly hope to trace
The *living* **Word,** the *Spirit,* and the *Grace.*

It matters not, whatever be the State
That full-bent Will and ftrong Defires create;
Where-e'er they fall, where-e'er they love to dwell,
They kindle **there their** *Heaven,* or their *Hell;*
'The chofen Scene furrounds them as their own,
All elfe is dead, infipid, or unknown.
However poor and empty be the Sphere,
'Tis **All,** if Inclination **centre there:**
Its own *Enthufiafts* each Syftem **knows,**
Down to lac'd *Fops,* and Powder-fprinkled *Beaux.*
Great *Wits,* **affecting,** what they call, *to think,*
That deep immers'd in Speculation fink,
Are great *Enthufiafts,* **howe'er** refin'd,
Whofe Brain-bred Notions fo inflame the Mind,
That, **during** the Continuance **of** its Heat,
The *Summum Bonum* is——its **own** Conceit:
Critics, **with all** their Learning recondite,
Poets, **that** fev'rally be-mufed write;

F

The

The *Virtuosos*, whether great or small;
The *Connoisseurs*, that know the Worth of all;
Philosophers, that dictate Sentiments,
And *Politicians*, wiser than Events;
Such, and such-like, come under the *same Law*,
Altho' their Heat be from a Flame of *Straw*;
Altho' in one Absurdity they chime,
To make religious Entheasm a Crime.

Endless to say how many of their Trade
Ambition, Pride, and Self-conceit have made.
If one, the chief of such a nùm'rous Name,
Let the great Scholar justify his Claim.
Self-love, in short, where-ever it is found,
Tends to its own *enthusiastic* Ground;
With the same Force that Goodness mounts above,
Sinks, by its own enormous Weight, Self-love——
By this the wav'ring *Libertine* is prest,
And the rank *Atheist* totally possest:
Atheists are dark *Enthusiasts* indeed,
Whose Fire enkindles like the smoking Weed:
Lightless, and dull, the clouded Fancy burns,
Wild Hopes, and Fears, still flashing out by Turns.
Averse to Heav'n, amid the horrid Gleam
They quest *Annihilation*'s monst'rous Theme,
On gloomy Depths of *Nothingness* to pore,
'Till *All* be none, and *Being* be no more.

The sprightlier *Infidel*, as yet more gay,
Fires off the next Ideas in his Way,

The

The dry fag **Ends of** ev'ry obvious Doubt;
And puffs and blows **for** fear they fhould go out.
Boldly refolv'd, againft Conviction fteel'd,
Nor inward Truth, nor outward Fact, to yield;
Urg'd with a thoufand Proofs, he ftands unmov'd
Faft by himfelf, and fcorns to be out-prov'd;
To his own Reafon loudly he appeals,
No Saint more zealous for what God reveals.

Think not that you are no Enthufiaft then:
All Men are fuch, as fure as they are Men.
The Thing itfelf is not at all to blame:
'Tis, in **each State** of human Life, **the fame.**
The fiery Bent, the driving of the **Will,**
That **gives** the Prevalence to Good, **or Ill.**
You need not go to *Cloifters,* or to *Cells,*
Monks, **or Field** *Preachers,* to fee where it dwells:
It dwells alike in *Balls* and *Mafquerades;*
Courts, Camps, and *Changes,* it alike pervades.
There be Enthufiafts, who love to fit
In Coffee-houfes, and cant out their **Wit.**
The firft **in moft** Affemblies **would you fee,**
Mark **out the** firft Haranguer, **and that's He:**
Nay 'tis what filent Meetings cannot hide,
It may be notic'd **by its mere** Outfide.
Beaux and *Coquets* would quit the magic Drefs,
Did not this mutual Inftinct both poffefs.
The *Mercer,* **Taylor,** *Bookfeller,* grows rich,
Becaufe fine Cloaths, fine **Writings** can bewitch.

A *Ch*

A *Cicero*, a *Shaftsbury*, a *Bayle*,
How quick would they diminish in their Sale?
Four Fifths of all their Beauties who would heed,
Had they not *keen Enthusiasts* to read?

That which concerns us therefore is to see
What Species of Enthusiasts we be;
On what Materials the fiery Source
Of thinking Life shall execute its Force:
Whether a Man shall stir up Love, or Hate,
From the mix'd Medium of this present State;
Shall choose with upright Heart and Mind to rise,
And reconnoitre Heav'n's primeval Skies;
Or down to Lust and Rapine to descend,
Brute for a Time, and *Demon* at its End.
Neither perhaps, the wary Sceptics cry,
And wait till Nature's River shall run dry;
With sage Reserve not passing o'er to Good,
Of Time, lost Time, are borne along the Flood;
Content to think such thoughtless Thinking right,
And common Sense enthusiastic Flight.

Fly from *Enthusiasm?* Yes, fly from Air,
And breathe it more intensely for your Care.
Learn, that, whatever Phantoms you embrace,
Your own essential Property takes Place:
Bend all your Wits against it, 'tis in vain,
It must exist, or sacred, or profane.
For Flesh, or Spirit, Wisdom from above,
Or from this World, an Anger, or a Love,

Must

Must have its Fire within the human Soul:
'Tis ours to fpread the Circle, or controul;

In Clouds of fenfual Appetites to fmoke,
While fmoth'ring Lufts the rifing Confcience choke;

Or, from ideal Glimmerings, to raife,
Showy and faint, a fuperficial Blaze;
Where fubtle Reafons with their lambent Flames,
Untouch'd the *Things*, creep round and round the *Names*;

Or—— with a true celeftial Ardor fir'd,
Such as at firft created Man infpir'd,
To will, and to perfift to will, the Light,
The Love, the Joy, that makes an Angel bright,
That makes a Man, in Sight of God, to fhine
With all the Luftre of a Life divine.

When true Religion kindles up the Fire,
Who can condemn the vigorous Defire?
That burns to reach the End for which 'twas giv'n,
To fhine, and fparkle in its native Heav'n?
What elfe was our creating Father's View?
His Image loft why fought he to renew?
Why all the Scenes of Love that Chriftians know,
But to attract us from this poor Below?
To fave us from the fatal Choice of Ill,
And blefs the free co-operating Will?

Blame not *Enthufiafm*, if rightly bent;
Or blame of Saints the holieft Intent,

The

The ftrong Perfuafion, the confirm'd Belief,
Of all the Comforts of a Soul the Chief;
That God's continual Will, and Work to fave,
Teach, and infpire, attend us to the Grave:
That they, who in his Faith and Love abide,
Find in his Spirit an immediate Guide:
This is no more a *Fancy*, or a *Whim*,
Than that we *live*, and *move*, and *are in Him*:
Let Nature, or let Scripture, be the Ground,
Here is the Seat of true Religion found.
An earthly Life, as Life itfelf explains,
The *Air* and *Spirit* of this World maintains:
As plainly does an heav'nly Life declare,
An heav'nly *Spirit*, and an holy *Air*.

What Truth more plainly does the Gofpel teach,
What Doctrine all its Miffionaries preach,
Than this, That ev'ry good Defire and Thought
Is in us by the Holy Spirit wrought?
For this the working *Faith* prepares the Mind;
Hope is expectant, *Charity* refign'd:
From this bleft Guide the Moment we depart,
What is there left to fanctify the Heart?
Reafon and Morals? And where live they moft?
In Chriftian Comfort, or in *Stoic* Boaft?
Reafon may paint unpractis'd Truth exact,
And Morals rigidly maintain——no Fact:
This is the *Pow'r* that raifes them to Worth,
That calls their rip'ning Excellencies forth.

Not

Not afk for this ?——May Heav'n forbid the vain,
The fad Repofe !——What Virtue can remain ?
What Virtue wanting, if, within the Breaft,
This Faith, productive of all Virtue, reft,
That God is always prefent to impart
His Light and Spirit to the willing Heart?

He, who can fay My willing Heart began
To learn this Leffon, may be chriften'd *Man;*
Before, a Son of *Elements* and *Earth;*
But now, a Creature of another Birth;
Whofe true regenerated Soul revives,
And Life from Him, that ever lives, derives;
Freed by compendious Faith from all the Pangs
Of long-fetch'd Motives, and perplex'd Harangues;
One Word of Promife ftedfaftly embrac'd,
His Heart is fix'd, its whole Dependence plac'd:
The Hope is rais'd, that cannot but fucceed,
And found *Infallibility* indeed :
Then flows the *Love* that no Diftinction knows
Of *Syftem*, *Sect*, or *Party*, *Friends*, or *Foes;*
Nor loves by halves; but, faithful to its Call,
Stretches its whole Benevolence to All;
It's univerfal Wifh, th' Angelic Scene,
That God within the Heart of Man may reign;
The true Beginning to the final Whole,
Of Heav'n, and heav'nly Life, within the Soul.

This Faith, and this Dependence, once deftroy'd,
Man is made helplefs, and the Gofpel void.

He

He that is taught to seek elsewhere for Aid,
Be who he will the Teacher, is betray'd:
Be what it will the System, he's enslav'd;
Man by Man's Maker only can be fav'd.
In this One Fountain of all Help to trust,
What is more easy, natural, and just?
Talk what we will of Morals, and of Blifs,
Our Safety has no other Source but this:
Led by this Faith, when Man forsakes his Sin,
The Gate stands open to his God within:
There, in the Temple of his Soul, is found,
Of inward central Life, the holy Ground;
The sacred Scene of Piety and Peace,
Where new-born Christians feel the Life's Increase;
Blessing, and blest, revive to pristine Youth,
And worship God in Spirit, and in Truth.

Had not the Soul this Origin, this Root,
What else were Man but a two-handed Brute?
What but a Devil, had he not possest
The Seed of Heav'n, *replanted* in his Breast?
The Spark of Potency, the Ray of Light,
His Call, his Help, his Fitness to excite
The Strength and Vigour of celestial Air,
Faith, and the Breath of living Christians, Pray'r:
Not the Lip-Service, nor the mouthing Waste
Of heartless Words, without an inward Taste;
But the true Kindling of desirous Love,
That draws the willing Graces from above;

The

The Thirſt of Good that naturally pants
After that Light and Spirit which it wants;
In whoſe bleſt Union quickly coincide,
To aſk, and have, to want, and be ſupply'd.
Then does the faithful Suppliant diſcern
More of true Good, more of true Nature learn,
Than from a thouſand Volumes on the Shelf,
In one meek Intercourſe with Truth itſelf.

All that the Goſpel ever could ordain,
All that the Church's daily Rites maintain,
Is to keep up, to ſtrengthen, and employ,
This lively Faith, this Principle of Joy;
This Hope and this Poſſeſſion of the End,
Which all her pious Inſtitutes intend;
Fram'd to convey, when freed from wordy Strife,
The Truth, and Spirit, of an inward Life;
Wherein th' eternal Parent of all Good
By his own Influence is underſtood,
That Man may learn infallibly aright,
Bleſt in his Preſence, ſeeing in his Light,
To gain the Habit of a Godlike Mind,
To ſeek his Holy Spirit, and to find.

In this *Enthuſiaſm*, advanc'd *thus high*,
'Tis a true Chriſtian Wiſh, to live, and die.

                    A PARA-

A PARAPHRASE

ON THE

LORD's PRAYER.

Our Father which art in Heaven——

FATHER——to think of his paternal Care
  Is a moſt ſweet Encouragement to Pray'r.
Our Father——all Men's Father; to remind
That we ſhould love, as Brethren, all Mankind.
Which art in Heaven——aſſures an heav'nly Birth
To all his loving Children upon Earth.

Hallowed be thy Name.

Name——is expreſſive of a real Thing,
With all the Pow'rs of which it is the Spring.
Thy Name——is therefore to be underſtood
Thy bleſſed Self, thou Fountain of all Good.
Be hallowed——be lov'd, obey'd, ador'd,
By inward Pray'r habitu'lly implor'd.

Thy Kingdom come——

Kingdom—— of Grace, at preſent, Seed and Root
Of future Glory's everlaſting Fruit.

Thy

Thy Kingdom——not the World's War-shifted Scene,
Of Pomp **and Show, but Love's all** peaceful Reign.
Come——rule within **our Hearts, by Grace divine,**
'Till all the Kingdoms of the World be thine.

*Thy Will be done in Earth **as it is in Heaven.***

Thy Will——to ev'ry Good **that boundlefs Pow'rs**
Can raife, **if we conform** to it with ours.
Be done in Earth——where Doing of his Will
Promotes **all Good,** and overcomes all Ill.
As 'tis in Heav'n——where all the Bleft above
Serve, **with one Will, the living Source of Love.**

*Give us this Day our daily **Bread.***

Give us——implies **Dependence, whilft we live,**
Not on ourfelves, but what He wills to **give.**
This Day——cuts off all covetous Defire
Of **more** and more, than real Wants require.
Our daily Bread——whatever we fhall need,
And rightly ufe, to make it *Ours* indeed.

And forgive us our Trefpaffes——

Forgive——betokens penitential Senfe,
And Hope for Pardon, of confefs'd Offence.
Us——takes in all, but hints the fpecial Part
Of ev'ry one, to look to his own Heart.

Our

Our Trespasses——which the forgiving Grace,
By our sincere Conversion, must efface.

As We forgive them that trespass against Us.

As We forgive——because the fairest Claim
To Mercy pray'd **for** is to shew the same.
And **we** who pray should all be minded thus,
To pardon them, *that trespass against Us.*
Without forgiving, **Chrift** was pleas'd to add,
Our own Forgiveness never **can be had.**

And lead us not into Temptation.

Temptation rises in this World, the Field
Of Good and Evil, and incites to yield.
Lead us not into it——becomes the Voice
Of all, who would not go to it by Choice.
Whose Resignation, **mix'd with meek Diftruft**
Of their own Strength, **is more securely juft.**

But deliver Us from Evil——

But——when Temptation will, of course, arise,
The Hand that leads can minifter Supplies.
Deliver Us——inftructs the Soul to place
Its firm Reliance on protecting Grace.
From Evil——from the greateft Evil, Sin;
The only one not to be fafely in.

For

For thine is the Kingdom, the Power, and the Glory.

Thine is the Kingdom————the effential Right
To fov'reign Rule, and Majefty, and Might.
Thine is the Pow'r————to blefs, and to **redeem;**
All elfe is weak whatever it may feem.
Thine is the Glory————manifeftly found
In all **thy** Works, the whole Creation **round.**

For Ever and Ever.

For Ever————from an unbeginning **Source,**
Almighty **Love** purfues its endlefs Courfe.
Through all its Scenes, Eternity difplays
New Wonders to our heav'nly Father's Praife.
King, Father, Leader, Judge, his **hallow'd Name**
Was, is, and ever will be, ftill the fame.

Amen.

Amen is Truth, **in** Hebrew, **and Confent**
To Truth receiv'd, **by its long Ufe, is meant.**
Jefus, Himfelf the **Truth,** the living **Way,**
The **faithful Witnefs,** teaches thus to pray.
Again fhould **we be** learning, and again,
'Till Life becomes a practical Amen.

An

A DIVINE PASTORAL.

I.

THE Lord is my Shepherd, my Guardian, and Guide;
   Whatsoever I want he will kindly provide:
Ever since I was born, it is he that hath crown'd
The Life that he gave me with Blessings all round:
While yet on the Breast a poor Infant I hung,
E'er Time had unloosen'd the Strings of my Tongue,
He gave me the Help which I could not then ask;
Now therefore to thank him shall be my Tongue's Task.

II.

  Thro' my tenderest Years, with as tender a Care,
My Soul, like a Lamb, in his Bosom he bare;
To the Brook he would lead me, whene'er I had need,
And point out the Pasture where best I might feed:
No Harm could approach me; for he was my Shield
From the Fowls of the Air, and the Beasts of the Field
The Wolf, to devour me, would oftentimes prowl,
But the Lord was my Shepherd, and guarded my Soul.

III.

  How oft in my Youth have I wander'd astray?
And still he hath brought me back to the right Way!

When,

When, loft in dark Error, no Path I could meet,
His Word, like a Lantern, hath guided my Feet:
What wond'rous Efcapes to his Kindnefs I owe?
When, rafh and unthinking, I fought my own Woe:
My Soul had, long fince, been gone down to the Deep,
If the Lord had not watched, when I was afleep.

IV.

Whenfoe'er, at a Diftance, he fees me afraid,
He fkips o'er the Mountain, and comes to my Aid;
Then leads me back gently, and bids me abide
In the midft of his Flock, and feed clofe by his Side:
How fafe in his Keeping, how happy and free,
Could I always remain where he bids me to be!
Yea bleft are the People, and happy thrice told,
That obey the Lord's Voice, and abide in his Fold.

V.

The Fold it is full, and the Pafture is green;
All is Friendfhip and Love, and no Enemy feen:
There the Lord dwells, amongft us, upon his own Hill;
With the Flocks all around him awaiting his Will:
Himfelf, in the Midft, with a provident Eye
Regarding our Wants, and procuring Supply;
An Abundance fprings up of each nourifhing Bud,
And we gather his Gifts, and are filled with Good.

VI. At

VI.

At his Voice, or Example, we move, or we ſtay;
For the Lord is himſelf both our Leader and Way:
The Hills ſmoke with Incenſe where'er he hath trod,
And a ſacred Perfume ſhows the Footſteps of **God**:
While bleſt, with **his Preſence, the Valleys beneath** .
A ſweet ſmelling Savour inceſſantly **breathe**:
The Delight is renew'd of each ſenſible Thing;
And behold in their Bloom all the Beauty **of Spring.**

VII.

Or, if a quite different Scene he prepare,
And we march thro' the Wilderneſs, barren and bare;
By his wonderful Works we ſee plainly enough,
That the Earth is the Lords, and the Fullneſs thereof:
If we hunger, and thirſt, and are ready to faint,
A Relief in due Seaſon prevents our Complaint;
The Rain, at his Word, brings us Food from the Sky,
And Rocks become Rivers when we are adry.

VIII.

From the fruitfulleſt Hill to the barreneſt **Rock**,
The Lord hath made all for the Sake of his Flock;
And the Flock, in Return, the Lord always **confeſs**
In Plenty their **Joy**, and their Hope in Diſtreſs:
He beholds in **our** Welfare his **Glory** diſplay'd,
And we find **ourſelves** bleſt in Obedience repay'd;

With

With a chearful Regard we attend to his Ways;
Our Attention is Pray'r, and our Chearfulnefs Praife.

IX.

The LORD is my Shepherd; what then fhall I fear?
What Danger can frighten me whilft He is near?
Not, when the Time calls me to walk thro' the Vale
Of the Shadow of Death, fhall my Heart ever fail;
Tho' afraid, of myfelf, to purfue the dark Way,
Thy Rod, and thy Staff, be my Comfort and Stay;
For I know, by thy Guidance, when once it is paft,
To a Fountain of Life it will bring me at laft.

X.

The LORD is become my Salvation and Song,
His Blefling fhall follow me all my Life long:
Whatfoever Condition He places me in,
I am fure 'tis the beft it could ever have been:
For The LORD He is good, and his Mercies are fure;
He only afflicts us in order to cure:
The LORD will I praife while I have any Breath;
Be content all my Life, and refign'd at my Death.

H   A Thankf.

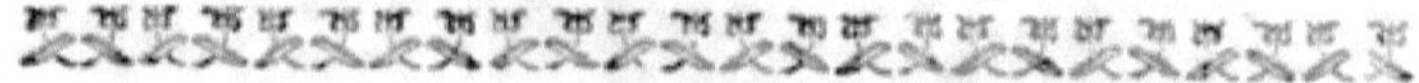

A Thankſgiving HYMN.

I.

O Come let us ſing to the Lord a new Song,
   And praiſe Him to whom all our Praiſes belong;
While we enter his Temple, with Gladneſs and Joy,
Let a Pſalm of Thankſgiving our Voices employ:
O come, to his Name, let us joyfully ſing;
For the Lord is a great and omnipotent King:
By his Word were the Heav'ns, and the Hoſt of them made,
And of all the round World the Foundation he laid.

II.

He plac'd, in the Center, yon beautiful Sun;
And the Orbs that, about him, due Diſtances run;
To receive, as they haſte their vaſt Rounds to complete,
Of a Luſtre ſo dazling, the Light and the Heat.
What Language of Men can the Brightneſs unfold
Of his Preſence, whoſe Creature they cannot behold?
What a Light is his Light! of its infinite Day
The Sun, by his Splendor, can paint but a Ray.

III.

The Sun, in the Evening, is out of our Sight,
And the Moon is enlighten'd to govern the Night:

His

His Power we behold, in yon high arched Roof,
When the Stars, in their Order, shine forth in its Proof:
While the Works, so immense, of thy Fingers we see,
And reflect on our Littlenefs, Lord, what are we?
Yet, while 'tis our Glory thy Name to adore,
Even Angels of Heav'n cannot boast any more.

IV.

Praife the Lord, upon Earth, all ye Nations and Lands,
Ye Seasons and Times, that fulfill his Commands;
Let his Works, in all Places, his Goodnefs proclaim,
And the People, who fee them, give Thanks to his Name:
For the Good, which he wills to communicate, brings
Into visible Form his invisible Things:
Their Appearance may change, as his Law fhall ordain,
But the Goodnefs that forms will for ever remain.

V.

What a World of good Things does all Nature produce,
Which the Lord, in his Mercy, hath made for our Ufe?
The Earth, by his Blessing bestow'd on its Soil,
By his Rain, and his Sunshine, gives Corn, Wine, and Oil:
Let Men to adore Him then thankfully join,
When fill'd with his Bread, or made glad by his Wine;
As in Wealth, fo in Gratitude, let them abound,
And the Voice of his Praife be heard all the World round.

H 2

VI. They

VI.

They, that o'er the wide Ocean their Bus'nefs purfue,
Can tell to his Wonders what Praifes are due:
When toft, to and fro, by the huge fwelling Wave,
They rife up to Heav'n, or fink down to the Grave;
Difmay'd with the Tempeft, that mocks at their Skill,
They cry to the Lord, and he maketh it ftill:
His Works in Remembrance ye Mariners keep,
And praife Him whofe Judgments are like the great Deep.

VII.

He ftilleth the Waves of the boifterous Sea;
And the Tumults of Men, more outrageous than they:
Thy Goodnefs, O Lord, let the People confefs,
Whom Wars do not wafte, nor proud Tyrants opprefs;
And devoutly contemplate thy wonderful ways,
Thou that turneft the Fiercenefs of Men to thy Praife:
Then Lands, in due Seafon, fhall yield their Increafe,
And the Lord give his People the Bleflings of Peace.

VIII.

The Lord he is high, far above all our Thought——
How then fhall we worfhip him fo as we ought?
What Tongue can exprefs, or what Words can fhew forth
The Praife which is due to his excellent Worth?
Ye Righteous, and ye that in Virtue excell,
Begin the glad Tafk which becomes you fo well;

The

The Lord fhall be pleas'd when he heareth your Voice,
And in his own Works fhall th' Almighty rejoice.

IX.

The Lord hath his Dwelling far out of our View,
And yet humbleth himfelf to behold what we do;
To his Works, all around him, his Mercies extend,
His Works have no Number, his Mercies no End;
He accepteth our Thanks, if the Heart do but pay;
Tho' we never can reach him, by all we can fay.
How juft is the Duty! how pure the Delight!
Since whilft we give Praifes we Honour him right.

X.

Praife the Lord, O my Soul! all the Pow'rs of my
    Mind,
Praife the Lord, who hath been fo exceedingly kind!
Who fpareth my Life, and forgiveth my Sin,
Still directeth the Way that I ought to walk in:
When I fpeak let me thank him; whenever I write,
The Remembrance of him let the Subject excite;
Guide Lord to thy Glory, my Tongue, and my Pen;
Yea, let ev'ry Thing praife Thee——Amen, and Amen.

An

An · H Y M N

ON THE

OMNIPRESENCE.

OH Lord! thou haſt known me, and ſearched me out,
  Thou ſee'ſt, at all Times, what I'm thinking about;
When I riſe up to Labour, or lye down to Reſt,
Thou markeſt each Motion that works in my Breaſt;
My Heart has no Secrets, but what thou can'ſt tell,
Not a Word in my Tongue, but thou knoweſt it well;
Thou ſee'ſt my Intention before it is wrought,
Long before I conceive it, thou knoweſt my Thought.

  Thou art always about me, go whither I will,
All the Paths that I take to, I meet with thee ſtill;
I go forth abroad, and am under thine Eye,
I retire to myſelf, and behold! thou art by;
How is it that thou haſt encompaſs'd me ſo
That I cannot eſcape thee, wherever I go?
Such Knowledge as this is too high to attain,
'Tis a Truth which I feel, tho' I cannot explain.

  Whither then ſhall I flee from thy Spirit, O Lord?
What Shelter can Space from thy Preſence afford?
If I climb up to Heav'n, 'tis there is thy Throne,
If I go down to Hell, even there thou art known;

If

If for Wings I fhould mount on the Mornings fwift Ray,
And remain in the uttermoft Parts of the Sea,
Even there, let the Diftance be ever fo wide,
Thy Hand would fupport me, thy right Hand would guide.

If I fay, peradventure, the Dark may conceal
What Diftance, tho' boundlefs, is forc'd to reveal,
Yet the Dark, at thy Prefence, would vanifh away,
And my Covering, the Night, would be turn'd into Day:
It is I myfelf only who could not then fee,
Yea, the Darknefs, O Lord, is no Darknefs to Thee:
The Night, and the Day, are alike in thy Sight,
And the Darknefs, to Thee, is as clear as the Light.

The COLLECT for ADVENT SUNDAY.

ALMIGHTY God, thy heav'nly Grace impart,
    And caft the Works of Darknefs from our Heart;
Send us thy Light, and arm us for the Strife
Againft all Evils of this mortal Life;
O'er which our SAVIOUR JESUS CHRIST, thy SON,
With great Humility the Conqueft won:
That when, in Glory, our victorious Head
Shall come to judge the Living and the Dead,
We may, thro' Him, to Life immortal fpring,
Wherein he reigns, the everlafting King;
The FATHER, SON, and SPIRIT may adore,
One glorious GOD TRIUNE, for evermore.

HYMNS

HYMNS

FOR

CHRISTMAS DAY.

I.

ON this aufpicious, memorable Morn,
    God and the Virgin's holy Child was born;
Offspring of Heav'n, whofe undefiled Birth
Began the Procefs of redeeming Earth;
Of re-producing Paradife again,
And God's loft Image in the Souls of Men.

II.

    Adam, who kept not his firft State of Blifs,
Rend'red himfelf incapable of this;
Nor could he, with his outward Helpmate Eve,
This pure, angelic, virgin Birth retrieve:
This, in our Nature, never could be done,
Until a Virgin fhould conceive a Son.

III.

    Mary, prepar'd for fuch a chafte Embrace,
Was deftin'd to this Miracle of Grace;

In

In her unfolded the myſterious Plan
Of Mans Salvation, **God's** becoming **Man;**
His Power, with her Humility combin'd,
Produc'd the finleſs Saviour of Mankind.

IV.

The Heighth and Depth of ſuch amazing **Love**
Nor can we meaſure, nor the Bleſt above;
Its Truth whoever reaſons right will own;
Man never could be ſav'd by Man alone:
Salvation is, if rightly we define,
Union **of** human Nature with divine.

V.

What Way to this, unleſs it had been trod
By the new Birth of an incarnate God?
Birth of a Life, that triumphs over Death,
A Life inſpir'd by God's immortal Breath;
For which Himſelf, to ſave us from the Tomb,
Did not abhor the Virgin Mother's Womb.

VI.

O may this Infant Saviour's Birth inſpire
Of real Life an humble, chaſte Defire!
Raiſe it up in us! form it in our Mind,
Like the bleſt Virgin's, totally refign'd!
A **mortal** Life from Adam we derive;
We are, in Chriſt, eternally alive.

I

On

On the S·A M E.

CHRISTIANS awake, falute the happy Morn,
   Whereon the SAVIOUR. of the World was born;
Rife, to adore the Myftery of Love,
Which Hofts of Angels chanted from above:
With them the joyful Tidings firft begun
Of GOD incarnate, and the Virgin's Son:
Then to the watchful Shepherds it was told,
Who heard th' Angelic Herald's Voice——*Behold!*
I bring good Tidings of a SAVIOUR's Birth
To you, and all the Nations upon Earth;
This Day hath GOD fulfill'd his promis'd Word;
This Day is born a SAVIOUR, CHRIST, the LORD:
In David's City, Shepherds, ye fhall find
The long foretold Redeemer of Mankind;
Wrapt up in fwaddling Cloaths, the Babe divine
Lies in a Manger; this fhall be your Sign.
He fpake, and ftraightway the Celeftial Choir,
In Hymns of Joy, unknown before, confpire:
The Praifes of redeeming Love they fung,
And Heav'ns whole Orb with Hallelujahs rung:
GOD's higheft Glory was their Anthem ftill;
Peace upon Earth, and mutual Good-will.
To *Bethlehem* ftraight th' enlightened Shepherds ran,
To fee the Wonder GOD had wrought for Man;
And found, with *Jofeph* and the bleffed Maid,
Her Son, the SAVIOUR, in a Manger laid.

Amaz'd,

Amaz'd, the wond'rous Story they proclaim;
The firſt Apoſtles of his **Infant Fame:**
While *Mary* **keeps,** and ponders in her **Heart,**
The heav'nly Viſion, which the Swains impart;
They to their Flocks, ſtill praiſing GOD, return,
And their glad Hearts within their Boſoms burn.

Let us, like theſe good Shepherds **then, employ**
Our grateful Voices to proclaim the Joy:
Like *Mary,* **let** us ponder **in our** Mind
GOD's wond'rous Love **in ſaving** loſt Mankind;
Artleſs, **and** watchful, **as theſe favour'd** Swains,
While Virgin Meekneſs **in the Heart remains:**
Trace we the Babe, who has retriev'd our Loſs,
From his poor Manger to his bitter Crofs;
Treading his Steps, aſſiſted by his Grace,
'Till Man's firſt heav'nly State again **takes** Place:
Then may we hope, th' Angelic Thrones among,
To ſing, redeem'd, a glad triumphal Song:
He that was born, upon this joyful Day,
Around us all, his Glory ſhall **diſplay;**
Sav'd **by his** Love, inceſſant we **ſhall ſing**
Of Angels, **and of Angel-Men,** the King.

ON

EPIPHANY.

I.

LED by the Guidance of a living Star,
    The Eastern Sages travel'd from afar
To feek the Saviour, by prophetic Fame
Defcrib'd to them as King of Jews by Name;
Whofe Birth, to Gentiles worthy of his Sight,
Was now declar'd by this angelic Light.

II.

    To its full Height th' Expectancy had grown
Of what the learned Foreigners made known;
When at Jerufalem the facred News
Was fpread by them to Herod, and the Jews;
Where is he born? For by his Star, they faid,
Thus far to worfhip him have we been led.

III.

    Herod, who had in his tyrannic Mind
No Thought of Empire, but of earthy Kind,
Jealous of this new King of Jewifh Tribes,
In Hafte affembl'd all the Priefts, and Scribes;

                                        Where

Where Chrift was to be born was his Demand——
In Bethlehem, they faid, in Juda's Land.

IV.

He call'd the Magi, privately again,
To learn from them the Time, precifely, **when**
The Star, which had conducted them, appear'd:
And, having all his wily Queftions clear'd,
Bad them to feek the Child, and from the View
Come, and **tell him,** that he might worfhip too.

V.

They journey'd on **to** the appointed Place,
Which Jewifh Priefts from Prophecy could trace:
Chear'd by the Star's Appearance **on** the Way,
That pointed where the Infant Saviour lay;
Meekly they ftep'd into his humble Shrine,
And **fell to** worfhipping the Babe divine.

VI.

The Virgin Mother faw them all prefer
Their Off'rings, Gold, and Frankincenfe, and Myrrh;
But warn'd of God his Father, in a Dream,
They difappointed Herod's murd'rous Scheme;
And, having feen the Object of **their** Faith,
Sought **their** own Country by **another** Path.

VII. Does

VII.

Does not Reflection juftly hence arife,
That in the Eaft, fo famous for the Wife,
The trueft Learning, Sapience, and Skill,
Was theirs, who fought, amidft the various Ill
Which they beheld, for that predicted Scene,
That fhould on Earth commence an heav'nly Reign?

VIII.

Thefe true Enquirers into Nature faw
That Nature muft have fome fuperior Law;
Some righteous Monarch, for the Good of all,
To rule with Juftice this diforder'd Ball;
Their humble Senfe of Wants, o'erlook'd by Pride,
Made them fo worthy of the Starlike Guide.

IX.

We read how, then, the very Pagan School
Was fill'd with Rumors of a Jewifh Rule:
Tho' Jews themfelves, as at this prefent Day,
Dreamt of a worldly domineering Sway;
The truly wife, or Jew, or Gentile, fought
A Chrift, the Object of an happier Thought.

X.

They beft could underftand prophetic Page,
Simple, or learn'd, the Shepherd, or the Sage:

Their

Their Eyes could fee, and follow **a true Light,**
That led them on **from** Prophecy **to** Sight:
Could own the Son who, by the Father's Will,
Should reign a King on Sion's holy Hill.

XI.

Of Treafures which the Wife were mov'd **to bring,**
If Gold prefented might confefs the King,
Incenfe to his Divinity relate,
And Myrrh denote his bitter, fuff'ring State,
They offer'd Types of the Theandric Plan
Of our Salvation, God's becoming Man.

XII.

In this redeeming Procefs all concur'd
To give fure Proof of the prophetic Word;
Jefus, Emanuel, the inward Light
Of all Mankind, who feek the **Truth aright,**
Forms in the **Heart** of all the Wife on Earth
The true Day Star, **the Token** of his Birth.

MEDITATIONS

FOR

Every Day in PASSION WEEK.

MONDAY.

GOD *in* CHRIST *is all Love.*

I.

BEHOLD the tender Love of God!——behold
  The Shepherd dying to redeem his Fold!
Who can declare it?——Worthy to be known——
What Tongue can speak it worthily?——His own:
From his own sacred Lips the Theme began,
The glorious Gospel of God's Love to Man.

II.

  So great, so boundless was it, that he gave
His only Son——and for what End?——To save;
Not to condemn; if Men reject the Light,
They, of themselves, condemn themselves to Night;
God, in his Son, seeks only to display,
In ev'ry Heart, an everlasting Day.

III. God

III.

God hath fo fhown his Love to us, fays *Paul*,
Even yet Sinners, that Chrift di'd for all:
Peter, that God's all gracious Aim is this,
By *Chrift*, to call us to eternal Blifs:
Of all th' infpir'd to underftand the View
Love is the Text——and Love the Comment **too;**

IV.

The Ground to build all **Faith, and Works upon;**
For *God is Love*——fays the **beloved** *John*——
Short Word——but Meaning infinitely wide,
Including **all** that **can** be faid befide;
Including all the joyful Truths above
The Pow'r of Eloquence——for——*God is Love.*

V.

Think on the Proof, that *John* from *Jefus* learn'd,
In this was **God's amazing** Love difcern'd,
Becaufe he fent his **Son to us;** that we
Might live thro' **him**——**how** plain it is **to fee**
That, if in **this, in ev'ry other** Fact,
Where God is **Agent, Love is** in the Act.

VI.

Effential Character, (whatever **word**
Of **diff'rent Sound in** Scripture has occurr'd)

Of

Of all that is afcrib'd to God; of all
That can by his immediate Will befall:
The Sun's bright Orb may lofe its fhining Flame,
But Love remains unchangeably the fame.

T U E S D A Y.

How CHRIST quencheth the Wrath of GOD in us.

I.

THE Saviour di'd, according to our Faith,
  To quench, attone, or pacify a Wrath——
But——*God is Love*——he has no Wrath his own;
Nothing in him to quench, or to attone:
Of all the Wrath, that Scripture has reveal'd,
The poor fall'n Creature wanted to be heal'd.

II.

  God, of his own pure Love, was pleas'd to give
The Lord of Life, that thro' him it might live;
'Thro' *Chrift*; becaufe none other could be found
To heal the human Nature of its Wound:
This great Phyfician of the Soul had, fure,
In him, who gave him, no Defect to cure.

III. He

III.

He did, **he** ſuffer'd ev'ry Thing, that we
From Wrath, by Sin enkindl'd, might be free,
The Wrath of God, in us, that is, the Fire
Of burning Life, without the Love-Deſire;
Without the Light, which *Jeſus* came to **raiſe**,
And change the Wrath into a joyful Blaze.

IV.

The Wrath is God's; but in himſelf unfelt;
As Ice, and Froſt are his, and Pow'r to melt:
Not even Man could any Wrath, **as** ſuch,
Till he had loſt his firſt Perfection, touch:
God has but one immutable good Will,
To bleſs his Creatures, and to ſave from Ill.

V.

Cordial, or bitter a Phyſician's Draught,
The Patient's **Health is** in his ord'ring **Thought**:
God's Mercies, or God's Judgments be the Name,
Eternal Health is his all-ſaving Aim.
Vengeance belongs to GOD———and ſo it ſhould———
For Love alone **can** turn it all to Good.

VI.

All that, in Nature, by his Act is done
Is to give Life; and Life is in his Son:

When

When his Humility, his Meekneſs finds
Healing Admiſſion, into willing Minds,
All Wrath diſperſes, like a gath'ring Sore;
Pain is its Cure, and it exiſts no more.

WEDNESDAY.

CHRIST satisfieth the Juſtice of GOD by fulfilling all
Righteouſneſs.

I.

JUSTICE demandeth Satisfaction——Yes;
  And ought to have it where Injuſtice is:
But——there is none in God——it cannot mean
Demand of Juſtice where it has full Reign:
To dwell in **Man it rightfully demands,**
Such as he came **from his Creator's Hands**

II.

  Man had departed from a righteous State,
Which he, at firſt, muſt have, if God create:
Tis therefore call'd God's Righteouſneſs; and muſt
Be ſatisfy'd by Man's becoming juſt:
Muſt exerciſe good Vengeance upon Men,
'Till it regain its Rights in them again.

III. This

III.

This was the Juftice, for which *Chrift* became
A Man, to fatisfy its righteous Claim;
Became Redeemer of the Human Race,
That Sin, in them, to Juftice might give Place:
To fatisfy a juft, and righteous Will
Is neither more, nor lefs, than to fulfill:

IV.

It was, in **God, the loving Will that fought**
The Joy **of having Man's Salvation wrought:**
Hence, in his Son, fo infinitely pleas'd
With Righteoufnefs fulfill'd, and Wrath appeas'd:
Not with mere Suff'ring, which he never wills,
But with mere Love, that triumph'd over Ills.

V.

'Twas tender **Mercy——by the Church confefs'd,**
Before fhe feeds the facramental **Gueft;**
Rememb'ring him, who offer'd up his Soul
A Sacrifice for Sin, full, perfect, whole,
Sufficient, fatisfactory——and all
That Words (how **fhort of** Merit!) can recall.

VI.

And **when** receiv'd his Body, and his Blood,
The Life enabling to be juft, and good,

Off'ring

Off'ring, available thro' him alone,
Body, and Soul, a Sacrifice her own:
From Him, from his, fo, Juftice has its due;
Itfelf reftor'd,——not any thing in Lieu.

THURSDAY.

Christ the Beginner and Finifher of the New Life
in Man.

I.

DEAD as Men are, in Trefpaffes and Sins,
    Whence is it in them that new Life begins?
'Tis that, by God's great Mercy, Love, and Grace,
The Seed of *Chrift* is in the Human Race;
That inward, hidden Man, that can revive,
And, dead in *Adam*, rife in *Chrift* alive.

II.

    Life natural, and Life divine poffefs'd,
Muft needs unite, to make a Creature blefs'd:
The firft, a feeling Hunger, and Defire
Of what it cannot of itfelf acquire;
Wherein the fecond, entering to dwell,
Makes all an Heav'n, that would be elfe an Hell.

III. As

III.

As only Light all Darkneſs can expell,
So was his Conqueſt over Death, and Hell,
The only poſſible, effectual Way
To raiſe to Life what *Adam*'s Sin could ſlay:
Death by the falling, by the riſing Man
The Reſurrection of the Dead began.

IV.

This Heav'nly Parent of the human Race
The Steps, that *Adam* fell by, could retrace;
Could bear the Suffrings requiſite to ſave;
Could die, a Man, and triumph o'er the Grave:
This, for our Sakes, incarnate Love could do;
Great is the Myſtery——and greatly true.

V.

Prophets, Apoſtles, Martyrs, and the Choir
Of holy Virgin Witneſſes, conſpire
To animate a Chriſtian to endure
Whatever Croſs God gives him, for his Cure:
Looking to *Jeſus*, who has led the way
From Death to Life, from Darkneſs into Day.

VI.

Unmov'd by earthly Good, or earthly Ill,
The Man *Chriſt Jeſus* wrought God's bleſſed Will:

Death, in the Nature of the Thing, that Hour
Wherein he di'd, loſt all its deadly Pow'r:
Then, then was open'd, by what he ſuſtain'd,
The Gate of Life, and Paradiſe regain'd.

FRIDAY.

How the Sufferings and Death of CHRIST are available
to Man's Salvation.

I.

WITH Hearts deep rooted in Love's holy Ground
  Should be ador'd this Myſtery profound
Of God's Meſſiah, ſuff'ring in our Frame;
The Lamb *Chriſt Jeſus*——bleſſed be his Name!
Dying, in this Humanity of ours,
To introduce his own Life-giving Pow'rs.

II.

  Herein is Love! deſcending from his Throne,
The Father's Boſom, for our Sakes alone,
What Earth, what Hell, could wrathfully unite
Of Ills, he vanquiſh'd with enduring Might;
Legions of Angels ready at Command,
Singly he choſe to bear, and to withſtand.

III. To

III.

To bear, intent upon Mankind's Relief,
Ev'ry Excefs of ev'ry Shame, and Grief;
Of inward Anguifh, paft all Thought fevere;
Such as pure Innocence alone could bear:
Dev'lifh Temptation, Treachery, and Rage,
Naked, for us, did Innocence engage.

IV.

Nail'd to a **Crofs it fuffer'd, and forgave;**
And fhow'd the Penitent **its Pow'r** to fave:
It's Majefty confefs'd by Nature's Shock;
Darknefs——and Earthquake——and the rented Rock,
And opening Graves——the Prelude to that Pow'r,
Which rofe in fuff'ring Love's momentous Hour.

V.

No other Pow'r could **fave, but _Jefus_ can;**
The living God **was** in the dying **Man:**
Who, perfected by Suff'rings, from the Grave
Rofe in the Fullnefs of all Pow'r to fave:
With that one bleffed Life of God to fill
The vacant Soul, that yieldeth up its Will.

VI.

To learn is ev'ry pious Chriftian's Part,
From his great Mafter, this moft holy Art;

L

This

This our high Calling, Privilege, and Prize,
With Him to fuffer, and with Him to rife·
To live——to die——meek, patient, and refign'd
To God's good Pleafure, with a Chrift-like Mind.

SATURDAY.

How CHRIST by his Death overcame Death.

I.

JESUS is crucifi'd——the previous Scene
 Of our Salvation, and his glorious Reign:
Myfterious Procefs! tho', by Nature's Laws,
Such an Effect demanded fuch a Caufe:
For none but He could form the grand Defign,
And raife, anew, the human Life divine.

II.

No lefs a Myftery can claim Belief,
Than what belongs to our redeeming Chief:
Divine, and fupernatural indeed
The Love that mov'd the Son of God to bleed;
But what he was, and did, in each Refpect,
Was real Caufe producing its Effect.

III. Children

III.

Children of *Adam* needs muſt ſhare his Fall;
Children of *Chriſt* can re-inherit All:
This was the one, and therefore choſen Way,
For Love to manifeſt its full Diſplay:
Abſurd the Thought of arbitrary Plans;
Nature's one, true Religion this——and Man's.

IV.

All that we know of God, and Nature too,
Proves the Salvation of the Goſpel true;
Where all unites in one conſiſtent Whole,
The Life of God renew'd within the Soul:
Renew'd by *Chriſt*——He only could reſtore
The Heav'n in Man to what it was before:

V.

Could raiſe God's Image, clos'd in Death by Sin,
And raiſe Himſelf, the Light of Life, therein:
The one ſame Light that makes angelic Bliſs;
That ſpreads an Heav'n thro' Nature's whole Abyſs:
The Light of Nature, and the Light of Men,
That gives the Dead his Pow'r to live again.

VI.

The *Way,* the *Truth,* the *Life*—— whatever Terms
Prefer'd, 'tis Him that ev'ry Good affirms;

The one true Saviour; all is Dung and Drofs,
In faving Senfe, but *Jefus* and his Crofs:
All Nature fpeaks; all Scripture anfwers thus——
Salvation is the Life of CHRIST *in us.*

EASTER COLLECT.

ALMIGHTY GOD! whofe bleffed Will was done
By Jefus Chrift, our Lord, thine only Son;
Death overcome, and open'd unto Men
The Gate of everlafting Life again;
Grant us, baptiz'd into his Death, to die
To all Affeétions, but to Things on high;
That when, by thy preventing Grace, we find
The good Defires to rife within our Mind,
Our Wills may tend as thine fhall ftill direét,
And bring the good Defires to good Effeét;
Thro' Him, the one Redeemer from the Fall,
Who liv'd and di'd, and rofe again for all.

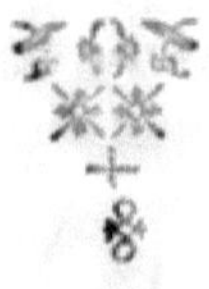

EASTER DAY.

I.

THE Morning dawns; the third approaching Day
  Can only fhow the Place where *Jefus* lay:
Angels defcend——Remember what he faid——
He is not here, but rifen from the dead;
Betray'd into the Hands of finful Men,
The Son of Man muft die, and rife again.

II.

  So fang the Prophets, ever fince the Fall;
Of Rites ordain'd the Meaning this, thro' all:
This, by the various Sacrifice of old,
Memorial Type, and Shadow, was foretold:
Even falfe Worfhip, carelefs what it meant,
Gave to this Truth an ignorant Confent.

III.

  Chrift is the Sum, and Subftance of the whole
That God has done, or faid, to fave a Soul:
To raife himfelf a Church; when that is done,
The World becomes the Kingdom of his Son:
An Heav'n reftor'd to the redeem'd, the born
Of him, who rofe on this aufpicious Morn.

He

IV.

He that was dead, in order to reſtore,
Behold! he is alive for evermore:
An heav'nly *Adam*, full impow'rd to give
The Life, that Men were firſt deſign'd to live:
Fountain of Life, come whoſoever will
To quench his Thirſt, and freely take his Fill.

V.

Mankind, in Him, are Life's predeſtin'd Heirs;
His riſing Glories the Firſt-fruits of theirs:
Hearts, that renounce the Slavery to Sin,
Feel of his Pow'r the living Warmth within:
Of ſtrength'ning Faith, of joyous Hope poſſeſt,
And Heav'n-producing Love, within the Breaſt.

VI.

The Breaſt——the Temple of the Holy Ghoſt,
When once enliven'd by this heav'nly Hoſt:
His Reſurrection, the ſure Proof of ours,
Will there exert his Death-deſtroying Pow'rs;
'Till all his Sons ſhall meet before his Throne
In glorious Bodies, faſhion'd like his own.

An

AN HYMN FOR EASTER DAY.

I.

THE LORD *is rifen!* He who came
 To fuffer Death, and conquer too,
Is *rifen;* let our Song proclaim
 The Praife to Man's REDEEMER due:

To Him whom GOD, in *tender* LOVE,
 Always, alike, to blefs inclin'd,
Sent to redeem us, from above;
 To *fave,* to *fanctify* Mankind.

CHORUS.

WORTHY of all Pow'r and Praife,
 HE who di'd, and rofe again;
Lamb of GOD, and flain to raife
 MAN, to Life redeem'd——AMEN.

II. That

II.

That Life which *Adam* ceas'd to live,
    When to this World he turn'd his Heart,
And to his Children could not give,
    The SECOND ADAM *can* impart.

We, on our *earthly* Parent's Side,
    Could but receive a Life of Earth;
The LORD from HEAVEN, He liv'd, and died,
    And rose to give us *Heav'nly* Birth.

CHO. *WORTHY of all Pow'r and Praise,* &c.

III.

This mortal Life, this living Death,
    Shews that in *Adam* we all die;
In CHRIST we have immortal Breath,
    And Life's *unperishing* Supply:

HE took our Nature, and sustain'd
    The *Mis'ries* of it's sinful State;
Sinless HIMSELF, for Us regain'd
    To Paradise an Open Gate.

CHO. *WORTHY of all Pow'r and Praise,* &c.

IV. As

IV.

As *Adam* rais'd a Life of Sin,
    So Christ, the Serpent-bruising Seed,
By God's Appointment could begin
    The Birth, in Us, of Life *indeed:*

He did begin; Parental Head,
    As *Adam* fell, so Jesus stood;
Fulfill'd all Righteousness, and said
    'Tis finish'd!——on the sacred Wood.

Cho. *WORTHY of all Pow'r and Praise*, &c.

V.

Finish'd *his* Work, to quench the Wrath,
    That Sin had brought on *Adam*'s Race;
To pave the *sole*, and certain Path
    From *Nature*'s Life, to that of *Grace:*

For Joy of *this*, God's only Son
    Endur'd the *Cross*, despis'd the *Shame*,
And gave the Victory, *so* won,
    For *imitating* Love to claim.

Cho. *Worthy of all Pow'r and Praise*, &c.

VI. To

VI.

To tread the Path that Jesus trod,
   Aided **by** him, be our Employ;
To *die* to Sin, and *live* to God,
   And yield him **the fair purchas'd Joy:**

To all the **Laws** that Love **has made**
   Stedfaft, unfhaken to attend;
He died, He rofe, *Himfelf* our Aid,
   Lo! I am with you to the End.

C H O R U S.

WORTHY of all Pow'r and Praife,
   HE who died and rofe again;
Lamb of GOD, and flain to raife
   MAN, to Life redeem'd——AMEN.

On

On WHITSUNDAY.

I.

JESUS, afcended into Heav'n again,
  Beftow'd this won'drous Gift upon good Men,
That various Nations, by his Spirit led,
All underftood what Galileans faid:
He gave the Word, who form'd the lift'ning Ear,
And Truth became in ev'ry Language clear.

II.

One Country's Tongue, to his Apoftles known,
To ev'ry pious Soul became its own:
The well difpos'd, from all the World around,
With holy Wonder, heard the Gofpel Sound;
Their Hearts prepar'd to hear it——God's Command
No Obftacle in Nature could withftand.

III.

Nature itfelf, if ev'ry Heart was right,
All jarring Languages would foon unite:
Her's is but one, intelligible Guide;
But Tongues are numberlefs where Hearts divide:
The Babel Projects bring them to their Birth,
And fcatter Difcord o'er the Face of Earth.

IV. The

IV.

The Prince of Peace now fending, from above,
His Holy Spirit of uniting Love,
By its miraculous Effufion, fhow'd
How great a Pow'r he promis'd, and beftow'd;
Pow'r to reverfe Confufion, and impart
One living Word to ev'ry honeft Heart.

V.

Deaf to its Influence the Wicked ftood,
And mock'd the juft Amazement of the Good;
For want of Senfe, afcribing to new Wine
Their joint Acknowledgments of Grace divine:
The World's devout Epitome was taught,
And hid from Pride the Miracle, when wrought.

VI.

Known to the Meek, but from the Worldly Wife,
From Scoffers hid, the wonderful Supplies
Of God's good Spirit, now as near to Men,
Whofe Hearts are open to the Truth, as then:
Bleft, in all Climates, all Conditions, they
Who hear this inward Teacher, and obey.

On TRINITY SUNDAY.

CO-EQUAL *Trinity* was always taught
  By the Divines moſt fam'd for pious Thonght:
The Men of Learning fill'd, indeed, the Page
With diſſonant Diſputes, from Age to Age;
But with themſelves, **ſo far as one can read,**
About **their** Schemes are not at all agreed;
When they oppos'd, by Reaſon, or by Wrath,
This grand Foundation **of** the Chriſtian Faith.

  For what more fundamental Point, **or** grand,
Than our aſcending Saviour's own **Command?**
" **Go and** baptize all Nations in the Name"——
Of Whom, or What? (**For** thence the ſureſt Aim
Of Chriſtian Doctrine muſt appear the moſt)
——The Name of FATHER, Son, **and HOLY** GHOST——
Our Lord's Interpretation here **we ſee,**
Of——" **Thou** ſhalt have no other **Gods but** Me"——

  For **can** the Phraſe, ſo highly ſacred, ſhow
The Name of **God to be omitted?** No;
By its eſſential **Trinity expreſt,**
It ſhow'd what Faith *Chriſt* will'd to be profeſt:
One God the *Jews* had **own'd;** and one Supreme,
With others lower, was the *Pagan* Theme;
How One was true, and how Supreme prophan'd,
Our Lord's *baptiſmal* Ordinance explain'd.

The

The one Divinity of Father, Son,
And Spirit, teaches Christian Thought to shun
Both *pagan*, and *rabbinical* Mistake,
And understand what holy Prophets spake;
Or in the ancient Writings, or the new,
To which this Doctrine is the sacred Clue;
That so conducts us to the saving Plan
Of true Religion, as no other can.

For, were the Son's Divinity deni'd,
The Father's must, of course, be set aside;
Or be a dark one——How can it be bright,
But by its own eternal, inborn Light?
The Glory of the Father is the Son,
Of all his Powers begotten, or begun,
From all Eternity; take Son away,
And what the Father can delight in, say.

The Love, paternally divine, implies
Its proper Object, whence it must arise,
That is, the Son; and so the filial too
Implies paternal Origin in View;
And hence the third distinctly glorious Tie
Of Love, which both are animated by:
All is one God, but He contains divine,
Living Relations, evidently *Trine*.

So far from hurting *Unity*, that hence
The Fullness rises of its perfect Sense;

And

And ev'ry barren, ſpiritleſs Diſpute,
Againſt its Truth, is pluck'd up by the Root:
The Faith is ſolid to repoſe upon,
Father, Word, Spirit, undivided One;
By whom Mankind, of threefold Life poſſeſt,
Can live, and move, and have its Being bleſt.

Not by *Three* Gods; **or** One ſupremely great,
With two *Inferiors;* **or the wild Conceit,**
God, *Michael*, *Gabriel;* or aught elſe, devis'd
For Chriſtians, **in no *Creature*'s** Name *baptiz'd;*
But **of** the whole inſeparable THREE,
Whoſe fertile Oneneſs cauſes **all to be;**
And **makes an Heav'n thro'** Nature's **whole Abyſs,**
By its Paternal, Filial, Spirit Bliſs.

On the S A M E.

I.

ONE *God the Father*——certainly this Term
    Does not a barren **Deity** affirm;
Without the Son; without the native Light,
By which its fiery Majeſty **is bright;**
Without the Spirit of the Fire, **and** Flame
Of Life divine, eternally the ſame.

II. More

II.

More One——than any Thing befide can be,
Becaufe of its infeparable Three;
Which Nothing can diminifh, or divide,
Tho' it fhould break all Unity befide;
For **This**, as felf-begetting, felf-begot,
And to itfelf proceeding, **it can not.**

III.

This total Onenefs of its threefold Blifs,
Life, Light, and Joy of Nature's vaft Abyfs,
No Tongue fo well can utter, but the Mind,
That feeks for fomewhat to object, may find;
No End of Queftions, if we muft conteft
A Truth, by Saints, **of** ev'ry Age, expreft.

IV.

The Church did always, always **will, agree**
In its one Worfhip **of** the Holy Three;
As taught, **by** *Chrift*, that Unity divine
Was **full** and perfect, that is, Unitrine:
He faid,——*Baptize all Nations, and proclaim*
Of Father, Son, and Holy Ghoft, The Name.

V.

The Holy! Holy! Holy! of the Hoft
Of Heav'n is Father, **Son**, and Holy Ghoft;

Not

Not Holy——Holier——and Holiest——
But one, **triune**, same Holiness confest;
One God, one Loving, and Beloved, Love;
On **Earth below** ador'd, in Heav'n above.

VI.

One living Fullness of all perfect Good;
Its own essential Fountain, Stream, and Flood:
And when, according to the Christian Creed,
Men worship God in Spirit, Word, and Deed;
Faith, Hope, and Love's Triunity of Grace,
Will find, in their **true**, single Heart, **a Place.**

A

CAUTION against DESPAIR.

DESPAIR is **a** cowardly Thing,
   And the Spirit suggesting it bad;
  In spite of my Sins I will sing,
That Mercy is **still to be had.**

  For he that has shown it so **far,**
As to give me a sensible Heart,
  How heinous soever they are,
Delights in the merciful Part.

By

By Affliction, so heavy to bear,
He searches the Wound He would cure;
  'Tis his, to be kindly severe,
'Tis mine, by his Grace to endure.

  O! comfort thyself in his Love,·
Poor sinful and sorrowful Soul,
  Who came, and still comes, from above,
To the Sick, that would fain be made whole.

  Who said, and continues to say,
In the Deep of a penitent Breast,
  Come Sinner, to me come away,
I'll meet thee, and bring thee to Rest.

  A Refusal to come is absurd;
I'll put myself under his Care;
  I'll believe his infallible Word,
And never, no never despair.

A Penitential SOLILOQUY.

WHAT! tho' no Objects strike upon the Sight!
  Thy sacred Presence is an *inward* Light!
What! tho' no Sounds should penetrate the Ear!
To list'ning Thought the Voice of Truth is clear!
Sincere Devotion needs no outward Shrine;
The Center of an *humble* Soul is thine!

There

There may I worſhip! and there may'ſt thou place
Thy Seat of Mercy, and thy Throne of Grace!
Yea fix, if CHRIST my Advocate appear,
The dread Tribunal of thy Juſtice there:
Let each vain Thought, let each impure Deſire
Meet, in thy Wrath, with a *conſuming* Fire.

Whilſt the kind Rigours of a righteous Doom
All deadly Filth of *ſelfiſh Pride* conſume,
Thou, Lord! can'ſt raiſe, tho' puniſhing for Sin,
The Joys of peaceful Penitence within:
Thy Juſtice and thy Mercy both are ſweet,
That make our *Suff'rings* and *Salvation* meet.

Befall me, then, whatever God ſhall pleaſe!
His Wounds are healing, and his Griefs give Eaſe:
He, like a true Phyſician of the Soul,
Applies the Medicine that may make it whole:
I'll do, I'll *ſuffer* whatſoe'er he wills;
I ſee his Aim thro' all theſe tranſient Ills.

'Tis to infuſe a *ſalutary* Grief,
To fit the Mind for *abſolute* Relief:
That purg'd from ev'ry *ſalſe* and finite Love,
Dead to the World, alive to Things above,
The Soul may riſe, as in its *firſt* form'd Youth,
And worſhip God in *Spirit* and in *Truth*.

An

An Encouragement to earneſt and im-
portunate PRAYER.

Luke 18, 1.   *And he ſpake a Parable unto them, to*
    this End, that Men ougʰt always to pray, and not to
    faint.

A Bleſſed Truth for Parable to paint,
　　That Men ſhould always pray, and never faint!
Juſt the Reverſe of this would Satan ſay,
That Men ſhould always faint, and never pray:
He wants to drive poor Sinners to Deſpair;
And Chriſt to ſave them by prevailing Pray'r.

　　The Judge, who feared neither God nor Man,
Deſpis'd the Widow when ſhe firſt began
Her juſt Requeſt; but ſhe, continuing on
The ſame Petition, wearied him anon;
He could not bear to hear her praying ſtill,
And did her Juſtice, tho' againſt his Will.

　　Can Perſeverance force a Man, unjuſt,
To execute, however loth, his Truſt?
And will not God, whoſe fatherly Delight
Is to ſave Souls, ſo precious in his Sight,
Hear his own Offspring's perſevering Call,
And give the Bleſſing which He has for all?

Yes,

Yes, to be fure, He will; **the** lying No
Is a downright Temptation of the Foe;
Who firft emboldens Sinners to prefume,
As if a righteous Judgment had no Room;
And, having led them into grievous Faults,
With the Defpair of Mercy, then, affaults.

Dear Soul, **if thou haft liften'd to the Lies**
Which, at the firft, the Tempter would devife,
Let him not cheat thee with a fecond Snare,
And drag thee into Darknefs, by Defpair;
Pray, againft all his **Wiles,** for God will hear,
And will avenge Thee of him, never fear.

He gives the Grace to forrow for thy Sin,
The Sign of kindling Penitence within;
Let not the Smoke difturb thee, for, no doubt,
The Light and Flame will follow, and break out;
And Love arife to overcome Reftraint,
That Thou may'ft always pray, and never faint.

A SOLI-

A SOLILOQUY,

On reading the 5th and 8th Verses of the 37th Pfalm.

*Leave off from Wrath, and let go **Difpleafure**: Fret not thyfelf,*
*elfe fhalt thou be moved to **do** Evil.* **V. 8.**

IN Pfalm, this Evening order'd to be read,
  Fret not thyfelf——the Royal Pfalmift faid.
His Reafon why, fucceeding Words inftill;
Or elfe, fays he, 'twill *move thee to do Ill*.
Now tho' I know that Fretting does no Good,
Its evil Movement have I underftood?

  Move to do Evil! then, dear Soul of mine
Stir it not up, if that be its Defign:
Its being vain is Caufe enough to fhun;
But if indulg'd fome Evil muft be done:
And thou, according to the holy King,
Muft be the Doer of this evil Thing.

  Men ufe thee ill——that Fault is theirs alone;
But if thou ufe thyfelf ill, that's thy own:
Meeknefs and Patience is much better Treafure;
Then *leave off* **Wrath,** and *let go* **all** *Difpleafure:*
Tho' thou art ever fo ill treated——yet——
Remember *David;* and forbear to *fret.*

Commit

*Commit thy Way unto the Lord, and put thy Trust in Him,
and He will bring it to pass.* V. 5.

Commit thy *Way unto the Lord*——Resign
Thyself intirely to the Will divine:
All real Good, all Remedy for Ill,
Lies in conforming to His blessed Will:
By all Advice that holy Books record,
Thou must *commit thy Way* **unto the Lord.**

And put thy Trust in Him—— all other Trust,
Plac'd out of Him, is foolish and unjust:
His loving **Kindness** is the only Ground,
Where **solid Peace** and Comfort **can be found:**
What **other Prospects either sink,** or swim,
Do thou stand Firm, and *put thy Trust in Him.*

And *He will bring thy Way to pass* —— the whole
Of all that thou canst wish for to thy Soul:
He wills to give it, and thy seeking Mind,
By Faith and Patience, cannot fail to find:
To Him, whatever good Desire **it has,**
Commit, and trust, and **He will bring** *to pass.*

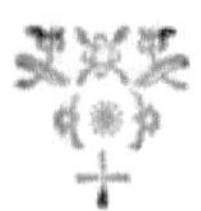

An EPISTLE

From the Author to his Sister, with the foregoing Soliloquy inclosed.

Dear Sister,
      If Soliloquy conduce,
(Meant, as the Name declares, for private Use)
To your Contentment——if such Kind of Fruit
Pleases your Taste, you're very welcome to't:
Tho' pluck'd, one Day in April, from the Ground,
It keeps, in Pickle, all the Seasons round.

'Tis Summer now, and Autumn comes anon;
Winter succeeds, and Spring when that is gone;
But be it Winter, Summer, Autumn, Spring,
To nurture Fretting is a simple Thing:
A Weed so useless, to the Use of Reason,
Can, absolutely, never be in Season.

Without much Nursing, that the Weed will grow,
I wish I had some Reason less to know;
Some less to see, how Folly, when it grew
In my own Ground, could cultivate it too;
Could hedge it round, and cherish, and suppose
That, being mine, the Thistle was a' Rose.

You know the Saying, of I know not whom,
" *Little Misfortunes serve 'till greater come;*"

And

And Saying, somewhere met with, I recall,
" *That 'tis the greatest to have none at all :*"
Rare Cafe perhaps; they reach, we often fee,
All Sorts of Perfons, Him, **Her, You, or Me.**

This being then, Experience fays, the Cafe,
What Kind of Conduct muft a Man embrace?
My 'Pothecary, as you think, replies——
Pray take 'em quietly, if you be wife;
Bitter they are, 'tis true, to Flefh and Blood;
But if they were not——they would do no Good.

One Time, when 'Pothecary Patience found
That his Perfuafion got but **little Ground,**
He call'd in Doctor Gratitude, **to try**
If his Advice **could make me** to comply;
I recommended **Patience,** Sir, faid he,
Pray will you fpeak, for he regards not me.

Patience! a Cuftard Lid——faid Dr. Grat,
His Cafe wants, plainly, fomething more than that;
'Tis a good Recipe——but **Cure is longer**
Than it fhould be; we muft have fomething ftronger;
A creeping **Pulfe !**——bare Patience will not do——
To get him Strength, he muft **be** thankful too.

He muft confider——and fo on he went,
To fhow Thankfgiving's marvellous Extent;
And what a true *Catholicon* it was;
And what great Cures it had but brought to pafs;

And

And how beſt Fortunes, wanting it, were curſt;
And how it turn'd to good the very worſt.

O what a deal he ſaid !——and in the Light,
Wherein he plac'd it, all was really right:
But like good Doctrine, of ſome good Divine,
Which, while 'tis preach'd, is admirably fine,
When Doctor Gratitude had left the Spot,
All that he ſaid was charming——and forgot.

Your Doctor's Potion, Patience, and the Bark,
May hit both mental, and material Mark;
One ſerves to keep the Ague from the Mind,
As t'other does, from its corporeal Rind:
There is, methinks, in their reſpective Growth,
A fair Analogy betwixt 'em both.

For what the Bark is to the growing Tree,
To human Mind, that, Patience ſeems to be;
They hold the Principles of Growth together,
And blunt the Force of Accident, and Weather:
Bar'd of its Bark, a Tree, we may compute,
Will not remain much longer on its Root.

And Mind in Mortals, that are wiſely will'd,
Will hardly bear to have its Patience peel'd:
Nothing, in fine, contributes more to Living,
Phyſic, or Food, than Patience and Thankſgiving;
Patience defends us from all outward Hap;
Of inward Life Thankſgiving is the Sap.

VERSES

VERSES written under a PRINT,

The Salutation of the B. VIRGIN.

SEE reprefented here, in Light and Shade,
  The Angels Vifit to the bleffed Maid;
To *Mary*, deftin'd, when the Time fhould come,
To bear the *Saviour* in her virgin womb;
Explaining to her the myfterious Plan
Of Man's Redemption——*his becoming Man*.

When ev'ry previous Wonder had been **done**,
The Virgin then was to conceive a Son;
And, to prepare her for the grand Event,
From God his Father *Gabriel* was fent,
To hail the chofen Organ of his Birth
Of *God with us*,——of JESUS upon Earth.

Unable to exprefs celeftial Things
Imagination adds expanded Wings
To human Form exact, and beauteous Face;
Which Angels have, but with angelic Grace,
Free from all Groffnefs and Defect; nor feen
But with a pure chafte Eye, divinely keen.

O 2

Such

Such *Mary*'s was, whofe Pofture here defign'd
The moft profound Humility of Mind;
Modeftly afking how the Thing could be;
And faying, when inform'd of Gcd's Decree,
Behold the Handmaid of the Lord! his Will
Let him, according to thy Word, fulfill.

What fair Inftruction may the Scene impart
To them, who look beyond the Painter's Art!
Who, in th' angelic Meffage from above,
See the Revealing of God's gracious Love
To ev'ry Soul, that yields itfelf to all
That pleafes Him, whatever may befall!

Whatever Circumftance of heav'nly Grace
Might be peculiar to the Virgin's Cafe,
'That holy Thing, that faves a Soul from Sin,
Of God's good Spirit muft be born *within:*
For all *Salvation* is, upon the whole,
The Birth of Jesus *in the human Soul.*

DITTO,

DITTO, under a PRINT

REPRESENTING

CHRIST in the Midst of the DOCTORS.

ENGAG'D, amidst the Doctors here, behold,
  In deep Difcourfe, a Child of twelve Years old;
Who fhow'd, whatever Queftion they prefer'd,
A Wifdom that aftonifh'd all who heard,
And found, in afking, or in anfw'ring Youth,
Of Age fo tender, fuch a Force of Truth.

  Obferve his mild, but penetrating Look;
Thofe bearded Sages poring o'er their Book:
That meek old Prieft, with placid Face of Joy;
That pharifaic Frowner at the Boy:
That penfive Rabbi, feeming at a Stand;
That ferious Matron, lifting up her Hand.

  A Group of Heads, as painting Fancy taught,
Hints at the various Attitude of Thought
In diff'rent Hearers, all intent upon
The wond'rous Graces that in Jefus fhon:
Each Afpect witneffing the fame Surprize,
From whence his Underftanding fhould arife.

  We know, at prefent, what the learned Jew,
Difputing in the Temple, little knew;

That

That, thro' this Child, in every Anfwer made,
God's own eternal Wifdom was difplay'd;
That their Meffiah, then, the Truths inftill'd
Which, grown to Man, He perfectly fulfill'd.

We know that his corporeal Prefence then
On Earth, as Man, was requifite for Men;
That, by his Spirit, He is prefent ftill,
And always was, to Men of upright Will:
To faving Truth, whatever Doctors fay,
His inward Guidance muft affure the Way.

Whether his Actions therefore be pourtray'd
In printed Letter, or in figur'd Shade,
The Books, the Pictures, that we read, or fee,
Should raife Reflection, in fome due Degree;
And ferve as Memorandums, to recall
The Teacher Jesus, in the Midft of All.

PASCAL's Character of Himfelf.

I Love and honour a poor humble State,
  Becaufe my Saviour *Jefus Chrift* was poor;
And Riches too, that help us to abate
The Miferies, which other Men endure.

I render back no Injuries again;
Becaufe I wifh the Doer's Cafe like mine;

In

In which, nor Good, nor Evil, as from Men
Is minded much, but from an Hand divine.

   I aim, fincerely, to be juft and true;
For my good Will to all Mankind extends:
A Tendernefs of Heart, I think, is due,
Where ftricter Ties unite me to my Friends.

   Whether in Converfation, or alone,
Still to my Mind God's Prefence I recall:
My Actions wait the Judgment of his Throne,
And 'tis to Him I confecrate them all.

   Thefe are my Thoughts, and briefly thus difplay'd;
I thank my Saviour for them ev'ry Day;
Who, of a poor, weak, finful Man, has made
A Man exempt from Vice's evil Sway.

   Such is the Force of his infpiring Grace!
For all my Good to that alone I owe;
Since, if my own corrupted Self I trace,
I'm Nothing elfe but Mifery and Woe.

ARMELLE

ARMELLE NICHOLAS's Account of Herself.

From the FRENCH.

TO the God of my Love, in the Morning, said she,
    Like a Child to its Parent, when waking I flee;
With a Longing to serve him, and please him, I rise,
And before him kneel down, as if seen by these Eyes:
I resign up myself to his absolute Will,
Which I beg that in me he would always fulfill;
That the Pray'rs of the Day, by whomever prefer'd,
For the Good of each Soul, may be also thus heard.

    If, oblig'd to attend on some houshold Affair,
I have scarce so much Time as to say the Lord's Pray'r,
This gives me no Trouble: my dutiful Part
Is Obedience to Him, whom I have at my Heart,
As well at my Work, as retiring to pray,
And his Love does not suffer in mine a Decay;
He has taught me Himself, that a Work, which I do
For his Sake, is a Pray'r very real and true.

    I dress in his Presence, and learn to confess
That his provident Kindness supplies me with Dress:
In the midst of all outward Employment I find
A Conversing with him of an intimate Kind:
How sweet is the Labour! his loving Regard
So supporting ones Mind, that it thinks nothing hard;

While

While the Limbs are at Work, in the feeking to pleafe
So belov'd a Companion, **the Mind** is at Eafe.

In his Prefence I eat and I drink; and reflect
How Food, of his Gift, is the growing Effect;
How his Love to my Soul is fo great, and fo good,
Juft as if it were fed with his own Flefh and Blood:
What a Virtue this Feeder, his Meat, and his Drink
Has to kindle one's Heart, I muft leave you **to** think;
He alone can exprefs it, no Language of mine,
Were my Life fpent in fpeaking, could ever define.

When perhaps by hard Ufage, **or** Wearinefs preft,
I myfelf am too apt to be fretful at beft,
Love fhows me, forthwith, how **I** ought to take Heed
Not to nurfe the leaft Anger, by Word or by Deed;
And He fets fuch a Watch at the Door of my Lips,
That of hafty crofs Words there is nothing that flips;
Such irregular Paffions, as feek to furprife,
Are crufh'd, and are conquer'd, as foon as they **rife.**

Or, if e'er I give Place to **an Humour fo bad,**
My Mind has no Reft 'till Forgivenefs be had;
I confefs all my Faults, as if He had not known,
And my Peace is renew'd, **by** a Goodnefs his own;
In a Manner fo free, as if, after my Sin,
More ftrongly confirm'd than **before it had** been:
By a Mercy fo tender my Heart **is** reclaim'd,
And the more to love Him by its Failing inflam'd.

P

Sometimes

Sometimes I perceive that he hideth his Face,
And I seem like a Person depriv'd of all Grace;
Then I say——'Tis no Matter, altho' thou conceal
Thyself as thou pleasest, I'll keep to my Zeal;
I'll love Thee, and serve Thee, however this Rod
May be sent to chastise, for I know Thou art God;
And with more Circumspection I stand upon Guard,
'Till of such a great Blessing no longer debar'd.

But a Suff'ring, so deep, having taught me to try
What I am in my Selfhood, I learn to rely
More firmly on Him, who was pleas'd to endure
The severest Extremes, to make way for our Cure:
To conform to his Pattern, as Love shall see fit,
My Faith in the *Saviour* resolves to submit;
For no more than my Self (if the Word may go free)
Can I live without Him, can He help loving me.

Well assur'd of his Goodness, I pass the whole Day,
And my Work, hard or easy, is felt as a Play;
I am thankful in Feelings, but, Pleasure or Smart,
It is rather Himself that I love in my Heart.
When they urge me to Mirth, I think, O! were it known
How I meet the best Company when I'm alone!
To my dear Fellow-creatures what ties me each Hour
Is the Love of my God, to the best of my Pow'r.

At the Hour of the Night, when I go to my Rest,
I repose on his Love, like a Child at the Breast;

And

And a sweet, peaceful Silence invites me to keep
Contemplating Him, **to my** dropping asleep:
Many Times a good **Thought,** by its gentle Delight,
Has with-held me from **Sleep,** a good Part of the Night,
In adoring his Love, that continues to share
To a poor, wretched Creature, so special a Care.

This——after my Heart was converted at last,
Is the Life I have led for these twenty Years past:
My Love has not chang'd, and my innermost Peace,
Tho' it ever seem'd full, has gone on to increase:
'Tis an infinite Love **that has** fill'd **me,** and fed
My still rising Hunger **to eat of its Bread;**
So satisfi'd still, as if such an Excess
Could have Nothing more added, **than what** I possess.

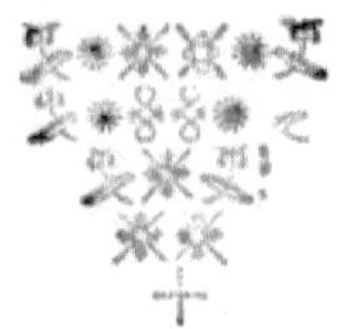

REFLEC-

REFLECTIONS

On the foregoing ACCOUNT.

HOW full a Proof of Heav'ns *all-present* Aid
 Was *good Armelle,* a simple Servant Maid!
A poor *French* Girl, by Parentage and Birth
Of low, and mean Condition upon Earth;
By Education ignorant indeed,
She, all her Life, could neither write nor read.

 But she had *that* which all the Force of Art
Could neither give, nor take away——an *Heart;*
An honest, humble, well difposed Will,
The true Capacity for higher Skill
Than what the World, with all its learned Din,
Could teach——she learn'd her Leffon from *within:*
Plain, single Leffon of effential Kind,
The *Love* of GOD's *pure Prefence* in her Mind.
Her artlefs, innocent, attentive Thought
Was at the *Source* of all *true* Knowledge taught:
There she could read the Characters impreft
Upon the Mind of ev'ry human Breaft;
The native Laws prefcrib'd to ev'ry Soul;
And *Love,* the one Fulfiller of the Whole.

 This *holy Love* to know, and practice well,
Became the sole Endeavour of *Armelle:* ·

Of

Of outward Things, the Management and Rule,
She wisely took from this *internal* School:
In ev'ry Work well done by *such* a Hand,
The Work was *servile*, but the Thing was *grand*.
There was a Dignity in all she did,
'Tho' from the World by meaner Labours hid;
If mean *below*, not so esteem'd *above*,
Where all the *Grand* of Labour is the *Love*:
In vain to boast Magnificence of Scene;
It is all *Meanness*, if the *Love* be *mean*.

St. CECILIA's HYMN.

O! Born of a Virgin, **most** lowly and meek,
   Thou sent **of** thy Father lost Creatures to seek,
Vouchsafe, in the Manner that pleaseth thee best,
To kindle thy Love, in my virginal Breast;
Let the Words of my Mouth, **and the Thoughts of my**
      Heart,
Obey the sweet Force, which thy Grace shall impart;
Whilst Angels assist me **to** offer my Vows
To **the God of my Life,** my Redeemer and Spouse.

  My Life, I esteem, O Creator divine,
As a loving Impression out-flowing from thine;
As an act of thy Bounty, **that** gives us a Part
Of the Light, Love and Glory, which thou thyself art:

May

May I always as little thy Pleasure oppose,
As the pure simple Nature from whence I arose;
And by thee, and for thee, created, fulfill
In Thought, Word and Deed, thy adorable Will.

By this blessed Will, howsoever made known,
With a dutiful Joy will I govern my own;
And, deaf to all tempting Inchantments of Sin,
I will hearken to Thee, my Redeemer within;
Thy Words will I ponder by Night, and by Day,
And the Light of thy Gospel shall mark out my Way:
'Till at length I arrive at the Honour I claim,
To live like a Virgin, baptiz'd in thy Name.

A
LETTER to a LADY,

OCCASIONED

By her desiring the Author to revise and polish the Poems of Bishop KEN.

YOUR Book again with Thanks——of worthy Men
   One of the worthiest was Bishop *Ken.*
Without Offence to Authors, far above
Ten Men of Learning is one Man of Love:
How many Bishops, and Divines renown'd,
Time after Time, the Catechism expound!

And

And which, of all, so help it to impart
Th' essential Doctrine, Purity of Heart?

His Choice of Poetry, when civil Rage
O'erturn'd a Throne, the last revolving Age;
When Churches felt, as well as States, the Shock
That drove the pious Pastor from his Flock;
His Choice of Subjects, not of Party kind,
But simply fit for ev'ry Christian Mind,
Are Proofs of gen'rous Virtue, and sublime,
And high Encomiums on the Force of Rhime.

His Rhimes, if those of *Dryden*, or of *Pope*,
Excel on Subjects of a diff'rent Scope,
It is because they only chose the Mold
Where Ore shone brightest, whether Lead, or Gold:
He, less concern'd for superficial Glare,
Made Weight, and Worth, his more especial Care,
They took the Tinsel of the fabl'd Nine,
He the substantial Metal from the Mine.

His Phrase (sometimes same Sentence may be past
On theirs) might have more artificial Cast;
But, in the main, his Pieces, as they stand,
Could scarce be alter'd by a second Hand:
Patchwork Improvements, in the modern Stile,
Bestow'd upon some venerable Pile,
Do but deface it——Poems to revise
That *Ken* has writ——another *Ken* must rise.

The

The Dedication, where the Cafe is fhown
Of a Greek Saint, of old, fo like his own;
The **Preface**, Introduction, and the View
To *Jefus*——Point which all his Works purfue——
Arife to Mind, and tempt to try the Cafe
Of reprefenting the imperfect Trace;
To make, as Memory can beft **recall**
It's leading Thoughts, one Preface out of all.

Imagine then the good old Man reclin'd
On Couch, or Chair, and mufing in his Mind,
How **to** adjuft the Prefatory Hint,
To all the Lines that he gave Leave to print;
Thinking on *Gregory*, whofe former Fate
Bore fuch Refemblance to his own of late;
Thinking on *Jefus*, **and** opprefs'd with **Pain,**
Inditing thus th' apologizing Strain.

    " **In all my Pains I court the facred Mufe,**
" Verfe is the only Laudanum I **ufe;**
" Verfe, and the Name of *Jefus,* in **the Line,**
" **The** Chriftian's univerfal Anodyne;
" **To** hymn his faving Love to all Mankind
" **Softens my** Grief, and recreates my Mind;
" Thy Glory, *Jefu,* while my Songs intend,
" May thy good Spirit blefs them to that End!

    " **Like** deftin'd *Jonah* caft into the Deep,
" **To fave** the Veffel from the ftormy Sweep,

                                                                            " And

" And, wafted providentially to **Shore,**
" I rifk the boift'rous Element no more ;
" But whilft alone I tread the diftant Strand,
" **Safe o'er the** Waves that all may come to Land,
" **Whom** once I call'd Companions on **the** Sea,
" **I** pray to *Jefus,* whom the Winds obey.

" Thus *Nazianzen Gregory,* of old,
" Whom Faction drove from his beloved Fold,
" Could will a *Jonah's* Lot, to be caft o'er,
" If his Difmiffion might the Calm reftore.
" However fhort of **this** illuftrious **Saint,**
" **Yet I can find, from Virtues that I want,**
" A Caufe **to pray that reigning Feuds may ceafe,**
" To hope in *Jefus* **for a calming Peace.**

" **The Saint,** expell'd **by a** tumultuous Rage,
" **Chear'd** with diviner Songs his drooping Age;
" With Will refign'd, in his retir'd Abode,
" On Chriftian Themes compos'd the various Ode:
" Thus, to my Clofet prompted to retire,
" Nothing on this Side Heav'n **do I** require;
" Employ'd in Hymns, **tho'** with unequal Skill,
" To confecrate **to** *Jefus* all my Will.

" With Pain and Sicknefs, when the Saint was griev'd,
" His anxious Mind a facred Song reliev'd;
" **Oft,** when opprefs'd, the Subject which he fang,
" **Mix'd** with Devotion, fweeten'd ev'ry Pang;

Q

" So,

" So, being banish'd by unruly Heat,
" With Hymns I feek to folace my Retreat;
" Be my Confinement ever fo extreme,
" The Love of *Jefus* is a fpecial Theme.

" When the Apoftate *Julian* decreed
" That Pagan Poets Chriftians fhould not read,
" The Saint, who knew the fubtle Edict's Caufe,
" Made Verfe to triumph o'er the Tyrant's Laws:
" May I, while Poetry is unreftrain'd,
" Tho' more in thefe, than pagan Times, profan'd,
" Show, that what real Charms it has belong
" To *Jefus*, Founder of the Chriftian Song.

" When *Gregory* was forc'd to leave his Flock,
" He chofe in Verfe the Gofpel to unlock;
" That flowing Numbers might th' Attention gain,
" So long forbidden to his preaching Strain:
" My Care for them, whom I was forc'd to leave,
" Taught, and untaught, what Doctrine to receive,
" Would hint in Rhimes, to all whom they fhall reach,
" What *Jefus* only, in themfelves, can teach.

" For fake of Peace did *Gregory* withdraw,
" And wifh'd more Leaders to obferve that Law;
" By which Refigners of Dominion, here,
" Purchafe much greater in the heav'nly Sphere:
" In Hopes of Peace, more joyfully I fhook
" Preferment off, than e'er I undertook;

" For

" For all the **Flock**, and banish'd Head befide,
" My **Comfort** is that *Jefus* can provide.

" **When** worldly Politics, and Luft of Rule,
" Prevail'd againft him in a Chriftian School,
" The Saint retir'd, and labour'd to difperfe
" Ungrateful Difcord by harmonious Verfe:
" Sharing his Fate, I fhare in his Defire
" Of Difcord drown'd, and of an hymning Lyre
" To tune **the Hopes** of Peace; and in the Name
" Of *Jefus*, rightly hop'd for, to proclaim.

" This Prince of Peace, this Origin divine,
" Vouchfafe to aid the well intended Line,
" To teach the Reader's Heart, and, by his Grace,
" Make thefe poor Labours ufeful in their Place.
" O might they raife, in any fingle Soul,
" One Spark of Love, one Glimpfe of the great **Whole**,
" **That** will poffefs it, when by Thee poffeft,
" *Jefus!* Th' eternal Song of all **the** bleft!"

A HINT to Chriftian POETS.

WHERE now the *Jove*, the *Phæbus*, and the *Nine*,
    Invok'd in Aid of Greek, and Roman Line;
The Verfe-infpiring Oracle, and Stream,
Delphos, and *Helicon*, and every Theme

Of

Of charming Fictions, which the Poets sung,
To shew the Beauties of a reigning Tongue?

   The **Wars of** Gods, and Goddesses, and Men,
Employ'd an *Homer's,* and a *Virgil's* **Pen:**
An *Epicurus* taught, that, with this Ball,
The Gods, at Ease, had no Concern at all:
And a *Lucretius* follow'd, to rehearse
His *Greek* Impieties, in *Latin* Verse.

   Such were the Bibles **of** the Pagan **Age,**
Sung at the Feast, and acted on the Stage;
Transform'd to pompous, or to luscious Ode,
As *Bacchus, Mars,* or *Venus* was the Mode:
Dumb Deities, **at Wit's** profuse Expence,
Worshipp'd with **Sounds that** echoed to no Sense.

   The *Christian* **Bard has, from a** *real* Spring
Of Inspiration, **other Themes to** sing;
No vain Philosophy, **no fabled Rhime,**
But sacred Story, simple and sublime,
By holy Prophets told; **to** whom belong
The Subjects worthy of the Pow'rs of Song.

   Shun then, ye born with Talents that may **grace**
The most important Truths, their hapless Case;
From ranting, high, theatrical Bombast,
To low Sing-song of meretricious Cast:
Shun ev'ry Step, by which a *Pagan* **Muse**
Could lead her Clients to the Stage, **or Stews.**

Let

Let no Examples tempt you to profane
The Gift——abhorrent of all hurtful Strain:
Contemn the vicious, tho' prevailing Fame,
That gains, by proftituting Verfe, a Name:
Take the forbearing Hint; and all the reft
Will rife fpontaneous in your purer Breaft.

ON THE

DISPOSITION of MIND,

REQUISITE FOR

Tlie right Ufe and Underftanding of the HOLY SCRIPTURES.

TO hear the Words of Scripture, or to read,
   With good Effect, requires a *threefold* Heed;
If incompleat, it only can produce
Hearings, and Readings, of no fort of Ufe.

   The firft INTENTION; or a fix'd Defign
To learn the Truth concerning Things divine;
If previous Difpofition be not good,
How fhall a ferious Point be underftood?

   The next ATTENTION; not the outward Part,
But the fair Liftening of an honeft Heart:

Sound

Sound may, and Figure, strike the Ear and Eye,
But Sense and Meaning to the Mind apply.

   The last RETENTION; or the keeping pure,
From hurtful Mixtures, what is clear and sure:
In vain the Purpose, and the Pains have been
To gain a Good, if not secur'd within.

   Without INTENTION Truth no more can stay,
Than Seed can grow upon a public Way;
The more it is affecting, plain, and grand,
The less will heedless Persons understand.

   Without ATTENTION 'twill have no more Fruit,
Than Seed on stony Ground, for want of Root;
That makes a Show with hasty Shoots awhile,
And then betrays the Barrenness of Soil.

   Without RETENTION all is lost at last,
Like Seed among the Thorns and Briars cast:
So worldly Cares, and worldly Riches both,
May mix with Truth, and choak it in its Growth.

   As Ground produces goodly Crops of Corn,
If good, and free from Footstep, Stone, or Thorn;
That of good Hearts has Properties as plain——
To *seek* the Truth, *receive* it, and *retain*.

On

On the same SUBJECT,

IN A

LETTER to Mr. PONTHIEU.

WE ought to read, my worthy Friend *Ponthieu*,
　　All holy Scriptures, with a Scripture View:
Writ for our Learning, as their Aim and Scope
Is Patience, Comfort, and the blessed Hope
Of everlasting Life, a Reader's Aim,
To understand them right, should be the same.

　The Prosecution of this happier Quest
If Doubts and Difficulties shall molest;
And huge Debates, on Passages obscure,
Be suffer'd to eclipse the plain and sure;
The more he reads, the more this rambling Art
Will fill his Head, but never touch his Heart;
With controversial Circumstances fill,
On which the Learned have employ'd their Skill,
With such Success, that scarce the plainest Text
Can be produc'd, but what they have perplext
In such a Manner, that, while all assign
To Scripture Page Authority divine,
The Compliment is rather paid, for Sake
Of such Constructions as they please to make.

　Down from the Pope to the obscurest Sect,
Too many Proofs are seen of this Effect;

Of

Of making one fame Scripture a Retreat
For ev'ry Party's oppofite Conceit:
Profaner Wits, obferving this, miftook,
And laid the Fault upon the Bible Book;
Taking the fame Variety of Ways,
By fancied Meanings for its ancient Phrafe,
To cry it down, as Sects were wont to ufe
To cry it up, for their peculiar Views.

 As this Excefs, from Age to Age, has grown
To fuch a monftrous Height within our own,
What a fincere, impartial, honeft Mind
In Search of Truth, does it require, to find!
What calm Attention, what unfeign'd Defire
To hear its Voice does Truth itfelf require!
In Scripture Phrafe, what an *unceafing* **Pray'r**
Should for its facred Influence prepare!
Becaufe, whatever Comments we recall,
The Difpofition of the Mind is all.

 'Tis in this Point (undoubtedly the main)
That facred Books do differ from prophane:
They do not afk, fo **much**, for letter'd Skill
To underftand them, as for fimple Will:
For as a fingle, or clear-fighted Eye
Admits the Light, like an unclouded Sky,
So is the Truth, by Scripture Phrafe defign'd,
Receiv'd into a well difpofed Mind;
By the fame Spirit, ready to admit
The written Word, as they poffefs'd who writ;

Who

Who writ, if Chriftians do not vainly boaft,
By Infpiration of The Holy Ghoft.

In Books fo writ this great Advantage lies,
That the firft Author of them never dies;
But is ftill prefent to inftruct, and fhow,
To them who feek him, what they need to know;
Still, by his chofen Servants, to unfold,
As He fees fit, the Myfteries of old;
To re-confirm what any facred Pen
Has writ, by Proof within the Hearts of Men.

This is the true and folid Reafon, why
No Difficulties, now objected, lie
Againft the Volumes writ fo long ago,
And in a Language that few People know;
Subject, as Books, to Errors and Miftakes,
Which oft tranfcribing, or tranflating makes;
While Manners, Cuftoms, Ufages of Phrafe
Well known of old, but not fo in our Days,
For many obvious Reafons, muft elude
The utmoft Force of criticifing Feud:
Still, all Editions verbally contain
The fimple, neceffary Truths and plain,
Of Gofpel Doctrine; and-the Spirit's Aid,
Which is the chief, is not at all decay'd.

Nor can it hurt a Reader to fufpend
His Judgement, where he does not comprehend

R

A darker

A darker Text; however it appear,
He knows it cannot contradict a clear:
So that with all the Helps, of ev'ry Kind,
The ſhorteſt, and the ſureſt, is to mind
When read, or heard, and inwardly digeſt
The plaineſt Texts, as Rules to all the reſt;
To pray for that Good Spirit, which alone
Can make its former Inſpirations known;
The promis'd Comforter, th' unerring Guide,
Who, by Chriſt's Word, was always to abide
Within His Church, not only in the paſt,
But in all Ages, while the World ſhould laſt;
A Church diſtinguiſh'd, in the ſacred Code,
By his perpetual Guidance and Abode.

   Such is the Teacher whom our Saviour choſe,
And writ no Books, as human Learning knows;
Loth as it is, of later Years, to preach,
That by this Teacher He will always teach;
Bleſs all the Means of Learning, or the Want,
To them who after His Inſtructions pant:
Of reading Helps, what holy Men expreſs'd,
When mov'd to write, are certainly the beſt;
But for the real, underſtanding Part,
The Book of Books is ev'ry Man's own Heart.

A STRIC-

A STRICTURE

ON THE

Bishop of Glocester's Doctrine of GRACE.

WRITING, or Scripture, facred or profane,
    Can only render Hiftory more plain
Of what was done, or faid, by God or Man,
Since the Creation of the World began:
Tho' ev'ry Word in facred Page be true,
To give *Account*, is all that it can do.

    Now an Account of Things, as done, or faid,
Is not a *living* Letter, but a *dead;*
A Picture only, which may reprefent,
But cannot give us what is really meant:
He that has got a Map into his Hand
May ufe the *Name*, but knows it is not *Land.*

    So in *the Bible* when we come to look,
(That is, by way of Eminence, *The Book)*
We muft not fancy that it can beftow
The Things themfelves, which we defire to know;
It can but yield, however true and plain,
Verbal Directions how we may obtain.

    Tho' a Prefcription be directly fure,
Upon the Patient's taking it, to cure,

R 2

No one imagines that the worded Bill
Becomes, itſelf, the Remedy for Ill;
The Med'cines taken, as the Bill directs,
Procure the ſalutiferous Effects.

Who then can place in any written Code
The Holy Ghoſt's, the Comforter's Abode?
* *Conſtant Abode———ſupreme Illumination* ———
What Copy can be *This*, or what Tranſlation?
The Spirit's Dwelling, by th' atteſting Pen
Of all th' inſpir'd, is in the Hearts of Men.

'Were *Books* his conſtant Reſidence indeed,
What muſt the Millions do who cannot *read?*
When they, who can, ſo vary in their Senſe,
What muſt diſtinguiſh true from falſe Pretence?
If they muſt follow where the learned guide,
What diff'rent Spirits in one Book abide?

Genius for *Paradox*, however bright,
Can not well juſtify this Overſight:
Better to own the Truth, for the Truth's Sake,
Than to perſiſt in ſuch a groſs Miſtake:
Books are but Books; th' illuminating Part
Depends on God's good Spirit, in the *Heart.*

The

---

* *For though, according to the Promiſe, his ordinary Influence occaſionally aſſiſts the faithful of all Ages; yet his conſtant Abode, and ſupreme Illumination, is in the ſacred Scriptures of the* **New Teſtament.** **P. 39.** *The Doctrine of Grace, &c. by the* Biſhop *of* Glouceſter.

The Comforter, Chrift faid, *will come unto,*
Abide with, dwell in, (not your *Books,* but) *you:*
Juft as abfurd an Ink and Paper Throne
For God's Abode, as one of Wood or Stone:
If to adore an Image be Idolatry,
To deify a Book is *Bibliolatry.*

ON THE

Converfion of St. PAUL.

IN *Paul*'s Converfion we difcern the Cafe
  Of human Talents, wanting heavenly Grace:
What Perfecutions, 'till he faw the Light,
Againft the Chriftian Church did he excite!
By his own Reafon led into Miftake,
Amongft the Flock what Havock did he make!
Within himfelf when, verily, he thought,
That, all the while, he did but what he ought.

  His Ufe of Reafon cannot be deni'd,
Nor legal Zeal, nor moral Life befide;
Blamelefs as any *Jew,* or *Greek* could claim,
Who fhow'd Averfion to the Chriftian Name;
His Fund of Learning fome are pleas'd to add;
And yet, with all th' Endowments which he had,
From Place to Place, with eager Steps, he trod,
To perfecute the real Church of God.

When

When to *Damascus*, for the like Intent,
With the High Prieft's Authority he went;
Struck to the Ground, by a diviner Ray,
The *reaf'ning, legal, moral* Zealot lay;
To the plain Queftion put by JESUS——*why
Perfecute me?* had only to reply,
What fhall I do?——his Reafon, and his Wrath
Were both convinc'd, and he embrac'd the Faith.

His outward loft, his inward Sight renew'd,
Truth in its native Evidence he view'd;
With three Days Faft he nourifh'd his Concern,
And, a new Conduct well prepar'd to learn,
Good *Ananias*, whom he came to bind,
Was fent to cure, and to baptife the Blind:
A deftin'd Martyr, to his *Jewifh* Zeal,
Of *Chriftian* Faith confers the facred Seal.

Of nobler Ufe his Reafon, while it ftood
Without a *Conference* with *Flefh* and *Blood*,
Still, and fubmiffive; when, within, begun
The Father's Revelation of the Son;
Whom, 'till the *Holy Spirit* rife to fhow,
No Pow'r of Thought can ever come to know;
The faving Myftery, obfcur'd by Sin,
Itfelf muft manifeft itfelf, *within*.

Thus, taught of God, *Paul* faw the Truth appear
To his enlighten'd Underftanding clear:

The

The Pow'r of *Chrift* himfelf, and nothing lefs,
Could move its Perfecutor to profefs:
He learn'd, and told it from the real Ground,
And prov'd, to all the *Chriftian* World around,
That true Religion had its true Foundation,
Not in Man's *Reafon*, but God's *Revelation*.

A CONTRAST

BETWEEN

Human Reafon and divine Illumination,

Exemplified in three different CHARACTERS.

AN humble Chriftian, to whofe inward Sight
God fhows the Truth, and then infpires to write;
Becaufe of deeper Certainties declar'd,
Than what the Mind perceives, when unprepar'd,
From them, who meafure all on which he treats,
By the fix'd Standard of their own Conceits,
Meets with Contempt; and very few will own
The real Truths, which he has really fhown.

A fharp Philofopher, who thinks to find
By his own Reafon, his own Strength of Mind,
Sublimer Things, that lie fo far beyond
The Scenes to which fuch Forces correfpond;

From

From them, who love to fpeculate like him,
And think all Light, but that of Reafon, dim,
Meets with Admirers; tho' he reafons wrong,
And draws the Dupes, if plaufible, along.

    Now, tho' a Searcher fhould no more defpife
The ufe of Reafon, than he fhould of Eyes;
Yet, if there be a ftill fuperior Light,
Than Faculty of Reafon has, or Sight;
Which all Religion feems to pre-fuppofe,
That God on fuch, as rightly feek, beftows;
In higher Matters how fhould he decide,
Who takes his Reafon, only, for his Guide?

    Such Words as Nature, Reafon, Common Senfe,
Furnifh all Writers with one fame Pretence;
Altho', in many an acknowledg'd Cafe,
They muft fall fhort, without fuperior Grace:
So that, in Things of more momentous kind,
Nature itfelf directs us not to mind,
If facred Truth be heartily defir'd,
The greateft Reaf'ners, but the moft infpir'd.

    Whence comes the Value for the Scripture Page,
So juftly due, fo paid thro' ev'ry Age?
Not writ by Men of Learning, and of Parts,
But honeft, humble, and enlighten'd Hearts:
Who, when they reafon'd, reafon'd very well;
But how enabl'd, let their Writings tell:

Not

Not one of all, but who afcribes the Force
Of Truth difcover'd to an higher Source.

Take thefe three Men, fo diff'rent in their Way,
For Inftance, *Behmen*, *Bolingbroke*, and *Hay*:
They all philofophize on facred Themes,
And build on Reafon, the two laft, their Schemes:
The firft affirms, that his *Principia* flow
From what God's Spirit gave him Pow'r to know;
As much a promis'd, as a certain Guide,
With *Chrift*'s Difciples *ever* to **abide.**

If *Bolingbrokian* Reafon muft prevail,
All *Infpiration* is **an** idle Tale:
Writers **by** that, from *Mofes* down to *Paul*,
I fpare to mention how he treats them all:
Now if he err'd, whence did that Error fpring?
His *Reafon* told him there was no fuch Thing;
Foundrefs, in her philofophizing Caft,
Of **all** his *firft* Philofophy, and *laft*.

Hay, better taught, and more ingenuous Spark,
Gropes with his Reafon betwixt Light and Dark;
Now, gentle Glimmerings of Truth difplays;
Now, loft in Fancy's intricater Maze,
A motley Mixture of fuch Things has got,
As Reafon **could** difcover, and could not:
Which all the Builders on its boafted Plan
Prove to be juft as manifold as Man.

S

This

This *Behmen* knew; and, in his humble Way,
Became enlighten'd by a fteadier Ray;
Firft taught himfelf, by what he heard and faw,
Of *Grace* and *Nature* he explain'd the Law;
That facred Spirit, from which both arofe,
Taught him, of both, the Secrets to difclofe
To them, who, ufing Eyes, and Reafon too,
Were fit for Truth in a diviner View.

He does not write from Reafon; nor appeals,
Of courfe, to what that Faculty reveals;
Yet, if the common Privilege be mine,
Reafon may fee, that Something more divine
Lies hid, in what the Books of *Behmen* teach,
Tho' it furpafs its apprehenfive Reach;
May fee, from what it really apprehends,
That all mere Reas'ners *Behmen* far tranfcends.

Fond of his Reafon as a Man may be,
He fhould confefs its limited Degree;
And, by its fair Direction, feek to find
A furer Guide to Things of deeper Kind:
The moft fharp-fighted feek for other Men,
Who may have feen what lies beyond their Ken;
And, in religious Matters, moft Appeals
Are made by Men to that, which *God* reveals.

How is it poffible to judge, aright,
Of heav'nly Things, but by an heav'nly Light?

Contemn'd

Contemn'd by *Bolingbroke*, by *Hay* confefs'd,
By *Behmen*, poffibly at leaft, poffefs'd:
Truly infpir'd, as pious Minds have thought,
Jacob was known to live as he had taught;
And at his laft departing Moment cry'd,
Now I *go hence to Paradife*——and di'd.

SOCRATES's REPLY,

CONCERNING

HERACLITUS's WRITINGS.

WHEN *Socrates* had read, as Authors note,
  A certain Book that *Heraclitus* wrote;
Deep in its Matter, and obfcure befide;
Ask'd his Opinion of it, he repli'd,
All that I underftand is good and true,
And what I don't is, I believe, fo too.

  Thus anfwer'd *Socrates*, whom Greece confeft
The wifeft of her Sages, and the beft;
By Juftice mov'd, and Candour, of a Piece
With that Philofopher's Repute in Greece:
Worthy of Imitation, to be fure,
When a good Writer is fometimes obfcure.

  All the haranguing, therefore, on the Theme
Of deep Obfcurity, in *Jacob Behme*,

Is

Is but itfelf obfcure; for he might fee
Farther, 'tis poffible, than you, or me:
Meanwhile, the Goodnefs of his plainer Page
Demands the Anfwer of the Grecian Sage.

    The *Stuff* **and** *Nonfenfe, Labyrinth* **and** *Maze,*
Madnefs, Enthufiafm, and fuch like Phrafe,
Its quick Beftowers are oblig'd to own,
Ought not to **move us, by its** eager Tone,
More than they ought, **in Reafon,** to be mov'd,
Should we fo paint a Work which they approv'd.

  . **He,** whom the fair Socratical Remark
Defcribes, was call'd σκοτεινος, or the *dark;*
Yet his wife Reader, from the Good in View,
Thought that his darker Paffages were true:
He would not judge of what, as yet, lay hid,
By what he did not fee, but what he did.

    The Books of *Behme,* as none are tied to read,
To blame unread they **have as little need:**
As they who read them moft, the moft commend,
Others, at leaft, may venture to fufpend;
Or think, with ref'rence to fuch Books as thefe,
Of Heraclitus, and of Socrates.

THOUGHTS

THOUGHTS upon HUMAN REASON,

OCCASIONED BY

Reading some extravagant Declamations in it's Favour.

YES, I have read them——but I cannot find
  Much Depth of Sense in Writers of this Kind:
They all retail, as they proceed along,
Or superficial Sentiments, or wrong:
Of Reason! Reason! they repeat the Cries,
And Reason's Use——which Nobody denies.

  All Sharers in it follow, I suppose,
Each one his Reason, as he does his Nose;
When he intends to reach a certain Spot,
Whether he finds the Road to it, or not:
With equal Sense a *Postulatum* begs
The Use of Reason, as the Use of Legs.

  Full well these rational Adepts declaim
On Points, at which their Reason can take Aim;
But when they talk beyond them, what Mistakes,
Of various Kind, their various Reason makes!
All are for one same Rule; and in its Use
All singly clear, and mutually abstruse.

What

What plainer Demonſtration can be had,
That their original Pretence is bad;
Who ſay——Their own, or human Reaſon's, Light
Muſt needs direct them to determine right?
What greater Proof of a ſuperior Skill
Needful to Reas'ners, reaſon how they will?

Senſe to diſcern, and Reaſon to compare,
Are Gifts that merit our improving Care;
But want an inward Light, when all is done,
As Seeds, and Plants do that of outward Sun:
Main Help neglected, taſteleſs Fruits ariſe;
And Wiſdom grows inſipid in the Wiſe.

Tho' all theſe Reaſon-Worſhippers profeſs
To guard againſt fanatical Exceſs,
Enthuſiaſtic *Heat*——their fav'rite Theme
Draws their Attention to the *cold* Extreme;
Their Fears of *torrid* Fervors freeze a Soul;
To ſhun the *Zone* they ſend it to the Pole.

The very Sound of rational, and plain,
Contents, where Senſe is neither of the twain,
A World of Readers; whoſe polite Concern
Is to be learned, without Pains to learn:
To pleaſe their Palates, with a modiſh Treat,
Cheap is the Coſt——and here is the *Receipt*——

" Let Reaſon, firſt, Imagination, Paſſions,
" Be clean dreſt up in pretty-worded Faſhions;

" Then

" Then let Imagination, Paffions, Reafon,
" Change Places round, at each commodious Seafon;
" 'Till Reafon, Paffions, and Imagination
" Have prov'd the Point, by their compleat Rotation.

O N

FAITH, REASON, and SIGHT,

CONSIDERED AS

The three diftinct Mediums of human PERCEPTION.

THERE is a threefold correfpondent Light,
   That fhines to *Faith*, to *Reafon*, and to *Sight:*
The firft, *Eternal;* bringing into View
Celeftial Objects, if the *Faith* be true;
The next, *Internal;* which the reas'ning Mind
Confults in Truths of an ideal Kind;
The third, *External;* and perceiv'd thereby
All *outward* Objects that affect the Eye.

   Each Light is good within its deftin'd Sphere;
Nor with each other do they interfere:
Faith does not reafon, *Reafon* does not fee,
Nor *Sight* extend beyond a fixt Degree:
Yet Faith in Light of a fuperior Kind
'Cannot be call'd irrational, or blind;

Becaufe

Becauſe an higher Certainty, diſplay'd,
Includes the Force of all inferior Aid.

As Body, Soul, and Spirit make a Man,
Each has the Help of its appointed Plan;
Sight, Hearing, Smell, and Taſte, and feeling Senſe,
What the *corporeal* Nature wants, diſpenſe:
Thinking, Comparing, Judging, and the whole
Of reaſoning Faculties, affiſt the *Soul:*
Faith, and whatever elſe may be expreſt
By Grace celeſtial, makes the *Spirit* bleſt.

To heal Defect, or to avoid Exceſs,
The greater Light ſhould ſtill correct the leſs;
And form, within the right obedient Will,
A *ſeeing, reaſ'ning,* and *believing* Skill:
While Body moves as outward Senſe directs;
And Soul perceives what Reaſon's Light reflects;
And Spirit, fill'd with Luſtre from above,
Obeys by Faith, and operates by Love.

A ſober Perſon, tho' his Eyes are good,
Slights not the Truths by Reaſon underſtood;
Nor juſt Concluſions, under the Pretence
Of Contradiction to his ſeeing Senſe;
Knowing the Limits too that Reaſon hath,
He does not ſeek to quench the Light of Faith;
But rationally grants, that it may teach
What human Stretch of Reaſon cannot reach.

As

As Sight to Reafon, in the Things that lie
Beyond the Ken of the corporeal Eye,
Unhurt, **uninjur'd, yields** itfelf of **courfe,**
So well-taught Reafon owns a higher Force;
By Faith enlighten'd, it enjoys a Reft
In clearer Light to find its own fuppreft;
Suffering no more, for want of its Difplay,
Than Moon and Stars in full meridian Day.

To make the reas'ning Faculty of Man
Do more, or lefs to help him, than it can,
Is equally abfurd; but worfe to flight,
Or want **the** Benefits of *Faith*, **than** *Sight:*
If he who fees no outward Light **be** blind,
How *difmal dark* muft be the *faithlefs* Mind!
The one is only natural Defect,
The other wilful, obftinate Neglect.

Pretence of Reafon for it is Pretence
Foolifh and fatal, in the faddeft Senfe;
For Reafon cannot alter what is true,
Or any more prevent, than Eyes can do;
Both, by the Limits which they feel, proclaim
The real Want **of** a celeftial Flame:
How is it poffible **to fee, in** fine,
The Things of God, without a *Light divine?*

T   A DIA.

A

DIALOGUE

BETWEEN

Rusticus, Theophilus, and Academicus,

ON THE

Nature, Power, and Use of human Learning, in Matters of Religion.

From Mr. Law's Way to divine Knowledge.

RUSTICUS.

YES, *Academicus*, you love to hear
   The Words of *Jacob Behmen* made so clear;
But the Truth is, the fundamental Good,
At which he aims, you have not understood;
Content with such good Notions as befit
Your learned Reason, and your searching Wit,
To make a Talk about, you gather still
More ample Matter for your Hear-say Skill:
You know your self, as well as I, that this
Is all your Joy in him; and hence it is
That you are so impatient, ev'ry Day,
For more and more of what his Pages say;
So vex'd, and puzzl'd, if you cannot find
Their Meaning open'd to your eager Mind;

Nor

Nor add new Notions, and a ſtronger Force,
To heighten ſtill your **Talent of** Diſcourſe.

With all your Value for his Books, as yet,
This Diſpoſition makes you to forget
How oft they tell you, and how well they **ſhow**,
That this inordinate Deſire *to know*,
This heaping **up** of Notions, one by one,
For ſubtle Fancy to deſcant upon,
While *Babel*, **as** you think, is overthrown,
Is building up a new one of your own;
Your *Babyloniſh* Reaſon is the Pow'r,
That ſeeks Materials **to erect its Tow'r:**
The very Scriptures, under ſuch **a Guide,**
Will **only nouriſh your** high-ſoaring Pride;
Nor will you penetrate, with all your Art,
Of *Jacob's* Writings the ſubſtantial Part.

The Works of *Behmen* would you underſtand?
Then, where he ſtood, ſee alſo that you ſtand;
Begin where he began; direct your Thought
To ſeek the Bleſſing only, that he ſought;
The Heart of God; that, by a right true Faith,
He might be ſav'd from Sin, and Satan's Wrath
While thus the humble Seeker ſtood reſign'd,
The Light of God broke in upon his Mind:
But you, devoted to the Pow'r, alone,
Of ſpeculative Reaſon, all your **own,**
Would reach his Ladder's Top at once, nor try
The **Pains** of riſing, Step by Step, ſo high——

But,

But, on this Subject, by your Looks, I fee
You'd rather hear *Theophilus* than me.

THEOPHILUS.

Why really, *Academicus*, the Main
Of all that *Rufticus*, fo bluntly plain,
Has here been faying, tho' it feem fo hard,
Hints Truth enough to put you on your Guard:
Much in the fame Miftake your Mind has been,
That many of my learned Friends are in;
Who, tho' Admirers, to a great Degree,
Of Truths in *Jacob Behmen*, which they fee,
Yet, of all People, have the leaft Pretence
To real Benefit receiv'd from thence:
Train'd up in Controverfy, and Difpute;
Accuftom'd to maintain, or to refute,
All Propofitions, only by the Light
Of their own Reafon judging what is right,
They take this Guide in Truths of ev'ry Kind,
Both where it fees, and where it muft be blind;
So that in Regions, where a Light divine
Demonftrates Truth, and Reafon cannot fhine,
The real Good is hidden from their View,
And fome fuch Syftem rifes up, in Lieu,
As Birth or Education, Mode or Place,
In Courfe of Life, has led them to embrace.

Thus with the learned *Papift*, in his Creed,
The learned *Proteftant* is not agreed;

Not

Not that, to either, Truth and Light have taught
To entertain fo oppofite a Thought;
But Education's contrary Supplies
Have giv'n them *proteftant*, and *popifh* Eyes;
And Reafon being the accuftom'd Light
Of both the Parties, and of either Sight,
Decifions *proteftant*, and *popifh* too,
Can find it Work enough, and Tools enoo,
To fhape Opinions of a diff'rent Growth,
Whilft Learning is an open Field to both;
And, of its Harveft, the inur'd to reap
With greater Skill can fhow the greater Heap.

ACADEMICUS.

So then I muft, as I perceive by you,
Renounce my Learning, and my Reafon too,
If I would gain the neceffary Lights
To underftand what *Jacob Behmen* writes:
I cannot yield, as yet, to fuch Advice;
Nor make the Purchafe at fo dear a Price:
I hope the Study of the Scripture Text
Will do for me; and leave me unperplext
With his deep Matters——Little did I know
That Learning had, in you, fo great a Foe.

THEOPHILUS.

Be not uneafy; Learning has in me
No Foe at all, not in the leaft Degree;

No more than has the Science, or the Skill,
To build an Houſe to dwell in, or a Mill
For grinding Corn——I think an uſeful Art
Of human Things the nobleſt, for my Part:
Knowledge of Books or Languages, or aught
That any Perſon has been duly taught,
I would not aſk him to renounce, or ſay
They might not all be uſeful, in their Way:
I would not blame, within its proper Place,
The Art of throwing Silk, or making Lace;
Or any Art, confin'd to its own Sphere;
But then the Meaſure of its Uſe is there:
Some we call liberal, and ſome we call
Mechanic; now the Circle of them all
Does but ſhow forth, in its moſt perfect Plan,
The natural Abilities of Man;
The Pow'rs, and Faculties of human Mind,
Whether the Man be well, or ill inclin'd:
The moſt unjuſt, and wicked Debauchee,
Regarding neither God, nor Man, may be,
In any one, or more, of all the Train,
Of greater Skill than others can obtain.

But now, Redemption of the human Race
By *Chriſt*, with all its Myſteries of Grace,
Is, in itſelf, as it has always been,
Of quite another Nature; nor akin
To Art, or Science, which, for worldly Views,
The natural, or outward Man, can uſe:

It

It is an inward Fitnefs to revive
That heav'nly Nature, which was once alive
In Paradife; that blifsful Life within
The human Creature, which was loft by Sin:
It breathes a Spark of Life, to re-create
The poor fall'n Man in his firft happy State;
By which, awaken'd into new Defires,
After his native Country he enquires;
How he may rife above this earthly Den,
And get into his Father's Houfe again.

This is Redemption; or the Life divine
Off'ring it felf, on one Hand, with Defign
That inward Man, who loft it, to reftore
To all the Blifs which he was in before;
And, on the other, 'tis the Man's Defire,
Will, Faith, and Hope, which earneftly afpire
After that Life; the Hunger, Thirft, and Call
To be deliver'd, by it, from the Fall.

Now whether Man, in this awaken'd Strife,
Breathe forth his Longings after this good Life,
In Hebrew, Greek, or any Englifh Sound,
Or none at all, but filent Sigh profound,
Can be of no Significancy; He,
That knows but one, or ufes all the three,
Neither to him, more diftant, or more near,
Will this redeeming Life of God appear:
Can you conceive it more to fhine upon
Men of more Languages, than Men of one?

He

He who can make a Grammar for *High Dutch,*
Or *Welch,* or *Greek,* can you suppose, as such,
In Faith, and Hope, and Goodness, will excell
A Man, that scarce his Mother Tongue can spell?
If this Supposal, then, be too absurd,
No Hurt is done, no Enmity incurr'd,
To Learning, Science, Reason, critic Wit,
By giving them the Places which they fit;
Amongst the Ornaments of Life below,
Which the most profligate as well may know,
(One of the most abandon'd vicious Will)
As one who, fearing God, escheweth Ill.

Therefore no Truths, concerning this divine
And heav'nly Life, can come within the Line
Of all this Learning; as exalted far
Above the Pow'r of Trial at its Bar;
Where both the Jury, and the Judges too,
Are born with Eyes incapable to view;
Living, and moving in this World's Demesne,
They have their Being in another Scene;
The Life divine no abler to descry,
Than into Heav'n can look an Eagle's Eye.

If you, well read in ancient Books, my Friend,
To publish *Homer's Iliad* should intend,
Or *Cæsar's Commentaries,* and make out
Some Things more plain —— you have the Skill no doubt;
As well provided for the Work, perhaps,
As one to make his Baskets, one his Traps;

But

But if you think that Skill in ancient Greek,
And Latin, helps you, **of it** self, to feek,
Find, and explain the Spirit, and the Senfe
Of what *Chrift* faid, it is a vain Pretence,
And quite unnatural; of equal Kind
With the Endeavour of a Man born blind,
Who talks about exhibiting the Sight
Of diff'rent Colours, beautifully bright.

Doctrines, wherein Redemption is concern'd,
No more belong to Men as being learn'd,
Than Colours do to him, who never faw
The Light, that gives to **all of them the Law:**
From like unnatural Attempt proceeds
That huge Variety of Sects, and Creeds,
Which, from the fame true Scripture, can deduce
What ferves each diff'rent Error, for its Ufe:
Papift, or *Proteftant, Socinian* Clafs,
Or *Arian,* can as eafily amafs
The Texts of Scripture, and by Reafon's Ray,
One as another, urge the endlefs Fray;
Retort Abfurdities, whenever preft,
Prove its own Syftem, and confute the **reft;**
Juft as blind Men, **in their Difputes,** can do
Each others Notions **of red,** green, or blue.

The Light of the celeftial inward Man,
That died in Paradife, when Sin began,
Is *Jefus Chrift;* and confequently, Men
By Him alone can rife to Life again:

U

He

He, in the Heart of Man, muſt ſow the Seed,
That can awaken heav'nly Life indeed:
Nothing but this can poſſibly admit
Return of Life, or in the leaſt be fit,
Or capable, or ſenſible of Pow'r
From *Jeſus Chriſt*, in his redeeming Hour:
The Light, and Life, which he intends to raiſe,
Have no Dependence upon Word, and Phraſe;
Life, in it ſelf, be it of Heav'n, or Earth,
Muſt have its whole Proceſſion from a Birth:
Would it not found abſurdly, in your Mind,
That, if a Man be naturally blind,
Care muſt be had to teach him Grammar well,
Or in the Art of Logic to excell;
That he will beſt obtain, when this is done,
Knowledge of Light and Colours from the Sun?
Yet not one Jot is it the leſs abſurd
To think that Skill in Greek, or Hebrew Word,
Of Man's Redemption can explain the Whole,
Or let the Light of God into his Soul.

   This Matter, *Academicus*, if you
Can ſet in a more proper Light——pray do.

A

Poetical Version of a Letter

FROM THE

Earl of Essex to the Earl of Southampton.*

My LORD,
    Untaught by Nature, or by Art,
To give the genuine Dictates of my Heart
The Glofs of Compliment, I never lefs,
Than now, fhould aim at that polite Excefs;
Now, that my wand'ring Thoughts are fix'd upon,
Not Martha's *many* Things, but Mary's *one*.

  'Tis not from any ceremonious **View,**
But to difcharge a real, needful Due
From Friend to Friend in Abfence, that I write
To mine, fecluded from his wonted Sight;
By Force oblig'd to give, and to receive
A long——perhaps, a laft departing Leave;

U 2

For

* A Copy of the original Letter may be feen in Cogan's Collection of Tracts from Lord Somer's Library, *Vol.* **4,** *P.* **132.** under the Title of "*A precious and moft divine Letter, from that famous and ever to be renowned Earl of Effex, (Father to the now Lord General his Excellence) to the Earl of Southampton, in the latter End of Queen Elizabeth's Reign.*

For small, by ev'ry Test of human Ken,
The Hopes of meeting, in this World, again.

   Under such Circumstances, I recall
My Friend, whose Honour, Person, Fortune, All,
So dear to me, make Bosom Wish to swell,
That he may always prosper, and do well;
Where'er he goes, whate'er he takes in Hand,
Under the Favour, Service, and Command
Of his protecting Providence, from whom
All Happiness, if truly such, must come.

   My Friend's Abilities, and present State
Of natural Endowments how I rate;
To God what Glory, to himself what Use,
The best Exertion of them might produce,
I shall not here express; enough to note
That, at such Times as I was most remote
From all dissembling, Witnesses enoo
Can vouch my speaking what I thought was true.

   The Truths, which Love now prompts me to remind
Your Lordship of, are of the following Kind:
First; that whatever Talents you possess,
They are *God*'s Gifts, whom you are bound to bless:
Next; that you have them, not as Things your own,
Tho' for your Use, yet not for yours alone;
But as an human Stewarty, or Trust,
Of which Account is to be giv'n, and just:

So

So that, in fine, if Talents are appli'd
To ferve the Spirit of the World, in Pride,
And vain Delights, as he, who rules the Scenes
Of guilty Joy, the Prince of Darknefs, means,
It is Ingratitude, Injuftice too,
Yea, 'tis perfidious Treachery in you:
For if a Servant, of your own, fhould dare
To ufe the Goods, committed to his Care,
To the Advantage of your greateft Foe,
What would you think of his behaving fo?
Yet how with *God* would you yourfelf do lefs,
Having from him whatever you poffefs,
And ferving with it, in the Donor's Stead,
That Foe to him by whom the World is led?

A ferious Thought if you can ever lend
To Admonition, from your trueft Friend;
If the Regard due to your Country fways;
Which you may ferve fo many glorious Ways;
If an all-ruling, righteous Pow'r above
Can raife your Dread of Juftice, or your Love
If you your felf will to your felf be true,
And everlafting Happinefs purfue,
Before the Joys of any worldly Scheme,
The fhort Delufions of a pleafing Dream,
Of which, whatever it may reprefent,
The Soul, foon wak'd, muft bitterly repent;
If thefe Reflections, any of them, find
Due Eftimation in your prudent Mind;

Take

Take an Account of what is done, and paft,
And what the Future may demand, forecaft:
The Leagues, whatever they import, repeal,
To which good Confcience has not fet the Seal:
And fix your Refolution firm, to ferve
Him, from whofe Will no loyal Thought can fwerve;
That gracious God, from whom, in very Deed,
All your Abilities and Gifts proceed;
Whether of bodily, or mental Trace;
Without, within; of Nature, **or of Grace.**

    Then He, who cannot poffibly deny
Himfelf, **or** give his Faithfulnefs the Lie,
Will honour his true Servant, and impart
That **real Peace of** Mind, that Joy of Heart,
Of which until you are become poffeft,
Your Heart, your Mind, fhall never be **at Reft;**
And when you are, by having well approv'd
The **one true Way,** it never fhall **be mov'd.**

    This, I forefee, your Lordfhip may object,
Is Melancholy's vaporous Effect;
That **I** am got into a Pris'ner's Stile;
Far enough from it all the jocund While
That I was free like you, and other Men;
And, Fetters gone, fhould be the fame again.

    To which **I** anfwer——fay it tho' you fhould,
Yet cannot I diftruft a God fo good;

Or

Or Mercy failing me, so greatly shown,
Or Grace forsaking, but by Fault my own:
So deeply bound to him, my Heart so burns
To make his Mercy suitable Returns,
That not to try, of all th' Apostate Class
Worse should I be than any ever was:
I have with such repeated, solemn Stress,
Avow'd the Penitence which I profess;
From Time to Time so call'd on not a few,
To witness, and to watch, if it was true,
That of all Hypocrites, if found to lie,
That e'er were born, the hollowest were I.

But should I perish in my Sins, and draw
Upon my self my own Damnation's Law,
Will it not be your Wisdom to embrace
God's offer'd Mercy, of a saving Grace?
To profit by Example, if you see
The fearful Case of miserable Me?

A longer Time was I a Slave to Sin,
And a corrupted World, than you have been;
Had many a too, too slowly answer'd Call,
That made still harder my Return from Thrall:
To come to *Christ* was requisite, I knew,
But softer Pace, I flatter'd me, would do;
The Journey's End contented I remain'd
To see, and own, tho' still 'twas unattain'd:
Therefore the same good Providence that call'd,
With a kind Violence, has pull'd and haul'd;

As

As public Eye may, outwardly, at leaft,
Have feen, and drag'd me to the Marriage Feaft.

Kind, in this World, Affliction's heavieft Load,
That, in another, Blifs might be beftow'd;
Kind the repeated Stripes, that fhould correct
Of too great Knowledge a too fmall Effect:
God grant your Lordfhip may, with lefs Alloy,
Feel an unfeign'd Converfion's inward Joy,
As I do now; and find the happy Way,
Without the Torments of fo long Delay!

To the Divines (and there were none befide
That nam'd Converfion to me) I repli'd——
Could my Ambition enter, and poffefs
Your narrow Hearts, your Meeknefs would be lefs;
Were my Delights, to which it gives the Rife,
Tafted by you, you would be lefs precife:
But you, my Lord, have the momentous Hint,
From one that knows the very utmoft Stint
Of all that can amufe you, whilft you live,
Of all Contentments which the World can give.

Think then, dear Earl, that I have ftak'd, and buoy'd
The Ways of Pleafure, fatally enjoy'd,
And fet them up, as Marks at Sea, for you
To keep true Virtue's Channel in your View:
Think, tho' your Eyes fhould long be fhut, and faft,
They *muft*, they *muft* be open'd at *the laft*:

Truth

Truth will compel you to confefs, like me,
That to the wicked *Peace* can *never* be.
With my own Soul, that Heav'n may deign to aid
My Heart's Addrefs, this Covenant is made;
My Eyes fhall never yield to Sleep, at Night,
Nor Thoughts attend the Bus'nefs of the Light,
'Till I have pray'd my God, that you may take
This plain, but faithful Warning, for his Sake,
With a believing Profit——then, in you
Your Friends, your Country will be happy too;
And all your Aims fucceed——Events fo bleft
Would fill with Comfort, not to be expreft,

   Your Lordfhip's Coufin, and true Friend——fo ti'd
That worldly Caufe can never once divide——

Essex.

The ITALIAN BISHOP.

An ANECDOTE.

THERE is no Kind of a fragmental Note,
   That pleafes better than an Anecdote;
Or Fact unpublifh'd; when it comes to rife,
And give the more agreeable Surprize:
From long Oblivion fav'd, an ufeful Hint
Is doubly grateful, when reviv'd in Print:

X

A late

A late and ſtriking Inſtance of this Kind
Delighted many an attentive Mind;
This Anecdote, my Taſk is, to rehearſe,
As highly fit to be confign'd to Verſe.

There liv'd a Biſhop, once upon a Time,
Where is not ſaid, but *Italy* the Clime;
An honeſt, pious Man, who underſtood
How to behave as a true Biſhop ſhould;
But thro' an Oppofition, form'd to blaſt
His good Defigns, by Men of diff'rent Caſt,
He had ſome tedious Struggles, and a Train
Of rude Affronts, and Inſults to ſuſtain;
And did ſuſtain; with calm unruffled Mind
He bore them all, and never once repin'd:
An intimate Acquaintance, one who knew
What Difficulties he had waded thro'
Time after Time, and very much admir'd
A Patience ſo provok'd, and ſo untir'd,
Made bold to aſk him, if he could impart,
Or teach the Secret of his happy Art;
Yes, ſaid the good old Prelate, that I can,
And 'tis a plain and practicable Plan;
For all the Secret, that I know of, lies
In making a right Uſe of my own Eyes.
Beg'd to explain himſelf, how that ſhould be——
Why, in whatever State I am, ſaid he,
I firſt look up to Heav'n; as well aware,
That to get thither is my main Affair.

I then

I then **look down** upon the Earth; and **think,**
In a fhort fpace of **Time,** how fmall a Chink
I fhall poffefs of its extenfive Ground;
And then I caft my feeing Eyes around,
Where more Diftrefs appears, on ev'ry Side,
Amongft Mankind, than I myfelf abide.
So that, reflecting on my own Concern,
Firft——where true Happinefs is plac'd, I learn:
Next——let the World, **to what it** will, pretend,
I fee where all its Good and Ill muft end.
Laft——how unjuft it is, as well as vain,
Upon a fair Difcernment, to complain.
Thus, looking up, and down, and round about,
Right **ufe** of Eyes may find **my** Secret out:
With Heav'n in view——his real **Home**——in fine,
Nothing on Earth fhou'd make a **Man** repine.

ON

RESIGNATION.

To a FRIEND in TROUBLE.

DEAR Child, know this, that He, who gave thee Breath,
  Almighty God, **is** Lord of Life and Death,
And all Things that concern them, fuch as thefe,
Youth, Health, or Strength; Age, Weaknefs, or Difeafe;

Wherefore,

Wherefore, whatever thy Affliction be,
Take it as coming from thy God to Thee:
Whether to teach thee Patience be its End,
Or to inftruct fuch Perfons as attend,
That Faith and Meeknefs, tried by Suff'rings paft,
May yield Increafe of Happinefs at laft:
Or whether it be fent for fome Defect,
Which He, who wants to blefs thee, would correct;
Certain it is, that if thou doft repent,
And take thy Crofs up patiently, when fent,
Trufting in Him, who fends it thee, to take
For *Jefus Chrift* his Son, thy Saviour's, Sake,
Wholly fubmitting to his bleffed Will,
Whofe Vifitation feeks thy Profit ftill;
All that thou doft, or ever canft endure,
Will make thy everlafting Joy more fure.

Take therefore what befalls thee in good Part,
As a Prefcription of Love's healing Art;
Whom the Lord loveth he chaftifeth too,
Saith Paul, and fcourgeth with a faving View;
It is the Mark, by which he owns a Child,
Without it, not fo honourably ftil'd:
Fathers according to the Flefh, when they
Correct them, Children rev'rence, and obey;
How much more juftly may that Father claim,
By whom we live eternally, the fame?
They oft chaftife thro' Humour of their own,
He always for our greater Good alone;

Chaft'ning,

Chaft'ning below, that we may rife above
Holy, and happy in our Father's Love.

    Thefe Things for Comfort, and Inftruction fit,
In Holy Scripture, for our Sakes, are writ,
That with a patient, and enduring Mind,
In all Conditions we may be refign'd;
And reverencing our Father, and our Friend,
Take what his Goodnefs fhall be pleas'd to fend.
What greater Good, confidering the Whole,
Than Chrift's own Likenefs in a Chriftian Soul
By patient Suff'ring? Think what Ills, before
He enter'd into Joy, our Saviour bore;
What Things he fuffer'd, to retrieve our Lofs,
And make his Way to Glory, thro' the Crofs,
The Way for us; he wanted none to make,
But for the poor loft human Sinner's Sake;
For them he fuffer'd more than Words can tell,
Or Thought conceive; reflect upon it well,
Dear Child! and whether Life, or Death remains,
Depend on Him to fanctify thy Pains;
To be Himfelf thy ftrong Defence, and Tow'r,
To make thee know and feel his faving Pow'r:
Still taught by Him repeat——*Thy Will be done!*
And truft in **God** thro' his beloved Son.

A POE-

A

Poetical Version of a Letter,

FROM

JACOB BEHMEN, to a FRIEND,

On the fame Occasion.

DEAR Brother in our Saviour *Chrift*——His Grace
    And Love premis'd, in your afflictive Cafe;
I have confider'd of it, and have brought
The Whole, with Chriftian fympathetic Thought,
Before the Will of the moft High, to fee
What it would pleafe Him to make known to me.

And thereupon, I give you, Sir, to know,
What a true Infight he was pleas'd to fhow,
Into the Caufe and Cure of all your Grief,
And prefent Trial; which I fhall, in brief,
Set down for a Memorial, and declare
For you to ponder with a ferious Care.

Firft then, the Caufe, to which we muft affign
Your ftrong Temptation, is the *Love divine;*
The Goodnefs fupernatural, above
All Utt'rance, flowing from the God of Love;

Seeking

Seeking the creaturely and human Will,
To free it from Captivity to Ill:

And then, the Struggle with so great a Grace,
In human Will, refusing to embrace;
Tho' tender'd to it with a Love so pure,
It seeks itself, and strives against a Cure;
From its own Love to transitory Things,
More than to God, the real Evil springs.

'Tis Man's own Nature, which, in its own Life,
Or Center, stands in Enmity and Strife,
And anxious, selfish, doing what it lists,
(Without God's Love) that tempts him, and resists:
The Devil also shoots his fi'ry Dart,
From Grace, and Love to turn away the Heart.

This is the greatest Trial; 'tis the Fight,
Which *Christ*, with his internal Love and Light,
Maintains within Man's Nature, to dispel
God's Anger, Satan, Sin, and Death, and Hell;
The human Self, or Serpent to devour,
And raise an Angel from it by his Pow'r.

Now if God's Love in Christ did not subdue,
In some Degree, this Selfishness in you,
You would have no such Combat to endure;
The Serpent then, triumphantly secure,
Would, unoppos'd, exert its native Right,
And no such Conflict in your Soul excite.

For

For all the huge Temptation and Diſtreſs
Riſes in Nature, tho' God ſeeks to bleſs;
The Serpent feeling its tormenting State,
(Which, of itſelf, is a mere anxious Hate)
When God's amazing Love comes in, to fill,
And change the ſelfiſh to a god-like Will.

Here *Chriſt*, the Serpent-bruiſer, ſtands in Man,
Storming the Devil's helliſh, ſelf-built Plan;
And hence the Strife within the human Soul;
Satan's to kill, and *Chriſt*'s to make it whole;
As by Experience, in ſo great Degree,
God, in his Goodneſs, cauſes you to ſee.

Now, while the Serpent's Head is bruis'd, the Heel
Of Chriſt is ſtung; and the poor Soul muſt feel
Trembling, and Sadneſs, while the Strivers cope,
And can do nothing but ſtand ſtill in Hope;
Hardly be able to lift up its Face,
For mere Concern, and pray to God for Grace.

The Serpent, turning it another Way,
Shows it the World's alluring, fine Diſplay;
Mocking its Reſolution to forego,
For a *new Nature*, the engaging Show;
And repreſents the taking its Delight
In preſent Scenes, as natural, and right.

Thus, in the Wilderneſs with *Chriſt* alone,
The Soul endures Temptation of its own;

While

While all the Glories of this World display'd,
Pleasures, and Pomps, surround it, and persuade
Not to remain so humble, and so still,
But elevate itself in own Self-will.

The next Temptation, which befalls of Course
From Satan, and from Nature's selfish Force,
Is when the Soul has tasted of the Love,
And been illuminated from above;
Still in its Self-hood it wou'd seek to shine,
And, as its own, possess the Light divine.

That is, the soulish Nature, take it right,
As much a Serpent, if without God's Light,
As *Lucifer*, this Nature still would claim
For *own Propriety* the heav'nly Flame;
And elevate its Fire to a Degree,
Above the Light's good Pow'r, which cannot be.

This domineering Self, this Nature Fire,
Must be transmuted to a Love Desire:
Now, when this Change is to be undergone,
It looks for some own Pow'r, and finding none,
Begins to doubt of **Grace**, unwilling quite
To yield up its self-willing Nature's Right.

It ever quakes for Fear, and will not die
In Light divine, tho' to be blest thereby:
The Light of Grace it thinks to be Deceit,
Because it worketh gently without Heat:

Y

Mov'd

Mov'd too by outward Reafon, which is blind,
And, of itfelf, fees nothing of this Kind.

Who knows, it thinketh, whether it be true
That God is in Thee, and enlightens too?
Is it not Fancy? for thou doft not fee
Like other People, who, as well as thee,
Hope for Salvation, by the **Grace of God**,
Without fuch Fear, and Trembling at his Rod.

Thus the poor Soul, accounted for a **Fool**,
By all the Reas'ners of a gayer School,
By all the graver People, who embrace
Mere verbal Promifes of future Grace,
Sighs from its deep internal Ground, and pants
For fuch enlight'ning Comfort as it wants;

And fain would **have**; but Nature can, alafs!
Do Nothing, of itfelf, to bring to pafs;
And is, thro' its own Impotence, afraid
That God rejects it, and **will give no Aid**;
Which, with regard to the Self-will, is true;
For God rejects it, to implant a new.

The **own** Self-will muft die away, and fhine,
Rifing **thro' Death, in** faving Will divine;
And, from **the** Oppofition which it tries
Againft **God's Will,** fuch great **Temptations** rife:
The Devil too is loth to lofe his Prey,
And fee his Fort caft down, if it obey.

For,

For, if the Life of *Chrift* within arife,
Self-Luft, and falfe Imagination dies;
Wholly **it cannot in this** prefent Life,
But by the Flefh maintains the daily Strife;
Dies, and yet lives; as they alone can tell,
In whom *Chrift* fights againft the Pow'rs of Hell.

The third Temptation is in Mind, and Will,
And Flefh and Blood, if Satan enter ftill;
Where the falfe Centers lie in Man, the Springs
Of Pride, and Luft, and Love of earthly Things;
And all the Curfes wifh'd **by other** Men,
Which are occafion'd by this Devil's Den.

Thefe in the Aftral Spirit make a Fort,
Which all the Sins concenter to fupport;
And **human** Will, efteeming for its Joy
What *Chrift*, to fave it, combates to deftroy,
Will not refign the Pride-erected Tow'r,
Nor live obedient to the Saviour's Power.

Thus I have giv'n you, **loving Sir,** to know
What our dear Saviour has been pleas'd to fhow
To my Confideration; **now, on** This,
Examine well what your Temptation is:
We muft *leave all*, and *follow Him*, He faid,
Right Chrift-like poor, like our redeeming Head.

Now, if Self-Luft ftick yet upon your Mind,
Or Love **of** earthly Things, of any Kind,

Then

Then, from thofe Centers, in their working Force,
Such a Temptation will rife up of Courfe:
If you will follow, when it does arife,
My Child-like Counfel, hear what I advife.

Fix your whole Thought upon the bitter Woe,
Which our **dear** Lord was pleas'd **to** undergo;
Confider the Reproach, Contempt, and Scorn,
The worldly State fo poor, and fo forlorn,
Which he was fo content to bear; and then,
His fuff'ring, dying for us finful Men.

And thereunto give up your whole Defire,
And Mind, and Will; and earneftly afpire
To be as like him as you can; to bear,
(And with a Patience bent to perfevere)
All that is laid upon you; and to make
His Procefs your's, and purely for his Sake;

For **Love** of **Him**, moft freely to embrace
Contempt, Affliction, Poverty, Difgrace;
All that can happen, fo you may but gain
His bleffed Love within you, and maintain;
No longer willing with a Self-defire,
But fuch as *Chrift* within you fhall infpire.

Dear Sir, I fear left fomething ftill amifs,
Averfe to him, caufe fuch a Strife **as this:**
He wills you, in his Death, with Him to die
To your own Will, and to arife thereby

In

In his arifing; and that Life to live,
Which he is ftriving in your Soul to give.

Let go all earthly Will; and be refign'd
Wholly to Him, with all your Heart and Mind;
Be Joy, or Sorrow, Comfort, or Diftrefs,
Receiv'd alike, for He alike can blefs,
To gain the Victory of Chriftian Faith
Over the World, and all Satanic Wrath.

So fhall you conquer Death, and Hell, and Sin;
And find, at laft, what *Chrift* in you hath been:
By fure Experience will be underftood,
How all hath happen'd to you for your Good:
Of all his Children this hath been the Way;
And Chriftian Love here dictates what I fay.

ON
BEARING the CROSS.
A DIALOGUE.

I.

TAKE up the Crofs which thou haft got,
   For Love of CHRIST, and bear it not
As *Simon* of *Cyrene* did,
Compell'd to do as he was bid.

" Pray,

II.

" Pray, am not I, who cannot free
" Myſelf, compell'd as much as he?
" I cannot ſhun it, and, of Courſe,
" Muſt bear this heavy Croſs by Force.

III.

What doſt thou get then by Diſguſt
At bearing that, which bear thou muſt?
Nothing abates the Force of Ill,
Like a *reſign'd* and *patient* Will.

IV.

" 'Tis true; but how ſhall I obtain
" Such an Abatement of my Pain?
" Compulſion tempts me to repine
" At *Simon*'s Caſe becoming mine.

V.

Look then at JESUS gone before;
Reflect on what thy SAVIOUR bore;
Bore, tho' he could have been ſet free,
Death on the Croſs, for *Love* of thee.

VI. " He

VI.

" He did fo——*Lord!* what fhall I fay?
" **Do** thou enable me to pray,
" **If** 'tis not poffible to fhun
" This bitter Crofs——*Thy Will be done!*

A

SOLILOQUY

ON THE

Caufe and Confequence of a doubting Mind.

I Mufe, I doubt, I reafon, and debate——
  Therefore, I am not in that perfect State,
In which, when its Creation firft began,
God plac'd **his own beloved Image,** Man;
From whofe high Birth, at once defign'd **for all,**
This ever **poring** Reafon proves a Fall.

  Whilft *Adam* **ftood in that** immortal Life,
Wherein pure **Truth excluded** Doubt and Strife,
He knew, he faw, by **a diviner Light,**
All that was good **for Knowledge, or** for Sight;
But when the Serpent-Subtlety of **Hell**
Brought him to doubt, and reafon——then he fell.

Fell,

Fell, by declining from an upright Will,
And funk into a State of Good and Ill:
The very State of fuch a World as this
Became a Death to his immortal Blifs:
Blifs, which his Reafon gave him not, before
The Lofs enfu'd, nor after could reftore.

From him defcending, all the human Race
Muft needs partake the Nature of his Cafe:
Juft as the Trunk, the Branches, or the Fruit,
Derive their Subftance from the parent Root:
What Life, or Death, into the Father came,
The Sons, tho' guiltlefs, could but have the fame.

If I am one, if ever I muft live
The blifsful Life, which God defign'd to give;
As Reafon dictates, or as fome Degree
Of higher Light enables one to fee,
It cannot rife from being born on Earth,
Without a fecond, new, and heav'nly Birth.

The Gofpel Doctrine, which affures to Men
The joyful Truth of being *born again*,
Demands the free Confent of ev'ry Will,
That feeks the Good, and to efcape the Ill:
In all the fav'd, right Reafon muft allow
Such Birth effected, tho' it knows not how.

Such was the Faith in Life's redeeming Seed,
Of poor fall'n Man the Comfort, and the Creed:

Such

Such was the Hope before, and fince the Flood,
In ev'ry Time and Place, of all the good:
'Till the *new Birth* of JESUS, from above,
Reveal'd below the Myftery of **Love.**

His Virgin Birth, Life, Death, and Re-afcent,
Explain what all God's Difpenfations meant——
God give me Grace to fhun **the** doubting Crime!
Since nothing follows intermediate Time,
But Life, or Death, eternally **to rule**
A *bleffed* Chriftian, **or a** *curfed* Fool.

A

PLAIN ACCOUNT

OF THE

Nature and Defign of true RELIGION.

I.

WHAT is Religion?——Why it is a Cure,
    Giv'n in the Gofpel, *gratis*, to the Poor,
By *Jefus Chrift*, the Healer of the Soul;
Which all who take are fure to be made whole;
And they who will not, all the Art of Man
May ftrive to cure them, but it never can.

Z

II.

Cure for what Malady?——For that of Sin,
From whence all other Maladies begin;
It had its Rife in *Adam*, firft of all,
And all his Sons, partaking of his Fall,
Want a *new Adam* to beget them free
From *Sin* and *Death;* and *Jefus Chrift* is He.

III.

How is it giv'n?——By raifing a *new Birth*
Of heav'nly Life, furviving that of Earth;
Which may, at any Time, at fome it muft,
Return its mortal Body to the Duft;
And then the Born of *God* in *Chrift* again
Will rife immortal, true angelic Men.

IV.

Why in the Gofpel?——Gofpel is, indeed,
In its true living Senfe, the *holy Seed,*
By God's great Mercy, firft, in *Adam* fown,
And firft, in *Chrift,* to full Perfection grown:
Fullnefs, from which all holy Souls derive,
And Bodies too, the Pow'r to be alive.

V.

Why GRATIS *giv'n?*——Becaufe the *Love-defire*
Of God, in *Chrift,* can never work for Hire:

It's

It's Nature is to love for Loving's Sake,
To give itſelf to ev'ry Will to take;
'To them it brings, amidſt the darkeſt Night,
It's *Life* and *Immortality to Light.*

VI.

Why to the Poor?——Becauſe *they* feel their Want,
Which Truſt in *Riches* is ſo loth to grant:
The Rich have *ſomething* which they call *their own;*
The Poor have *nothing,* but to *Chriſt* alone
They owe Themſelves, and pay him what they owe,
And what Religion is——They only know.

ON THE
TRUE MEANING
OF THE
Scripture Terms LIFE and DEATH,

When applied to MEN.

TRUE *Life,* according to the Scripture Plan,
  Is God's own Likeneſs in his Image Man;
This was the Life that *Adam* ceas'd to live,
Or loſt by Sin; and therefore could not give:
So that his Offspring, all the born on Earth,
Want a *new* Parent of this heav'nly Birth.

Z 2

This

This, *Chriſt* alone, God's *Image* moſt *expreſs*,
The *ſecond* Adam, gives them to poſſeſs;
Becoming Man, reverſing human Fall,
And raiſing up the *firſt*, true Life in all;
Healing our Nature's deadly Wound within,
And quenching Wrath, or Death, or Hell, or Sin.

For all ſuch Words deſcribe one evil Thing,
Or Want of **Good; that** has one **only Spring,**
The *Love* of God, in *Chriſt*, which form'd **at firſt**
A *bleſſed* Adam, and redeem'd a **curſt**
By his *own* Act——Good *only* was deſign'd
For *Adam*, and, in him, for all Mankind.

He fell from Good, miſuſing his free Will,
Into this World, **this Life of Good and Ill;**
From whence, the willing to be ſav'd revive
Thro' Faith and Penitence, in *Chriſt* alive;
A *ſecond* Death ſucceeds, if they refuſe;
For *chuſing* Creatures muſt have what they *chuſe*.

Not bare *Exiſtence*, when **we go from hence,**
Is *Immortality*, in Scripture Senſe;
For thus, alike immortal, are confeſt
The good, the bad; the ruin'd, and the bleſt;
Whoſe *inbred* Tempers hint the Reaſon, why
They *live* for ever, **or** for ever *die*.

God's Likeneſs, Light and Spirit **in the Soul,**
Make, **as at firſt, its** bleſt immortal Whole;

'Tis

'Tis *Death* to want them; vain is **all** Difpute;
The Gofpel only reaches to the Root:
All the **infpir'd have** underftood it thus;
Immortal *Life* is that of CHRIST *in Us.*

ON THE

Ground of True and Falfe Religion.

EXPLAIN Religion by **a** thoufand Schemes,
  Still *God* and *Self* will be **the two** Extremes;
In Him the one true **Good of** it is found;
In Self, of all Idolatry, **the Ground:**
Falfe Worfhip, paid at all its various Shrines,
One fame Departure from his Love defines.

By Love to Him *bleft* Angels kept their State;
Which the *Apoftate* loft by curfed Hate;
Setting up *Self* in the ALMIGHTY's Room,
It funk them down into its dreadful Gloom:
On Separation from his Love, the Source
Of all Felicity was loft of Courfe.

By Love to Him, the firft created Man
Was highly bleft; 'till *Selfifhnefs* began,
'Tho' Serpentine Delufion, to arife,
And tempt above God's Wifdom to be wife;

Whea

When he had chosen to prefer his own,
The naked, miserable *Self* was known.

Hence we inherit such a Life as this,
Dead, of itself, to *paradisic* Bliss:
Hence all our Hopes of a diviner Birth
Depend on *Christ*, and his Descent on Earth;
Subduing Self, as *Adam* should have done,
And loving God thro' his beloved Son.

The *Mediator* betwixt God and Men,
Who brings their Nature back to Him again,
Sav'd from all sinful Self, or deadly Wrath,
Or hellish Evil, by the Pow'r of *Faith*
Working by *Love*, of which it is the Strength;
And must attain the full true Life at Length.

Born of this holy, *Virgin* Seed divine,
To a *new* Life within this mortal Shrine,
The faithful breathe a Spirit from above,
And make of Self a Sacrifice to Love:
By *Christ* redeem'd they rise from *Adam*'s Fall,
From Earth to Heav'n, where God is all in all.

PETER's

P E T E R's
DENIAL of his MASTER.

I.

THO' all forsake thee, Master, yet not I;
  I'll go to Prison with thee, or to die,
Said *Peter*——yet how soon did he deny!

II.

A striking Proof, that, even to good Will,
The Help of Grace is necessary still,
To save a Soul from falling into Ill.

III.

His Master told him how the Case would be,
But *Peter* could not see himself, not He;
'Till Grace withdrew, that he might come to see.

IV.

Peter, so valiant on a selfish Plan,
Quite frighted by a Servant Maid, began
To curse, and swear, and did not know the Man.

V. 'Twas

V.

'Twas thus that *Satan fifted him like Wheat,*
And made him think his Courage was fo great;
While JESUS pray'd that he might fee the Cheat.

VI.

High-minded in himfelf, he fell——How low,
The Cock inftructed him, foretold to crow:
His real Self then *Peter* came to know.

VII.

He that would *die* with him, tho' all forfook,
Diffolv'd in Tears, when JESUS gave a Look;
And learn'd Humility by Love's Rebuke.

VIII.

Leffon for us is plain from *Peter's* Cafe,
That real Virtue is the Work of *Grace,*
And of its Height *Humility* the Bafe.

O N

ON THE

Cause, Consequence, and Cure

of

SPIRITUAL PRIDE.

SUPPOSE an Heater burning in the Fire
  To be alive, to will, and to defire;
To reafon, feel, and have, upon the whole,
What we will call an underftanding Soul;
Confcious of pow'rful Heat within its Mold,
And Colour bright above the burnifh'd Gold.

  Suppofe that *Pride* fhould catch this Heater's Heart,
And from the Fire perfuade it to depart;
To fhow itfelf, and make it to be known,
That it can raife a Splendor of its own;
An own rich Colour, an own potent Heat,
Without Dependence on the Fire, compleat.

  It leaves, in Profpect of fo fine a Show,
The fiery Bofom where it learnt to glow;
Cools by Degrees, till all its golden Hue
Is vanifh'd, and its Pow'r of heating too;
Its own, once hidden, Nature domineers,
And the dark, cold, felf-iron Lump appears.

A a

Transfer

Transfer this feign'd, imaginary Pride,
To that which really does, too oft, betide;
When human Souls, endu'd with Grace divine,
Become ambitious, of themfelves, to fhine;
And, proud of Qualities which Grace beftows,
Forfake its Bofom for felf-fhining Shows.

And, thence conceive the natural Effects
Of Pride, in either fingle Men, or Sects;
That for Variety of felfifh Strife
Forfake the one, true Caufe of all true Life;
The heav'nly Spirit-fire of Love, within
Whofe facred Bofom all their Gifts begin.

From which, if Reafon, Learning, Wit, or Parts,
Tempt their Ambition to withdraw their Hearts,
There muft enfue, whatever they may mean,
The Difappearance of the glowing Scene;
From the moft gifted vanifhing of Courfe,
When dif-united from its real Source.

As only Fire can poffibly reftore
The Heater's Force, to what it was before;
So that of Love alone confumes the Drofs
Of wrathful Nature, and repairs its Lofs;
It will again unite with all Defire,
That cafts itfelf into the holy Fire.

THE

THE
BEGGAR and the DIVINE.

IN some good Books **one** reads of **a Divine,**
    Whose memorable Cafe deserves a Line;
Who, to serve God the best, and shortest Way,
Pray'd, for eight Years together, every Day,
That in the Midst of Doctrines and of Rules,
However taught and practis'd by the Schools,
He would be pleas'd to bring him to a Man
Prepar'd to teach him the compendious Plan.

    He was himself a *Doctor*, and well read
In all the Points to which Divines were **bred;**
Neverthelefs, he thought, that what concern'd
The most illiterate, as well as learn'd,
To **know** and practife, must be something still
More independent on such kind of Skill:
True Christian Worship had, within its Root,
Some simpler Secret, clear of all Difpute;
Which, **by** a living Proof that he might know,
He pray'd for some Practitioner to show.

    One Day, posseſs'd with an intenfe Concern
About the Lefſon which he fought to learn,
He heard a Voice that founded in his Ears——
" Thou has **been** praying for a Man eight Years;

A a 2

" Go

" Go to the Porch of yonder Church, and find
" A Man prepar'd according to thy Mind."

Away he went to the appointed Ground;
When, at the Entrance of the Church, he found
A poor old Beggar, with his Feet full fore,
And not worth Two-pence all the Cloaths he wore.
Surpris'd to fee an Object fo forlorn——
" My Friend," faid he, " I wifh thee a good Morn——
" Thank thee," repli'd the Beggar, " but a bad
" I don't remember that I ever had——
Sure he miftakes, the Doctor thought, the Phrafe——
" Good Fortune, Friend, befall thee all thy Days !——
" Me, faid the Beggar, many Days befall,
" But none of them unfortunate at all——
" God blefs thee, anfwer plainly, I requeft——
" Why, plainly then, I never was unbleft——
" Never? Thou fpeakeft in a myftic Strain,
" Which more at large I wifh thee to explain.——

" With all my Heart——Thou firft didft condefcend
" To wifh me kindly a good Morning, Friend;
" And I repli'd, that I remember'd not
" A bad one ever to have been my Lot:
" For, let the Morning turn out how it will,
" I praife my God for ev'ry new one ftill:
" If I am pinch'd with Hunger, or with Cold,
" It does not make me to let go my Hold;
" Still I praife God——Hail, Rain, or Snow, I take
" This bleffed Cordial, which has Pow'r to make

" The

" The fouleſt Morning, to my Thinking, fair;
" For Cold and Hunger yield to Praiſe and Pray'r.
" Men pity me as wretched, or deſpiſe;
" But whilſt I hold this noble Exerciſe,
" It chears my Heart to ſuch a due Degree,
" That ev'ry Morning is ſtill good to me.

" Thou didſt, moreover, wiſh me lucky **Days,**
" And I, by reaſon of continual Praiſe,
" Said that I had none elſe; for come what wou'd
" On any Day, I knew it muſt be good
" Becauſe God ſent it; Sweet or Bitter, Joy
" Or Grief, by this angelical employ,
" Of **praiſing him,** my Heart was at its Reſt,
" And took whatever happen'd for the beſt;
" So that my own Experience might ſay,
" It never knew of an unlucky Day.

" Then didſt thou pray——God bleſs thee——and **I** ſaid
" I never was unbleſt; for being led
" By the good Spirit of imparted Grace
" To praiſe his Name, and ever to embrace
" His righteous Will, regarding that alone,
" With total Reſignation of my own,
" I never could, in ſuch a State as this,
" Complain for want of Happineſs or Bliſs;
" Reſolv'd, in all Things, that the Will divine,
" The Source of all true Bleſſing, ſhould be mine."

The

The Doctor, learning from the Beggar's Cafe
Such wond'rous Inftance of the Pow'r of Grace,
Propos'd a Queftion, with Intent to try
The happy Mendicant's direct Reply——
" What wouldft thou fay, faid he, fhould God think fit
" To caft thee down to the infernal Pit?

" He caft me down? He fend me into Hell?
" No——He loves me, and I love Him too well:
" But put the Cafe he fhould, I have two Arms
" That will defend me from all hellifh Harms,
" The one, Humility, the other, Love;
" Thefe I would throw below him, and above;
" One under his *Humanity* I'd place,
" His *Deity* the other fhould embrace;
" With both together fo to hold him faft,
" That he fhould *go* wherever he would *caft*,
" And then, whatever thou fhalt call the Sphere,
" Hell, if thou wilt, 'tis Heav'n if he be there.

Thus was a great Divine, whom fome have thought
To be the juftly fam'd *Taulerus*, taught
The holy Art, for which he us'd to pray,
That to ferve God the moft compendious Way,
Was to hold faft a loving, humble Mind,
Still praifing Him, and to his Will refign'd.

FRAGMENT of an HYMN,

ON THE

GOODNESS of GOD.

O Goodneſs of God! more exceedingly great
    Than Thought can conceive, or than **Words can**
       repeat;
Whatſoever we fix our Conceptions upon
It has ſome Kind of Bounds, but thy **Goodneſs** has none:
As it never **began**, ſo it never can end,
But to all thy Creation will always extend;
All Nature partakes of its proper Degree,
But the Self-blinded Will that refuſes to ſee.

    Whenſoever new Forms of Creation began,
Thy Goodneſs adjuſted the beautiful Plan;
Adjuſted the Beauties of Body and Soul,
And plac'd in the Center the Good of the whole;
That ſhon, like a Sun, **the** Circumference round,
To produce all the **Fruits of** beatifi'd Ground;
To diſplay, in each poſſible Shape and Degree,
A Goodneſs eternal, eſſential to Thee.

    Bleſt Orders of Angels ſurrounded thy Throne,
Before any Evil was heard of, or known;
'Till a Self-ſeeking Chief's unaccountable Pride
Thine immutable Rectitude falſely beli'd;

                    And

And defpifing the Goodnefs that made him fo bright,
Would become independent, and be his own Light;
And indue'd all his Hoft to fo monftrous a Thing,
As to act againft Nature's omnipotent King.

    Then did Evil begin, or the Abfence of **Good**,
Which from Thee could not come——from a Creature it
      could;
Who, made in thy Likenefs, all happy and free,
Could only be good, as an Image of Thee:
When an Angel profan'd his angelical Truft,
And departed from Order, moft righteous and juft;
Self-depriv'd of the Light, that proceeds from thy Throne,
He fell to the Darknefs, by Nature, his own.

    For Nature, itfelf, is a Darknefs exprefs,
If a Splendor from thee does not fill it and blefs;
An Abyfs of the Pow'rs of all *creaturely* Life,
Which are, in themfelves, but an impotent Strife,
Of Action, Re-action, and Whirling around,
'Till the Rays of thy Light pierce the jarring Profound;
'Till thy Goodnefs compofe the dark, natural Storm,
And enkindles the Blifs of Light, Order, and Form.

    Thy unchangeable Goodnefs, when Wrath was begun,
Soon **as e'er** it beheld what an Angel had done,
Exerted itfelf in reftoring anew,
A celeftial Abode, and Inhabitants too;
Made a temporal World in the defolate Place,
And thy Likenefs, a Man, to produce a new Race;

That

That the Evil brought forth might in Time be fuppreft,
And a new Hoft of Creatures fucceed to be bleft.

When the Man, whom thy Counfel defign'd to have
    ftood,
Fell into this Mixture of Evil and Good;
And, againft thy kind Warning, confented to tafte
Of the Fruit, that would lay his own *Paradife* wafte;
Thy Mercy then fought his Redemption from Sin,
And implanted the Hope of a *Saviour* within;
Of a Man to be born, in the Fullnefs of Time,
To fupply his **Defect,** and abolifh his Crime.

All **the** Hopes of good Men, fince the Ruin began,
Were deriv'd **from the** Grace of this wonderful Man:
His Life, in the Promife, has fecretly wrought
Its intended Effect, in their penitent Thought,
Who believ'd in thy Word, in whatever Degree
They knew, or knew not, how his Coming would be:
A true Faith in a Saviour was one, and the fame,
Both before his bleft Coming, as after he came.

Patriarchal, *Mofaic, prophetical* Views,
The Defire of all Nations, **or** *Gentiles,* **or** *Jews,*
Who obey'd, in the **midft** of their natural Fall,
The Degree of his Light, which enlighten'd them all,
Still center'd **in** him, the MESSIAH, the Man
Who fhould execute fully **thy** merciful Plan;
And impart the true Life, which thy Goodnefs defign'd,
By creating a Man, to defcend to Mankind.

B b

When

When this Son of thy Love was incarnate on Earth,
And the WORD was made *Flesh* by a Virginal Birth,
Thy Angelical Host usher'd in the great Morn,
With the *Tidings* of *Joy*, that a SAVIOUR was born;
Of Joy to all People, who, round the whole Ball,
Should partake of the Goodness, that came to save all;
To erect, upon Earth, a true Kingdom of Grace,
And of Glory to come, for whoe'er would embrace.

UNIVERSAL GOOD

THE

OBJECT of the DIVINE WILL,

AND

EVIL the necessary Effect of the CREA-TURE'S Opposition to it.

THE God of Love, delighting to bestow,
  Sends down his Blessing to the World below:
A grateful Mind receives it, and above
Sends up Thanksgiving to the God of Love:
This happy Intercourse could never fail,
Did not a false, perverted Will prevail.

For Love divine, as rightly understood,
Is an unalterable Will to Good:

Good

Good is the Object of His bleſſed Will,
Who never can concur to real Ill;
Much leſs *decree, predeſtinate, ordain*——
Words oft employ'd to take his Name **in vain.**

But he permits it to be done, ſay you——
Plain then, I anſwer, that He does not *do;*
That, having will'd created Angels free,
He ſtill permits, or wills them ſo to be;
Were his Permiſſion aſk'd, before they did
An evil **Action,** he would ſoon forbid.

Before **the Doing he forbids indeed,**
But diſobedient Creatures take no heed:
If He, according to your preſent Plea,
Withdraws his Grace, and *ſo* they diſobey,
The Fault is laid on Him, not them at all;
For who can ſtand whom He ſhall thus let fall?

Our own Neglect muſt be the previous Cauſe,
When **it is** ſaid, the *Grace of God withdraws;*
In the ſame Senſe, as when the brighteſt Dawn,
If we will ſhut our Windows, is withdrawn;
Not that the Sun is ever the leſs bright,
But that **our** Choice is not to ſee the Light.

Free to receive the Grace, or to reject,
Receivers only can be God's *elect;*
Rejecters of it *reprobate* alone,
Not by divine *Decree,* but by their *own:*

B b 2

His

His Love to *all*, his Willing none to fin,
Is a Decree that never could begin.

It is the Order, the eternal Law,
The true free Grace, that never can withdraw;
Obfervance of it will, of courfe, be bleft,
And Oppofition to it felf-diftreft;
To them, who love its gracious Author, all
Will work for Good, according to St. *Paul.*

An eafy Key to each abftrufer Text,
That modern Difputants have fo perplext;
With arbitrary Fancies on each Side,
From God's pure Love, or Man's Freewill deny'd;
Which, in the Breaft of Saints, and Sinners too,
May both be found felf-evidently true.

ON THE

Difinterefted LOVE of GOD.

THE Love of God with genuine Ray
 Inflam'd the Breaft of good *Cambray;*
And banifh'd from the Prelate's Mind
All Thoughts of interefted Kind:
He faw, and Writers of his Clafs,
(Of too neglected Worth, alas!)

Difinterefted

Difinterefted Love to be
The Gofpel's **very A. B. C.**

When our *redeeming Lord* began
To practice it himfelf, as Man;
And, for the Joy then fet before
His loving View, fuch Evils bore;
Endur'd the Crofs, defpis'd the fhame——
Had he an interefted Aim?
Surely the leaft Examination
Shews, that the **Joy** was our Salvation.

For us he **fuffer'd, to make known**
The Love that feeketh **not its own;**
Suffer'd, what nothing but fo pure
A Love could poffibly endure:
No lefs a Sacrifice than this
Could bring poor Sinners back to Blifs;
Or execute the faving Plan
Of reuniting God and Man.

This Love was *Abra'm's* Shield and Guard;
Was his exceeding great Reward;
This Love the patriarchal Eye,
And that of *Mofes* could defcry;
In this difinterefted Senfe
They fought Reward, or Recompenfe,
City, or Country, Heav'n above,
The Seat of Purity and Love.

This

This the high Calling, this the Prize,
The Mark of *Paul*'s fo fteady Eyes;
For, with the felf-forgetting *Paul*,
Pure **Love** of God in *Chrift* was all:
The **Text** of the beloved *John*
Has all, that Words can fay, in one;
For GOD IS LOVE——compendious Whole
Of all the Bleffings of a Soul.

What Helps to this a Soul may want,
Pure Love is ready ftill to grant;
But with a View to wean it ftill
From felfifh, mercenary Will:
Of all Reward, all Punifhment,
This is the End, in God's Intent,
To form, in Offsprings of his own,
The Blifs of loving His alone.

Sole Rule of all Affection due
Both to ourfelves, and others too;
Meaning of ev'ry Scripture Text,
By interefted Love perplext:
Promife, or Precept, Gofpel Call,
Or legal Love, fulfils them all;
From Bafe arifing up to Spire,
Superior both to Fear and Hire.

Love of difinterefted Kind,
The Man who thinks it too refin'd

May,

May, by ambiguous Language, ftill
Perfift in metaphyfic Skill;
Even the juftly fam'd *Cambray*,
In fuch a Cafe, could only pray,
That *Love* itfelf would only dart
Some feeling Proof into his Heart.

On the fame SUBJECT.

I.

I Love my God, and freely too,
  With the fame Love that he imparts;
   That He, to whom all Love is due,
Engraves upon pure loving Hearts.

II.

  I love, but this celeftial Fire
Ye ftarry **Pow'rs! Ye** do not raife :
  No Wages, no Reward's Defire,
Is in the purely fhining Blaze.

III.

  Me, nor the **Hopes of heav'nly Blifs,**
Or Paradific Scenes excite;
  Nor Terrors of the dark **Abyfs,**
Of Death's eternal Den, affright.

IV. No

IV.

No bought, and paid-for Love be mine,
I will have no Demands to make ;
  Difinterefted, and divine
Alone, that Fear fhall never fhake.

V.

  Thou, my *Redeemer*, from above,
Suffering to fuch immenfe Degree,
  Thy Heart has kindled mine to Love,
That burns for Nothing but for *Thee*.

VI.

  Thy Scourge, thy Thorns, thy Crofs, thy Wounds,
Are ev'ry one of them a Source,
  From whence the Nourifhment abounds
Of endlefs Love's unfading Force.

VII.

  Thefe facred Fires, with holy Breath,
Raife in my Mind the gen'rous Strife ;
  While, by the Enfigns of thy Death
Known, I adore the LORD of LIFE.

VIII. Extinguifh

VIII.

Extinguish all celestial Light,
The Fire of Love will not go out;
  The Flames of Hell extinguish quite,
Love will pursue its wonted Rout.

IX.

Be there no Hope if it persist——
Persist it will, nor ever cease;
  No Punishment if 'tis dismist——
What caus'd it not will not decrease.

X.

Should'st thou give Nothing for its Pains,
It claims not any Thing as due;
  Should'st thou condemn me, it remains
Unchang'd by any selfish View.

XI.

Let Heav'n be darken'd if it will,
Let Hell with all its Vengeance roar;
  My God alone remaining, still
I'll love Him, as I did before.

ON

Meaning of the Word WRATH,

As applied to GOD in Scripture.

THAT *God is Love*——is in the Scripture said;
   That He is *Wrath*——is no where to be read;
From which, by literal Expreſſion free,
" *Fury.* (he ſaith himſelf) *is not in me:*"
If Scripture, therefore, muſt direct our Faith,
Love muſt be He, or in Him; and not Wrath.

And yet the Wrath of God, in Scripture Phraſe,
Is oft expreſs'd, and many diff'rent Ways:
His Anger, Fury, Vengeance, are the Terms,
Which the plain Letter of the Text affirms;
And plain, from two of the Apoſtle's Quire,
That *God is Love*——and *a conſuming Fire.*

If we conſult the Reaſons that appear,
To make the ſeeming Difficulty clear,
We muſt acknowledge, when we look above,
That God, as God, is overflowing Love:
And wilful Sinners, when we look below,
Make (what is call'd) the Wrath of God to flow.

Wrath, as St. *Paul* ſaith, *is the treaſur'd Part*
Of an impenitently harden'd Heart:

When

When Love reveals its own eternal Life,
Then Wrath and Anguiſh fall on evil Strife;
Then lovely Juſtice, in itſelf all bright,
Is burning Fire to ſuch as hate the Light.

If Wrath and Juſtice be indeed the ſame,
No Wrath in God——is liable to blame;
If not; if righteous Judges may, and muſt,
Be free Themſelves from Wrath, if they be juſt,
Such Kind of Blaming may, with equal Senſe,
Lay on a Judge the Criminal's Offence.

God, in Himſelf unchangeable, in fine,
Is one, eternal Light of Love divine;
In Him there is no Darkneſs, ſaith St. *John*,
In Him no Wrath——the Meaning is all one:
'Tis our own Darkneſs, Wrath, Sin, Death, and Hell,
Not to love Him, who firſt lov'd us ſo well.

THE

Foregoing Subject more fully illuftrated,

IN A

Comment on the following Scripture.

*GOD fo loved the World, that He gave his only begotten
Son, that whofoever believeth in Him fhould not perifh, but
have everlafting Life.* St. John, 3, 16.

I.

GOD fo loved the World!——by how tender a Phrafe
    The Defign of his Father our Saviour difplays!
Love, according to Him, when the World was undone,
Was the Father's fole Reafon for giving his Son.
No *Wrath in the Giver* had *Chrift* to atone,
But to fave a poor perifhing World from *it's own.*
A Belief in the Son carries with it a Faith,
That the Motive paternal was Love, and not Wrath.

II.

  Ev'ry good, perfect Gift, cometh down from above,
From the Father of Lights, thro' the Son of his Love:
As in Him there is no Variation or Change,
Neither "*Shadow of turning*", it well may feem ftrange
That

That, when Scripture affures us fo plainly, that He,
His Will, Grace, **or Gift, is fo** perfectly free,
Any Word fhould be ftrain'd to inculcate a Thought
Of a Wrath in **his** Mind, or a Change to be wrought.

III.

All Wrath is the Product of creaturely Sin;
In immutable Love it could never begin;
Nor, indeed, in a Creature, 'till oppofite Will
To the Love of its GOD had brought forth fuch **an Ill;**
'To the Love that **was** pleas'd to communicate Blifs
In fuch endlefs **Degrees, thro'** all Nature's Abyfs;
Nor could Wrath have been known, had not Man left
     the State,
In which Nature's GOD was pleas'd **Man to create.**

IV.

He faw, when this World in **its** Purity ftood,
Every Thing he had made, **and** " *behold! it was good;* "
And the Man, its one Ruler, before his fad Fall,
As the Image of GOD, **had** the Goodnefs **of All:**
When He **fell, and** awakned Wrath, Evil, and Curfe
In himfelf **and the World, was** GOD become worfe?
Who **fo lov'd the World** ftill, that, when **Wrath was**
     begun,
To redeem the loft Creature, he gave his own Son——

V. Freely

V.

Freely gave Him; not mov'd or incited thereto
By a previous *appeasing*, or payment of Due
To his *Wrath*, or his *Vengeance*, or any such Cause
As should *satisfy* Him for the Breach of his Laws:
This Language the Jew *Nicodemus* might use;
But our *Saviour's* to Him had more excellent Views;
" God so *loved* the World," (are his Words,) " that He
    gave
" His only-begotten" in order to save.

VI.

Love's prior, unpurchas'd, unpaid-for Intent
Was the Cause, why the only-begotten was sent,
That thro' Him we might live; and the Cause why He
    came,
Was to manifest Love, ever one and the same;
Full Conquest of Wrath ever striving to make,
And blotting Transgressions out for *it's own sake*;
Wanting no *Satisfaction* itself, but to give
Itself, that the World might receive it, and live——

VII.

Might believe on the Son, and receive a new Birth
From the Love, that in *Christ* was incarnate on Earth;
When a Virgin brought forth, without help of a Man,
The Restorer of G O D's true, original Plan;

The

The one Quencher **of Wrath**, the Atoner **of** Sin,
And the " *Bringer of Justice and Righteousness in*;"
The Renewer, in Man, of a Pow'r, and a Will
To satisfy Justice——that is, to fulfill.

VIII.

There is nothing that Justice and Righteousness **hath**
More opposite to it, than Anger and Wrath;
As repugnant to all that **is** equal and right,
As Falshood **to** Truth, **or as** Darkness to Light.
Of G O D, in Himself, **what** the Scripture affirms
Is Truth, **Light, and Love**——plain significant Terms;
In his Deity, therefore, **there** cannot befall
Any Falshood, or Darkness, **or Hatred at all.**

IX.

Such Defect can be found in that Creature alone,
Which against his good Will seeks to set up it's **own;**
Then, to G O D, and his Justice, it **giveth the Lie,**
And it's Darkness and Wrath are discover'd **thereby:**
What, before, was subservient to Life, **in due Place,**
Then usurps the **Dominion,** and Death is the Cafe;
Which the Son **of G O D only** could ever subdue,
By doing all that **which Love** gave Him to do.

X.

If the **Anger** of G O D, Fury, Wrath, waxing hot,
And the **like human** Phrases that Scripture has got,

Be

Be infifted upon, why not alfo the reft,
Where G O D, in the Language of Men, is expreft
In a Manner, which, all are oblig'd to confefs,
No Defect in his Nature can mean to exprefs ?
With a GOD, who is LOVE, ev'ry Word fhould agree;
With a GOD, who hath faid, " *Fury is not in me.*"

XI

The Diforders in Nature, for none are in G O D,
Are intitled his Vengeance, his Wrath, or his Rod,
Like his Ice, or his Froft, his Plague, Famine, or Sword——
That the Love, which directs them, may ftill be ador'd :
Directs them, till Juftice, call'd his, or call'd ours,
Shall regain, to our Comfort, it's primitive Pow'rs ;
The true, faving Juftice, that bids us endure
What Love fhall prefcribe, for effecting our Cure.

XII.

By a Procefs of Love, from the Crib to the Crofs,
Did the only-begotten recover our Lofs;
And fhew in us Men how the Father is pleas'd,
When the Wrath in our Nature by Love is appeas'd ;
When the Birth of His Chrift, being formed within,
Diffolves the dark Death of all Selfhood and Sin ;
Till the Love that fo lov'd us, becomes, once again,
From the *Father* and *Son*, a Life-*Spirit* in Men.

THE

T H E
T R U E   G R O U N D S

O F

Eternal and immutable RECTITUDE.

TH' eternal Mind, ev'n *Heathens* underſtood,
   Was infinitely *powerful*, **wiſe**, and **good:**
In their Conceptions, who conceiv'd aright,
Theſe three eſſential Attributes **unite:**
They ſaw, that, wanting any of the three,
Such an all-perfect Being could not be.

   For Pow'r, from Wiſdom ſuff'ring a Divorce,
Would be a fooliſh, **mad,** and frantic Force:
If **both** were join'd, and wanted Goodneſs **ſtill,**
They would concur **to** more pernicious Ill:
However nam'd, **their** Action **could but tend**
To Weakneſs, **Folly,** Miſchief **without End.**

   Yet ſome of old, and ſome of preſent Hour,
Aſcribe to God an arbitrary Pow'r;
An abſolute Decree; a mere Command,
Which Nothing **cauſes,** Nothing can withſtand:
Wiſdom and Goodneſs ſcarce appear in Sight;
But **all is** meaſur'd by reſiſtleſs Might.

D d

The

The verbal Queſtion comes to this, in fine,
Is Good, or Evil, made by *Will divine*,
Or ſuch by *Nature?* Does Command enact
What ſhall be right, and then 'tis ſo in Fact?
Or is it right, and therefore, we may draw
From thence the Reaſon of the righteous Law?

Now, tho' 'tis Proof, indiſputably plain,
That all is right, which *God* ſhall once ordain;
Yet, if a Thought ſhall intervene between
Things and Commands, 'tis evidently ſeen
That Good will be commanded: Men divide
Nature, and Laws, which really coincide.

From the divine, eternal Spirit ſprings
Order, and Rule, and Rectitude of Things;
Thro' outward Nature, his apparent Throne,
Viſibly ſeen, intelligibly known:
Proofs of a boundleſs Pow'r, a Wiſdom's Aid,
By Goodneſs us'd, eternal, and unmade.

Cudworth perceiv'd, that what Divines advance
For Sov'reignty alone is Fate, or Chance:
Fate, after Pow'r had made its forcing Laws;
And Chance, before, if made without a Cauſe:
Nothing ſtands firm, or certain, in a State
Of fatal Chance, or accidental Fate.

Endleſs Perfections, after all, conſpire,
And to adore excite, and to admire;

But

But to plain Minds, the plaineſt Pow'r above
Is native Goodneſs, to attract our Love:
Center of all its various Power, and Skill,
Is one divine, immutable Good Will.

ON THE

NATURE and REASON

OF ALL

OUTWARD LAW.

The Sabbath was made for Man; not Man for the Sabbath.
Mark 2, 27.

FROM this true Saying one may learn to draw
  The real Nature of all outward Law;
In ev'ry Inſtance, rightly underſtood,
Its Ground, and Reaſon, is the human Good:
By all its Changes, ſince the World began,
Man was not made for Law; but Law for Man.

Thou ſhalt not eat (the firſt Command of all)
Of Good and Ill, was to *prevent* his Fall:
When he became unfit to be alone,
Woman was form'd out of his Fleſh and Bone:
When both had ſinn'd, then Penitential Grief,
And ſweating Labour, was the Law Relief.

D d 2

When

When all the World had finn'd, fave one good Sire,
Flood was the Law that fav'd its Orb from Fire:
When *Fire* itfelf upon a *Sodom* fell,
It was the Law to ftop a growing Hell:
So on——The Law with Riches, or with Rods,
Come as it will, is *good*, for it is God's.

Men who obferve a Law, or who abufe,
For felfifh Pow'r, are blind as any *Jews*;
On Sabbath, conftru'd by *rabbinic* Will,
God muft not fave, and Men muft feek to kill;
Such Zeal for Law has *pharifaic* Faith,
Not as 'tis good, but as it worketh Wrath.

JESUS, the perfect Law-fulfiller, gave
The Victory that taught the Law to fave;
Pluck'd out its Sting, revers'd the cruel Cry,
——*We have a Law by which he ought to die*——
Dying for Man, this Conqueft he could give,
I have a Law by which he ought to live.

Whilft in the Flefh, how oft did he reveal
His faving Will, and god-like Pow'r to heal!
They whom Defect, Difeafe, or Fiend poffeft,
And pardon'd Sinners by his Word had Reft;
He, on the *Sabbath*, chofe to heal, and teach;
And *Law*-proud *Jews* to flay him for its Breach.

The Sabbath, never fo well kept before,
May juftify one Obfervation more;

Our

Our *Saviour* heal'd, as pious Authors fay,
So many Sick upon the *Sabbath* Day,
To fhew that *Reft*, and *Quietnefs* of Soul,
Is beft for one who wants to be made whole;

Not to indulge an Eagernefs too great,
Of outward Hurry, or of inward Heat;
But with an humble Temper, and refign'd,
To keep a Sabbath in a hopeful Mind;
In *Peace*, and *Patience*, meekly to endure,
'Till the *good Saviour*'s Hour is come, *to cure*.

DIVINE LOVE,

THE

Effential Characteriftic of true RELIGION.

RELIGION's Meaning when I would recall,
   Love is to me the plaineft Word of all;
Plaineft; becaufe that what I *love*, or *hate*,
Shews me directly my internal State:
By its own Confcioufnefs is beft defin'd,
Which way the *Heart* within me ftands inclin'd.

On what it lets its Inclination reft,
To that its real Worfhip is addrefs'd:
What ever Forms or Ceremonies fpring
From Cuftom's Force, *there* lies the real Thing:

Jew

Jew, *Turk*, or *Christian*, be the Lovers Name,
If fame the Love, Religion is the fame.

Of all Religions if we take a View,
There is but one that ever can be true;
One *God*, one *Christ*, one *Spirit*, none but He;
All elfe is *Idol*, whatfoe'er it be;
A Good that our Imaginations make,
Unlefs we love it purely for his Sake.

Nothing but grofs Idolatry alone
Can ever love it, merely, for its own:
It may be good, that is, may make appear
So much of God's *one* Goodnefs to be clear;
Thereby to raife a true, religious Soul
To Love of *Him*, the one eternal whole;

The one unbounded, undivided Good,
By all his Creatures partly underftood:
If therefore Senfe of its apparent Parts
Raife not his Love or Worfhip in our Hearts,
Our felfifh Wills or Notions we may feaft,
And have no more Religion than a Beaft.

For brutal Inftinct can a Good embrace,
That leaves behind it no reflecting Trace;
But thinking Man, whatever be his Theme,
Should worfhip Goodnefs in the great Supreme;
By inward Faith, more fure than outward Sight,
Shou'd eye the Source of all that's good, and right.

Religion

Religion then is *Love's* celestial **Force**,
That penetrates thro' all to its true Source;
Loves all along, but with proportion'd Bent,
As Creatures further the divine Ascent;
Not to the Skies or Stars; but to the part
That will be always uppermost ―― the *Heart*.

There is the Seat, as holy Writings tell,
Where the most High Himself delights to dwell;
Whither attracting the desirous Will
To its true Rest, he saves it from all Ill;
Gives it to find, in his *Abyssal* Love,
An Heav'n *within*, in other Words, *above*.

O N

Works of Mercy and Compassion,

CONSIDERED

As the Proofs of True Religion.

OF true Religion, Works of Mercy seem
    To be the plainest Proof, in *Christ's* Esteem;
Who has himself declar'd what he will say
To all the Nations, at the Judgement Day:
Come, or *depart*, is the predicted Lot
Of brotherly Compassion shewn, or not.

Then,

Then, they who gave poor hungry People Meat,
And Drink to quench the thirsty Suff'rer's Heat;
Who welcom'd in the Stranger at the Door,
And with a Garment cloath'd the naked Poor;
Who visited the Sick to ease their Grief,
And went to Pris'ners, or bestow'd Relief——

These will be deem'd *religious* Men, **to whom**
Will found——*ye blessed of* **my Father, come,**
Inherit ye the Kingdom, and partake
Of all the Glories founded for your Sake:
Your *Love to others I was pleas'd to see,*
What you have *done to them was done to me.*

Then, they who gave the hungry Poor no Food;
Who with no Drink the parch'd with Thirst bedew'd;
Who **drove the helpless** Stranger from their Fold,
And let the Naked perish **in the Cold;**
Who to the Sick no friendly **Visit paid,**
Nor gave to Pris'ners any needful Aid——

These will be deem'd of *irreligious* Mind;
And hear the——*Go, ye Men of cursed Kind,*
To endless Woes, which ev'ry harden'd Heart
For its own Treasure has prepar'd——*depart:*
Shewn *to a* Brother, *of the least Degree,*
Your *merciless* Behaviour *was to* **me.**

Here, all ye learned, full of all Dispute,
Of true and false Religion lies **the Root:**

The

The Mind of *Chrift*, when he became a Man,
With all its Tempers, **forms** its real Plan;
The *Sheep* from *Goats* diftinguifhing full well——
His Love is *Heav'n;* and Want of it is *Hell.*

V E R S E S

Defigned for an INFIRMARY.

DEAR loving Sirs! behold, **as ye pafs by,**
The poor fick People **with a** pitying Eye:
Let Pains, and **Wounds,** and Suff'rings of each Kind,
Raife **up** a juft Compaffion **in your** Mind:
Indulge a gen'rous Grief at fuch a Sight,
And then beftow your *Talent,* or your *Mite.*

Thus to beftow is really to obtain
The fureft Bleffing upon honeft Gain:
To help th' afflicted, in fo great **a Need,**
By your Supplies, is to be rich indeed:
The Good, the Pleafure, the Reward of Wealth
Is to procure your Fellow-creatures Health.

In other Cafes, Men may form a Doubt,
Whether their Alms be properly laid out;
But in the Objects, **here,** before **your** Eyes,
No fuch Diftruft can poffibly arife;

Too

Too plain the Miseries! which well may melt
An Heart, sincerely wishing them unfelt.

The Wise consider this terrestrial Ball,
As Heav'n's design'd INFIRMARY for all,
Here came the GREAT PHYSICIAN of the Soul,
To *heal* Man's Nature, and to make him *whole*:
Still, **by his SPIRIT, present** with all those,
Who lend an Aid to lessen human Woes.

A godlike Work; who forwards it is sure,
That ev'ry Step advances his own Cure:
Without Benevolence, the View to Self
Makes worldly Riches an unrighteous Pelf;
While blest thro' Life, the Giver, for his Love,
Dies to receive its huge Reward above.

To them who tread the certain Path to Bliss,
That leads thro' Scenes of Charity like this,
Think what the Saviour of the World will say——
" *Ye blessed of my Father, come your Way*;
" *'Twas done to me, if done to the distrest*:
" *Come, ye true Friends, and be for ever blest.*

A N

HYMN to JESUS.

I.

COME, Saviour *Jesus!* from above,
  Assist me with thy heav'nly Grace;
  Withdraw my Heart from worldly **Love,**
And for thy Self prepare the **Place.**

II.

  Lord! let thy sacred Presence fill,
And set my longing Spirit free;
  That pants to have no other **Will,**
But **Night** and Day to think on thee.

III.

  Where'er thou leadest, I'll pursue,
Thro' all Retirements, or Employs;
  But to the World I'll bid adieu,
And all its vain delusive Joys.

IV. That

IV.

That Way with humble Speed I'll walk,
Wherein my *Saviour's* Footsteps shine;
  Nor will I hear, nor will I talk
Of any other Love but thine.

V.

To Thee my longing Soul aspires;
To Thee I offer all my Vows:
  Keep me from false and vain Desires,
My God, my Saviour, and my Spouse!

VI.

Henceforth, let no profane Delight
Divide this consecrated Soul!
  Possess it Thou, who hast the Right,
As Lord and Master of the Whole.

VII.

Wealth, Honours, Pleasures, or what else
This short-enduring World can give,
  'Tempt as they will, my Heart repells,
To Thee alone resolv'd to live.

VIII. Thee

VIII.

Thee one may love, and thee alone,
With inward Peace, and holy Blifs;
  And when thou tak'ft us for thy **own,**
Oh! what an Happinefs is this!

IX.

Nor Heav'n, nor **Earth** do I defire,
Nor Myfteries **to be reveal'd;**
  'Tis Love that fets my **Heart on Fire:**
Speak thou **the Word, and I am** heal'd.

X.

All other Graces I refign;
Pleas'd to receive, pleas'd to **reftore:**
  Grace is thy *Gift,* it fhall be mine
The GIVER **only** to adore.

AN
HYMN on SIMPLICITY.
From the GERMAN.

I.

JESU! teach this Heart of mine
   True *Simplicity* to find;
Child-like, innocent, divine,
   Free from *Guile* of ev'ry Kind:
And fince, when amongft us vouchfafing to live,
So pure an Example it pleas'd Thee to give;
O! let me keep ftill the bright Pattern in View,
And be, after thy Likenefs, right fimple and true.

II.

When I read, or when I hear
   Truths that kindle good Defires;
How to act, and how to bear
   What Heav'n-inftructed Faith requires;
Let no fubtle Fancies e'er lead me aftray,
Or teach me to comment thy Doctrines away;
No Reas'nings of felfifh Corruption within,
Nor Slights by which Satan deludes us to Sin.

III. Whilft

III.

Whilſt I pray before thy **Face,**
 Thou! who art my higheſt Good!
O! confirm to me the Grace,
 Purchas'd by thy precious Blood:
That, with a true filial Affection of Heart,
I may feel what a real Redeemer thou art;
And, thro' thy Atonement to Juſtice above,
Be receiv'd, as a Child, by the Father of Love.

IV.

Give me, with a Child-like Mind,
 Simply to believe thy Word;
And to do whate'er I find
 Pleaſes beſt my deareſt Lord:
Reſolving to practice thy gracious Commands;
To reſign myſelf wholly up into thy Hands:
That, regarding Thee ſimply in **all my Employ,**
I may cry, *Abba! Father!* with dutiful **Joy.**

V.

Nor within me, **nor** without,
 Let *Hypocriſy* reſide ;
But whate'er I go about,
 Mere *Simplicity* be Guide:
Simplicity guide me in Word, and in Will;
Let me live——let me dye——in Simplicity ſtill:

Of

Of an Epitaph made me let this be the Whole——
Here lies a true Child, that was simple of Soul.

VI.

JESU ! now I fix my Heart,
    Prince of Life ! and Source of Bliss !
Never from Thee to depart,
    'Till thy Love shall grant me this :
Then, then, shall my Heart all its Faculties raise,
Both *here,* and *hereafter,* to sing to thy Praise :
O ! joyful ! my Saviour says, *so let it be !*
AMEN, *to my Soul,*——HALLELUJAH ! to *Thee* !

A

FAREWELL to the WORLD.

From the FRENCH.

I.

WORLD adieu, thou real Cheat !
    Oft have thy deceitful Charms
Fill'd my Heart with fond Conceit,
    Foolish Hopes, and false Alarms :
Now I see, as clear as Day,
How thy Follies pass away.

II. Vain

II.

Vain thy entertaining Sights;
   Falfe thy Promifes renew'd;
All the Pomp of thy Delights
   Does but flatter and delude:
Thee I quit for Heav'n above,
Object of the nobleft Love.

III.

Farewell Honour's empty Pride!
   Thy own nice, uncertain Guft,
If the leaft Mifchance betide,
   Lays thee lower than the Duft:
Worldly Honours end in Gall,
Rife to Day, To-morrow fall.

IV.

Foolifh Vanity, farewell!
   More inconftant than the Wave;
Where thy foothing Fancies dwell,
   Pureft Tempers they deprave:
He, to whom I fly from thee,
JESUS CHRIST, fhall fet me free.

F fV. Never

V.

Never shall my wandering Mind
 Follow after fleeting Toys;
Since in God alone I find
 Solid and substantial Joys:
Joys that, never overpast,
Thro' Eternity shall last.

VI.

Lord, how happy is a Heart,
 After Thee while it aspires!
True and faithful as thou art,
 Thou shalt answer its Desires:
It shall see the glorious Scene
Of thy everlasting Reign.

***

An H Y M N.
From the F R E N C H.

I.

HOW charming! to be thus confin'd
 Within this lovely Tow'r;
Where, with a calm, and quiet Mind,
 I pass the peaceful Hour:
Stronger than Chains of any Kind
 Is Love's enduring Pow'r.

II. These

II.

Thefe very Ills **are** my Delight;
  My Pleafures rife from Pains;
The Punifhments, that moft affright,
  Become my wifh'd-for Gains:
Whatever Torments they **excite,**
  Pure-fighing Love remains.

III.

Pain is no Object of my Fear,
  Tho' **Help is not in View;**
Sure as **I am, from** Evils here,
  That Bleffings will enfue:
To fov'reign Beauty it is clear,
  That fov'reign Love is due.

IV.

I fuffer; but along with Smart
  Is Grace and Virtue fent:
Prefence of GOD, who takes my Part,
  So fweetens all Event!
He is the Patience of my Heart,
  The Comfort, and Content.

F f 2

THE

THE

Soul's Tendency towards it's true Centre.

I.

STONES towards the Earth defcend;
    Rivers to the Ocean roll;
Every Motion has fome End:
    What is thine, beloved Soul?

II.

Mine is, where my Saviour is;
    There with him I hope to dwell:
Jesu is the central Blifs;
    Love the Force that doth impel.

III.

Truly, thou haft anfwer'd right:
    Now may Heav'ns attractive Grace,
Tow'rds the Source of thy Delight,
    Speed along thy quick'ning Pace!

IV. Thank

IV.

Thank thee for thy gen'rous Care:
  Heav'n, that did the Wish inspire,
Through thy instrumental Pray'r,
  Plumes the Wings of my Desire.

V.

Now, methinks, aloft I fly:
  Now, with Angels bear a Part:
Glory be to God on High!
  Peace to ev'ry Christian Heart!

THE

Desponding SOUL's WISH.

I.

MY Spirit longeth for thee,
  Within my troubled Breast;
Altho' I be unworthy
  Of so divine a Guest.

II.

Of ſo divine a Gueſt,
    Unworthy tho' I be;
Yet has my Heart no Reſt,
    Unleſs it come from Thee.

III.

Unleſs it come from Thee,
    In vain I look around;
In all that I can ſee,
    No Reſt is to be found.

IV.

No Reſt is to be found,
    But in thy bleſſed Love;
O! let my Wiſh be **crown'd,**
    And ſend it from above!

The ANSWER.

I.

CHEAR up deſponding Soul;
    Thy Longing, pleas'd, **I ſee;**
'Tis Part of that great Whole,
    Wherewith I long'd for thee.

II. Wherewith

II.

Wherewith **I long'd for** thee,
   And left my Father's Throne;
From Death to fet thee free,
   To claim thee for my own.

III.

To claim thee for my own,
   I fuffer'd on the Crofs:
Oh! were my Love but **known,**
   No Soul could fear its **Lofs.**

IV.

No Soul could fear its Lofs,
   But, fill'd with Love divine,
Would *die* on its *own* Crofs,
   And *rife* for ever *mine.*

An

An HYMN to JESUS.

From the Latin of St. BERNARD.

I.

JESU! the Soul that thinks on Thee,
    How happy does it feem to be!
What Honey can fuch Sweets impart,
As does thy Prefence to the Heart!

II.

    No Sound can dwell upon the Tongue,
Nor Ears be ravifh'd with a Song,
Nor Thought by pondering be won,
Like that of God's beloved Son.

III.

    JESU! the Penitent's Retreat,
The wearied Pilgrim's Mercy Seat:
If they that *feek* thee are careft,
How are the *Finders* of thee bleft!

IV.

    JESU! the Source of *Life* and *Light*,
That mak'ft the Mind fo bleft and bright;

Fullnefs

Fullnefs of Joy Thou doft infpire
Beyond the Stretch of all Defire.

V.

This can no Tongue that ever fpoke,
Nor Hand exprefs by figur'd Stroke:
It is *Experience* that muft prove
The Pow'r of JESUS, and his Love.

A PARAPHRASE

ON THE

PRAYER, ufed in the CHURCH LITURGY,

For all Sorts and Conditions of Men.

I.

IT will bear the repeating again and again,
  Will the Pray'r for all Sorts and Conditions of Men;
Not to this, or that Place, Name, or Nation confin'd,
But embracing, at once, the whole Race of Mankind;
With a Love univerfal inftructing to call
On the one great creating Preferver of All;
That his Way may be known upon Earth, and be found
His true faving Health, by the Nations all round.

II. He,

II.

He, who willeth all **Men** to be fav'd, and partake
Of the Blifs, which diftinguifh'd their primitive Make;
To arife to that Life, by a fecond new Birth,
Which *Adam* had loft, at his *Fall* upon Earth;
Will accept ev'ry Heart, whofe unfeigned Intent
Is to **pray for that** Bleffing, which he himfelf meant,
When he gave **his** own Son, for whoever fhould will
To efcape, by his Means, from the Regions of Ill.

III.

But tho' all the **whole** World, in a Senfe that is good,
To be God's Houfe, or Church, may be well underftood;
And the Men who dwell on it, his Children. for whom
It has pleas'd him that *Chrift* the Redeemer fhould come;
Yet his Church muft confift, in all faving Refpect,
Of them who receive him, **not** them who reject;
And his **true,** real Children, or People, are they,
Who, **when** call'd by **the Saviour,** believe and obey.

IV.

Now this excellent Pray'r, in this Senfe of the Phrafe,
For the Catholic Church more efpecially prays;
That **it may** be fo conftantly govern'd, and led
By the *Spirit* of God, and of *Jefus* **its** Head,
That all fuch as are taught to acknowledge its Creed,
And profefs to be *Chriftians,* may be **fo** indeed;

May

May hold the one Faith, in a Peace without Strife,
And the Proof of its Truth, a right practical Life.

V.

No partial Distinction is here to be sought;
For the Good of Mankind still enlivens the Thought;
Since God, by the Church, in its Catholic Sense,
Salvation to all is so pleas'd to dispense,
That the farther her Faith, and her Patience increase,
More Hearts will be won to the Gospel of Peace;
'Till the World shall come under Truth's absolute Sway,
And the Nations, converted, bring on the great Day.

VI.

Mean while, tho' Eternity be her chief Care,
The Suff'rers in Time have a suitable Share:
She prays to the fatherly Goodness of God,
For all whom Affliction has under its Rod;
That inward, or outward, the Cause of their Grief,
Mind, Body, Estate, He would grant them Relief,
Due Comfort, and Patience, and finally bless
With the most happy Ending of all their Distress.

VII.

The Compassion, here taught, is unlimited too,
And the Whole of Mankind the petitioning View:

As

As none can forefee, whether Chriftian, or not,
What Afflictions may fall in this World to his Lot;
The Church, which confiders whofe Providence fends,
Prays that all may obtain its beneficent Ends;
And whenever the Suff'rings, here needful, are paft,
By Repentance and Faith, may be fav'd at the laft.

VIII.

The particular Mention of fuch, as defire
To be publickly pray'd for, as made in our Quire,
Infers to all others God's merciful Grace;
Tho' we hear not their Names, who are in the like Cafe;
It excites our Attention to Inftances known,
Of Relations, or Neighbours, or Friends of our own;
For the Pray'r, in its Nature, extends to all thofe,
Who are in the fame Trouble, Friends to Us, or Foes.

IX.

All which fhe entreats, for his Sake, to be done,
Who fuffer'd to fave them, *Chrift Jefus*, his Son;
In refpect to the World, the Redeemer of All;
To the Church of the Faithful, moft chiefly, faith *Paul*;
And to them, who fhall fuffer, whoever they be,
In the *Spirit* of *Chrift*, in the higheft Degree:
How ought fuch a Goodnefs all Minds to prepare,
For an hearty *Amen* to this Catholic Pray'r!

X. The

X.

The Church is indeed, in its real Intent,
An Affembly, where Nothing but Friendfhip is meant;
And the utter Extinction of Foefhip, and Wrath,
By the Working of Love, in the Strength of its Faith:
This gives it its holy, and catholic Name,
And truly confirms its apoftolic Claim;
Showing what the one Saviour's one Miffion **had been,**
——*Go and teach all the World*——ev'ry Creature **therein.**

XI.

In the Praife ever due to the Gofpel of Grace,
Its Univerfality holds the firft Place:
When an Angel proclaim'd its glad Tidings, **the Morn**
That the Son of the Virgin, the *Saviour* was born;
Which fhall be to all People was faid to compleat
The angelical Meffage, fo good, and fo great;
Full of *Glory* to *God*, in the Regions above,
And of *Goodnefs* to *Men*, is fo boundlefs a Love.

XII.

This fhort Supplication, or Litany, read,
When the longer with us is not wont to be faid,
Tho' brief in Expreffion, as fully imports
The Will to all Bleffings, for Men of all Sorts;

Same

Same brotherly Love, by which Chriftians are taught
To pray without ceafing, or limiting Thought;
That Religion may flourifh upon its true Plan,
Of *Glory* to God, and *Salvation* to Man.

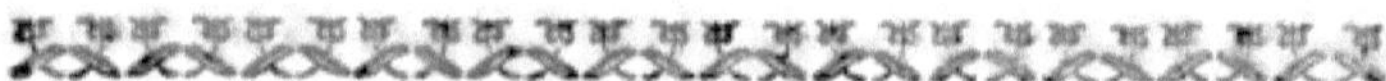

THE

PRAYER of RUSBROCHIUS.

I.

O Merciful Lord! by the Good which Thou art,
 I befeech Thee to raife a true Love in my Heart
For Thee, above all Things; Thee only; and then
To extend to all Sorts, and Conditions of Men:
Religious, or fecular; Kindred, or not;
Or near, or far off, or whatever their Lot;
That be any Man's State rich or poor, high or low,
As myfelf I may love him, Friend to me, or Foe.

II.

 May pay to all Men a becoming Refpect,
Not prone to condemn them for feeming Defect;
But to bear it, if true, with a Patience exempt
From the proud, furly Vice of a fcornful Contempt:
If fhown to myfelf, let me learn to endure,
And obtain, by its Aid, my own Vanity's Cure;

Nor

Nor, however difdain'd, in the fpitefulleft Shape,
By a finful Return ever think to efcape.

III.

Let my pure, fimple Aim, in whatever it be,
Thro' Praife, or Difpraife, be my Duty to Thee:
With a fixt Refolution, ftill eyeing that Scope
To admit of no other Fear, be it, or Hope,
But the Fear to offend Thee, the Hope to unite,
In thy Honour and Praife, with all Hearts that are right,
Wifhing all the World well; but intent to fulfill,
Be they pleas'd, or difpleas'd, thy adorable Will.

IV.

Preferve me, Dear Lord, from Prefumption and Pride,
That upon my own Actions would tempt to confide:
Let me have no Dependence on any but Thine,
With a right Faith and Truft in thy Merits divine:
Still ready prepar'd, in each requifite Hour,
Both to will, and to work, as thou giveft the Pow'r;
But may only thy Love flame thro' all my whole Heart,
And a falfe felfifh Fire not affect the leaft Part.

V.

To this End, let thine Arrow pierce deeply within,
Letting out all the Filth, and Corruption of Sin;

All

All that in the moſt ſecret Receſſes may lurk,
To prevent, or obſtruct, thy Intention or Work:
O! give me the Knowledge, the Feeling and Senſe,
Of thy all-bleſſing Pow'r, Wiſdom, Goodneſs immenſe!
Of the Weakneſs, the Folly, the Malice alone,
That, reſiſting thy Will, I ſhould find in my own!

VI.

Never let me forget, never, while I draw Breath,
What Thou haſt done for me, thy Paſſion, **and Death!**
The Wounds, and the Griefs, of thy Body, **and Soul,**
When aſſuming our Nature thou madeſt it whole:
Taughteſt how to engage in thy conquering Strife,
And **regain the** Acceſs to its true divine Life:
Let the Senſe of ſuch Love kindle all my **Deſire,**
To be thine my Life thro'; thine to die and expire.

VII.

To Hearts, in the Bond of thy Charity Knit,
Ev'ry Thing becomes **eaſy to do,** or omit;
The Labour is pleaſant, the ſharpeſt Degree
Of Suff'ring can find Conſolation in Thee:
That which Nature affords, or an Object terrene,
When **it does not divert** from a perfecter Scene,
Is receiv'd with all Thanks, if thou pleaſeſt to grant,
By a Mind, if thou pleaſeſt, as willing to want.

VIII. The

VIII.

The Amufements, on **which** it once fet fuch a Store,
Are now as infipid, as grateful before;
With **a much** greater Comfort it gives **up** each Toy,
Than the fondeft Poffeffor could ever enjoy:
If e'er I propos'd fuch unfuitable Ends
To the Thought of religious, or fecular Friends,
Expel the vain Images, Fancies of Good,
And in their Heart, and mine, make Thyfelf underftood.

IX.

Extinguifh, O Lord, **let not** any one take
A Complacence in me, which is not for thy Sake;
In me too root out the Refpect, of all Kind,
Which does not arife from thy Love in my Mind:
No Sorrow be fpar'd, **no** Affliction, no Crofs,
That may further this Love, or recover its Lofs;
This is always thy Meaning; O let it be mine
To confefs Myfelf guilty, repent, and refign.

X.

With a real Contempt **of all** Self-feeking Views,
To embrace, for **my** Choice, what thy Wifdom fhall chufe;
Looking up ftill **to Thee,** to receive all Event
Which it wills, **or** permits, with **a** thankful Content:
Not regarding what **Men** fhall do **to me,** or why,
But the provident Aim of thine all-feeing Eye;

H h

Ever

Ever watchful o'er them who perſiſt, in each Place,
To rely on its Preſence——O give me thy Grace!

XI.

Tho' unworthy to aſk it, poor Sinner! I truſt
In the Merits, and Death of a Saviour ſo juſt;
Whom the Father, well pleas'd in his ſatisfi'd Will,
The Deſign to ſave Sinners ſaw rightly fulfil:
In me let thy Grace, O Redeemer within,
Re-eſtabliſh his Juſtice, and purge away Sin;
That freed from its Evils, in me, may be ſhown
The Effect of thy all-ſaving Merits alone.

XII.

May Death, and its Conſequence, ſtill in my Eyes,
So remind me to live, that it may not ſurprize:
May the horrible Torments excite a due Dread,
Which impenitent Sinners bring on their own Head:
May I never ſeek Peace, never find a Delight,
But when I purſue what is good in thy Sight:
Whatſoever I do, ſuffer, feel to befall,
Be Thou the ſole Cauſe, the one Reaſon of all!

A PRAYER.

A PRAYER,

FROM

Mr. LAW's Spirit of Prayer.

OH heav'nly Father! gracious God above!
    Thou boundless Depth of never-ceasing Love!
Save me from *Self*, and cause me to depart
From sinful Works of a long-harden'd Heart;
From all my great Corruptions set me free;
Give me an Ear to hear, an Eye to see,
An Heart and Spirit to believe, and find
Thy Love in *Christ*, the Saviour of Mankind.

    Made for Thyself, O God, and to display
Thy Goodness in me, manifest, I pray,
By Grace adapted to each wanting Hour,
Thy holy Nature's Life-conferring Pow'r:
Give me the Faith, the Hunger, and the Thirst,
After the Life breath'd forth from thee, at first;
Birth of thy holy Jesus in my Soul;
That I may turn, thro' Life's succeeding Whole,
From ev'ry outward Work, or inward Thought,
Which is not Thee, or in thy Spirit wrought.

      On ATTEN-

On ATTENTION.

SACRED Attention! true effectual Prayer!
   Thou doſt the Soul for Love of Truth prepare.
Bleſt is the Man, who, from Conjecture free,
To future Knowledge ſhall aſpire by thee:
Who in thy Precepts ſeeks a ſure Repoſe,
Stays till he ſees, nor judges till he knows:
Tho' firm, not raſh; tho' eager, yet ſedate;
Intent on Truth, can its Inſtruction wait:
Aw'd by thy powerful Influence to appeal
To Heaven, which only can itſelf reveal;
The Soul in humble Silence to reſign,
And human Will unite to the divine;
Till fir'd at length by Heaven's enlivening Beams
Pure, unconſum'd the faithful Victim flames.

A P R A Y E R,

USED BY

FRANCIS the Firſt, when he was at War
with the Emperor CHARLES the Fifth.

ALMIGHTY Lord of Hoſts, by whoſe Commands
   The guardian Angels rule their deſtin'd Lands;
And watchful, at thy Word, to ſave or ſlay,
Of Peace or War adminiſter the Sway:

Thou,

Thou, who, againſt the great Goliah's Rage
Didſt arm the Stripling David to engage;
When, with a Sling, a ſmall unarmed Youth
Smote a huge Giant, in Defence of Truth;
Hear us, we pray thee, if our Cauſe be true,
If ſacred Juſtice be our only View;
If Right and Duty, not the Will to War,
Have forc'd our Armies to proceed thus far,
Then turn the Hearts of all our Foes to Peace,
That War, and Bloodſhed in the Land may ceaſe:
Or, put to Flight by providential Dread,
Let them lament their Errors, not their Dead.
If ſome muſt die, protect the righteous all,
And let the guilty, few as may be, fall.
With pitying Speed the Victory decree
To them, whoſe Cauſe is beſt approv'd by thee;
That ſheath'd on all Sides the devouring Sword,
And Peace, and Juſtice to our Land reſtor'd,
We all together, with one Heart, may ſing
Triumphant Hymns to thee, th' Eternal King.

A COM;

A COMMENT

ON THE

FOLLOWING PASSAGE, in the general CONFESSION OF SINS,

Uſed in the CHURCH-LITURGY.

—— *According to thy Promiſes declared unto Mankind in Chriſt Jeſu our Lord.*

ACCORDING to thy Promiſes —— hereby,
 Since it is certain that God cannot lie,
The truly penitent may all be ſure
That Grace admits them to its open Door;
And they, forſaking all their former Sin,
However great, will freely be let in.

 Declar'd —— by all the Miniſters of Peace,
God has aſſur'd Repentance of Releaſe;
An intervening Penitence, we ſee,
Could even Change his poſitive Decree;
As in the *Niniviter;* if any Soul
Repent, the Promiſe is the ſure Parole.

 Unto Mankind —— not only to the Jews,
Chriſtians, or Turks, in Writings which they uſe;
Writ

Writ on the Tablet of each confcious Heart,
Repent———*from all Iniquity depart*———
Not for no Purpofe; for the plain Intent
Is Reftoration, if a Soul repent.

In *Chrift*———by whom true Scripture has affur'd
Redeeming Grace for Penitents procur'd;
The fainter Hopes, which Reafon may fuggeft,
Are deeply, by the Gofpel's Aid, impreft:
'Twas always hop'd for was the promis'd Good,
But, by his Coming, clearly underftood.

Jefu———Jehovah's manifefted Love,
In *Chrift*, th' Anointed Saviour from above;
The Demonftration of the faving Plan,
For all Mankind, is God's becoming Man:
No Truth more firmly afcertain'd than this———
Repent, be faithful, and reftor'd to Blifs.

Our Lord———our new, and true parental Head;
Our *fecond Adam*, in the firft when dead;
Who took our Nature on him, that in Men
His Father's Image might fhine forth again:
Sure of Succefs may Penitents implore
What God, thro' Him, rejoices to reftore.

F O R

FOR THE

DUE IMPROVEMENT

OF A

FUNERAL SOLEMNITY.

AROUND the Grave of a departed Friend,
   If due Concern has prompted to attend,
Deep, on our Minds, let the affecting Scenes
Imprint the Leffon, which Attendance means :
For who can tell how foon his own *Adieu*
The folemn Service may, for Him, renew?

   He that believes on Me (what *Chrift* had faid
The Prieft proclaims) *fhall live tho' he were dead :*
To ev'ry Heart This is the gracious Call,
On which depends its everlafting All ;
The ever hoping, loving, working Faith,
That faves a Soul from Death's devouring Wrath.

   The patient *Job*, by fuch a Faith within,
Strengthning his Heart, could fay——*This mortal Skin
Deftroy'd, I know that my Redeemer lives*——
In Flefh and Blood, which his Redemption gives——
Job, from the Duft, expected to arife,
And ftand before his God with feeing Eyes.

The

The royal Pfalmift faw this Life of Man,
How vain, how fhort, at its moft lengthen'd Span;
Confcious in Whom the Human Truft fhould be,
" *Truly my Hope*, he faid, *is ev'n in Thee*"———
And pray'd for its recover'd Strength, *before*
He went from hence, here to be feen no more.

The myftic Chapter is rehears'd, **wherein**
Paul fings the Triumph **over** Death, and Sin;
The glorious Body, freed from earthy Leav'n,
Image and Likenefs of the Lord from Heav'n;
For fuch th' abounding in his Work fhall gain;
Labour, we know, *that never is in vain.*

Hence comes the fure and certain Hope, to rife
In *Chrift*; tho' Man, as born of Woman, dies:
True Life, which *Adam* di'd to, at his Fall,
And *Chrift,* the finlefs *Adam,* can recall,
By a new, heav'nly Birth, from Him, revives,
And breathes, again, God's holy Breath of Lives.

A Voice from Heav'n bad hearing *John* record,
Blefs are the dead, the dying in the Lord———
In them, the Pray'r, which Man's Redeemer will'd
That Men fhould pray, is perfectly fulfill'd:
This perfect Senfe the Words, that we **repeat**,
Require, to make the pray'd-for Good compleat.

Thanks then are due for all the faithful dead,
Departed hence, to be with *Chrift* their Head;

And

And Pray'r, unfainting, for his —— *Come, ye bleſt* ——
Come, ye true Children, enter into Reſt;
Live in my Father's Kingdom, and in mine,
In Grace, and Love, and Fellowſhip divine.

O N
CHURCH COMMUNION,
In SEVEN PARTS;
From a LETTER of Mr. LAW's.
PART FIRST.

I.

RELIGION, Church Communion, or the Way
   Of public Worſhip, that we ought to pay,
As it regards the Body, and the Mind,
Is of external, and internal Kind;
The one confiſting in the outward Sign,
The other in the inward Truth divine.

II.

This inward Truth intended to be ſhown,
So far as outward Signs can make it known,

Is

Is that which gives external Modes a Worth,
Juſt in Proportion as they ſhew it forth;
Juſt as they help, in any outward Part,
The real, true Religion of the Heart.

III.

Now what this is, excluſive of all Strife,
Chriſtians will own to be an inward Life,
Spirit, and Pow'r, a Birth, to ſay the Whole,
Of Chriſt himſelf, brought forth within the Soul;
By this all true Salvation is begun,
And carried on, however it be done.

IV.

Chriſtianity, that has not Chriſt within,
Can by no Means whatever ſave from Sin;
Can bear no Evidence of Him——the End,
On which the Value of all Means depend:
Chriſtian Religion ſignifies, no doubt,
Like Mind within, like Show of it without.

V.

The Will of God, the Saving of Mankind,
Was all that Chriſt had in his inward Mind;
All that produc'd his outward Action too,
In Church Communion while a perfect Jew;

Like

Like moſt of his Diſciples, till they came,
At *Antioch*, to have a Chriſtian Name.

VI.

If Chriſt has put an End to Rites of old,
If new recall what was but then foretold,
The one true Church, the real heav'nly Ground,
Wherein alone Salvation can be found,
Is ſtill the Same; and, to its Saviour's Praiſe,
His inward Tempers outwardly diſplays;

VII.

By hearty Love, and correſpondent Rites
Ordain'd, the Members to the Head unites,
And to each other——in all ſtated Scenes,
The Life of Chriſt is what a Chriſtian means;
Tho' Change of Circumſtance may alter thoſe,
In this he places, and enjoys Repoſe.

VIII.

Church Unity is held, and Faith's Increaſe,
By that of Spirit, in the Bond of Peace,
And Righteouſneſs of Life; without this Tie
Forms are in vain preſcrib'd to worſhip by,
Or Temples model'd; Hearts, as well as Hands,
An holy Church, and catholic demands.

PART

PART SECOND.

I.

IF once eſtabliſh'd the eſſential Part,
  The inward Church, the Temple of the Heart,
Or Houſe of God, the Subſtance, and the Sum
Of what is pray'd for in——*Thy Kingdom come*——
To make an outward Correſpondence true,
We muſt recur to Chriſt's Example too.

II.

  Now, in his outward Form of Life, we find
Goodneſs demonſtrated of ev'ry Kind;
What he was born for, that he ſhow'd throughout;
It was the Buſ'neſs that he went about;
Love, Kindneſs, and Compaſſion to diſplay
Tow'rds ev'ry Object coming in his Way.

III.

  But Love ſo high, Humility ſo low,
And all the Virtues which his Actions ſhow;
His doing Good, and his enduring Ill,
For Man's Salvation and God's holy Will,
Exceed all Terms——his inward, outward Plan
Was Love to God, expreſs'd by Love to Man.

IV. Mark,

IV.

Mark of the Church, which he eſtabliſh'd, then,
Is the ſame Love, ſame Proof of it to Men;
Without, let Sects parade it how they liſt,
Nor Church, nor Unity can e'er ſubſiſt;
The Name may be uſurp'd, but Want of Pow'r
Will ſhew the Babel, high or low the Tow'r.

V.

And where the ſame Behaviour ſhall appear
In outward Form, that was in Chriſt ſo clear,
There is the very outward Church, that He
Will'd all Mankind to ſhew, and all to ſee;
Of which whoever ſhews it, from the Heart,
Is both an inward, and an outward Part.

VI.

What Excommunication can deprive
A pious Soul, that is in Chriſt alive,
Of Church Communion? or cut off a Limb
That Life, and Action both unite to Him?
For any Circumſtance of Place, or Time,
Or Mode, or Cuſtom, which infers no Crime?

VII.

If He be That which his beloved *John*
Calls him,——*The Light enlight'ning ev'ry one*

That

That comes into the World——will he exclude
One from his Church, whofe Mind he has renew'd
To fuch Degree, as to exert, in fact,
Like inward Temper, and like outward Act?

VIII.

Invifible, and vifible Effect,
Of true Church Memberfhip, in each Refpect,
Let the one Shepherd from above behold;
The Flocks, howe'er difpers'd, are his one Fold;
Seen by their Hearts, and their Behaviour too,
They all ftand prefent in his gracious View.

PART THIRD.

I.

A Local Union, on the other Hand,
  Tho' crouded Numbers fhould together ftand,
Joining in one fame Form of Pray'r, and Praife,
Or Creed exprefs'd in regulated Phrafe,
Or aught befide——tho' it affume the Name
Of Chriftian Church, may want the real Claim.

II.

For if it want the Spirit, and the Sign,
That conftitute all Worfhip, as divine,

The

The Love within, the Teſt of it without,
In vain the Union paſſes for devout;
Heartleſs, and tokenleſs if it remain,
It ought to paſs, in Strictneſs, for profane.

III.

At firſt, an Unity of Heart and Soul,
A Diſtribution of an outward Dole,
And ev'ry Member of the Body fed,
As equally belonging to the Head,
With what it wanted, was, without Suſpenſe,
True Church Communion, in full Chriſtian Senſe.

IV.

Whether averſe the Many, or the Few,
To hold Communion in this righteous View,
Their Thought commences Hereſy, their Deed
Schiſmatical, tho' they profeſs the Creed;
Ways of diſtributing, if new, ſhould ſtill
Maintain the old communicative Will;

V.

Broken by ev'ry loveleſs, thankleſs Thought,
And not behaving as a Chriſtian ought;
By want of Meekneſs, or a Show of Pride
Tow'rds any Soul for whom our Saviour di'd;

While

While this continues, Men may pray, and preach
In all their Forms, but none will heal the Breach.

VI.

Whatever Helps an outward Form may bring
To Church Communion, it is not the Thing;
Nor a Society, as fuch, nor Place,
Nor any thing befides uniting Grace:
They are but Acceffories, at the moft,
To true Communion of the Holy Ghoft.

VII.

This is th' effential Fellowfhip, the Tie
Which all true Chriftians are united by;
No other Union does them any Good,
But that which Chrift cemented with his Blood,
As God and Man; that, having loft it, Men
Might live in Unity with God again.

VIII.

What He came down to bring us from above
Was Grace and Peace, and Law-fulfilling Love;
True Spirit-Worfhip, which his Father fought,
Was the fole End of what He did, and taught;
That God's own Church and Kingdom might begin,
Which Mofes and the Prophets ufher'd in.

K k

PART

❧❧❧❧❧❧❧❧❧❧❧❧❧❧❧❧❧❧❧❧❧❧❧❧❧❧❧

PART FOURTH.

I.

" THE Church of Chrift, as thus you reprefent,
"   And all the World is of the fame Extent:
" *Jews*, *Turks*, or *Pagans* may be Members too;
" This, fome may call a dreadful myftic Clue,
" A Combination of the Quaker Schemes
" With latitudinarian Extremes."

II.

They may; but Names, fo ready at the Call
Of fuch as want them, have no Force at all
To overthrow momentous Truths, and plain,
The very Points of Scripture, and the main;
Such as diftinguifh, in the cleareft View,
Th' enlighten'd *Chriftian* from the half-blind·*Jew.*

III.

What did the Sheet let down to *Peter* mean,
Who call'd the *Gentiles* common, or, unclean?
Let *Peter* anfwer——*God was pleas'd to fhow*
That I fhould call no Man whatever fo;
In ev'ry Nation he that ferves him right
Is clean, accepted, in his equal Sight.

If

IV.

If *Peter* said so, who will question *Paul?*
He, in a Manner, made this Point his all;
The real Sense of what has here been said
In mystic *Paul* is plainly to be read;
Nothing but obstinate Dislike to Terms
Obscures what all the Testament affirms.

V.

The *Jews* objected, to his Gospel Clue,
A——*What Advantage therefore hath the* Jew?
Or, of what Use is to be circumcis'd?
So may some *Christians* say——to be baptis'd?——
May form like Questions, like Conclusions draw,
And urge the Church, as they did, and the Law.

VI.

Th' Apostle's Reas'ning from the common Want
Of God's free Grace, its universal Grant
By Jesus Christ, its Reach to all Mankind,
For whom the same Salvation was design'd,
Shows that his Church, as boundless as his Grace,
x tends itself to all the human Race.

VII.

With pious *Jews* of old *our King* impli'd
The one true King of all the Earth beside;

. K k 2

Whose

Whofe regal Right, tho' he was pleas'd to call
Jacob his Lot, extended over all;
Tho' *Ifrael* gloried in acknowledg'd Light,
It's Virtue was not bounded by their Sight.

VIII.

So will a *Chriftian* Piety confefs
A Church of Chrift, with Boundaries no lefs;
Will fpeak, as ev'ry confcious Witnefs ought,
To what it knows, but fcorn the partial Thought
Of Grace, or Truth, or Righteoufnefs confin'd
To Modes and Cuftoms of external Kind.

PART FIFTH.

I.

THE Church confider'd only as poffeft
   Of *England, Rome, Geneva*——and the reft——
Notion of Church fo popularly rife,
Such Caufe of endlefs Enmity and Strife,
Did but arife in a fucceeding Hour,
When *Chriftians* came to have a worldly Pow'r.

The firft Apoftles fpread, from Place to Place,
The Gofpel News of univerfal Grace;

Inviting

Inviting all to enter, by Belief,
Into the Church of their redeeming Chief;
Entrance acceſſible in ev'ry Part,
And ſhut to Nothing but a faithleſs Heart.

III.

But when the **Princes** of the World became,
And Kings, Protectors of the Chriſtian Name,
Pow'r made ambitious Paſtors, Eaſe remiſs,
And Churches dwindl'd into *that* and *this*;
The one, divided, **came to want, of** courſe,
Supports quite foreign to its native Force.

IV.

Contentions roſe, all tending to create
Still **new** Alliances of Church and State;
Form'd, and reform'd, and turn'd, and overturn'd,
As Force prevail'd, and human Paſſion burn'd;
Old Revolutions when by new diſſolv'd,
Both Church and State accordingly revolv'd.

V.

Such is the Mixture of an human Sway,
In all external Churches at this Day;
To the ſame Changes liable, anew,
That Forms of Government are ſubject to;

While

While the one Church, in its true Senfe, in Name
And Thing, remains unchangeably the fame.

VI.

The private Chriftian, bearing Chrift in Mind,
Whofe Kingdom was not of a worldly Kind,
Has little, or has no Concern at all,
With thefe external Changes that befall;
Let Providence permit them, or prevent,
With Truth and Spirit he remains content.

VII.

Not that he thinks that Evil, more or lefs,
Is, in its Nature, alter'd by Succefs;
The Good is good, tho' fuff'ring a Defeat,
The Bad but worfe, if its Succefs be great;
He meafures neither by th' Event that's paft,
For what they were at firft they are at laft.

VIII.

But, by the Spirit of the Gofpel, free,
Whatever State of Government it be,
That God has plac'd him under, to fubmit,
So in the Church he thinks the Freedom fit,
Whilft, on Occafion of the outward Part,
He can prefent what God requires——An Heart.

PART

PART SIXTH.

I.

THE Heart is what the God of it demands,
   Who dwelleth not in Temples made with Hands:
When Hands have made them, if no Hearts are found,
Difpos'd aright to confecrate the Ground,
Vainly is Worfhip faid to be divine,
While in the Breaft its Object has no Shrine.

II.

   But if it has, in that devoted Breaft,
A right Intention, furely, will be bleft;
Tho' Forms, prefcrib'd by Paftors in the Chair,
Should be adjufted with lefs perfect Care;
Tho', in fome Points, the Services affign'd
Differ from thofe of apoftolic Kind.

III.

   What outward Church, or Form, fhall we felect,
That is not chargeable with fome Defect?
Each is prepar'd, in all the reft, to grant
A Superfluity, or elfe a Want,
Or both; a Diftance from Perfection wide,
Retorted on itfelf by all befide.

IV. What

IV.

What fafer Remedy than pure Intent
To feek the Good by any of them meant?
Which He, who mindeth only what the Heart
Brings of its own, is ready to impart;
No human Pow'r, fhould it enjoin amifs
A ceremonious Rite, can hinder this.

V.

Even in Sacrament, what frequent Storms
Has Superftition rais'd about the Forms?
In Rites baptifmal, which the true Refult?
Immerfion? Sprinkling? Infants? or th' adult?
In the Lord's Supper, does the Celebration
Make *Trans*, or *Con*, or *Non*-fubftantiation?

VI.

Thefe, and a World of Controverfies more
Serve to enlarge the bibliothecal Store;
While Champions make Antiquity their Boaft,
And all pretend to imitate it moft;
Prone to neglect, for criticifing Pique,
Effential Truths eternally antique.

VII.

Thus inward Worfhip lies in low Eftate,
Oppreft with endlefs Volumes of Debate

About

About the outward ; foon as old ones die,
All undecided. comes a new Supply
Of needlefs Doubts to a religious Soul,
Whofe upright Meaning diffipates the Whole.

VIII.

Clear of all worldly, interefted Views,
The one Defign of Worfhip it purfues;
Turns all to Ufe that public Form allows,
By off'ring up its ever private Vows
For the Succefs of all the Good defign'd
By Chrift, the common **Saviour** of Mankind.

PART SEVENTH.

I.

A Chriftian, in fo catholic a Senfe,
  Can give to none, but partial **Minds**, Offence:
Forc'd to live under fome divided Part,
He keeps intire the **Union** of the Heart;
The facred Tie of Love; by which alone,
Chrift faid, that his Difciples would be known.

II.

He values no Diftinction, as profeft
By way of Separation from the reft;

Oblig'd

Oblig'd in **Duty,** and inclin'd by Choice,
In all the Good of any to rejoice;
From ev'ry Evil, Falshood, or Mistake,
To wish them free, for common Comfort's Sake.

III.

Freedom, to which the most undoubted Way
Lies in Obedience (where it always lay)
To Christ himself; who, with an inward Call,
Knocks at the Door, that is, the Heart of all;
At the Reception of this heav'nly Guest,
All Good comes in, all Evil quits the Breast.

IV.

The free Receiver, then, becomes content
With what God orders, or does not prevent:
To them that love Him, all Things, he is sure,
Must work for Good; tho' how may be obscure:
Even successful Wickedness, when past,
Will bring, to them, some latent Good at last.

V.

Fall'n as divided Churches are, and gone
From the Perfection of the Christian one,
Respect is due to any, that contains
The venerable, tho' but faint Remains

Of

Of ancient **Rule, which** had not, in **its** View,
The Letter only, **but the Spirit too.**

VI.

When that Variety of new-found Ways
Which People fo run after, in our Days,
Has done its utmoft——when *Lo here, Lo there*,
Shall yield to inward Seeking, and fincere;
What was, at firft, may come to be again
The Praife of Church Affemblies **amongft Men.**

VII.

Mean while, in that to which we now belong,
To mind in public Leffon, Pray'r, and Song,
Teaching, and Preaching, what conduces beft
To **true** Devotion in the private Breaft,
Willing encreafe of Good to ev'ry Soul,
Seems to be our Concern upon the Whole.

VIII.

So God, and Chrift, and holy Angels ftand
Dispos'd to ev'ry Church, **in** ev'ry Land;
The Growth of Good ftill helping to compleat,
Whatever Tares be fown amongft the Wheat:
Who would not wifh to have, and to excite,
A Difpofition fo divinely right?

A DYING

A DYING SPEECH.

From Mr. L A W.

IN this unhappily divided State,
    That Christian Churches have been in of late,
One must, however catholic the Heart,
Join, and conform to some divided Part:
The *Church* of *England* is the Part, that I
Have always liv'd in, and now choose to dye;
Trusting, that if I worship God with her,
In Spirit, and in Truth, I shall not err;
But as acceptable to Him be found,
As if, in Times for one pure Church renown'd,
Born, I had also liv'd, in Heart and Soul,
A faithful Member of the unbroken Whole.

    As I am now, by God's good Will, to go
From this disorder'd State of Things below;
Into his Hands, as I am now to fall,
Who is the great Creator of us all;
God of all Churches that implore his Aid,
Lover of all the Souls that he hath made;
Whose Kingdom, that of universal Love,
Must have its blest Inhabitants above,
From ev'ry Class of Men, from all the good,
Howe'er descended from one human Blood;

So,

So, in this loving Spirit, I defire,
As in the midft of all their facred Quire,
With Rites prefcrib'd, and with a Chriftian View,
Of all the World to take my laft Adieu;
Willing in Heart and Spirit to unite
With ev'ry Church, in what is juft and right,
Holy and good, and worthy, in its Kind,
Of God's Acceptance from an honeft Mind:
Praying, that ev'ry Church may have its Saints,
And rife to that Perfection which it wants.

Father! *thy Kingdom come!* thy facred Will
May all the Tribes of human Race fulfill!
Thy Name be prais'd by ev'ry living Breath,
AUTHOR of LIFE, and VANQUISHER of DEATH!

A C O M M E N T

ON THE

FOLLOWING SCRIPTURE.

In the Beginning was the Word.

John, 1ft and 9th.

IN the Beginning was the Word——faith JOHN——
   The Life, the Light, the Truth, for all are one;
One all-creating Pow'r, all-wife, all-good,
In which, at firft, the whole Creation ftood;

Moving,

Moving, and acting in the Pow'r alone;
How bright, how perfect, and no Evil known!
How bleſt was Natures univerſal Plan,
And the fair Image of his Maker, MAN!

The Word, the Pow'r, is *Chriſt;* th' Eternal Son
Of **God,** by whom the Father's Will is done;
Each is the other's Glory; and the Love
From both the Bliſs of all the bleſt above:
Angels in Heav'n ſtand ready to obey,
And, as the Word directs them, ſo do they;
So muſt we Men, born here upon this Earth,
If ever we regain the heav'nly Birth;

Loſt by poor *Adam,* in the fatal Hour
Of luſting after Knowledge without Pow'r;
When, yielding to Temptation, tho' forbid
To eat what was not good for **him,** he did:
The Pow'r of Life conſenting **to** forego,
For what was told **him,** would be Death to know,
He di'd to his celeſtial State, **and** then
Could but convey an earthly one **to Men.**

From which to riſe, and in true Life to **live,**
What but the *Word,* wherein was Life, could **give?**
Ingrafted, as an holy Seed within,
And **born to** ſave the human Soul from Sin:
The *Word* made Man by Virgin Birth, and free
From Sin's Dominion, JESUS CHRIST is He;

Whom,

Whom, of pure Love, the Father sent to save,
And finish Man's Redemption from the Grave.

This second *Adam*, Healer of the Breach
Made by the first, nor Sin, nor Death could reach;
He conquer'd both; and, in the glorious Strife,
Became **the** Parent of an endless Life
To all **who** ever did, or shall aspire
To Life, and Spirit from this heav'nly Sire;
And cultivate the Seed which he hath sown
In ev'ry Heart, 'till the **new** Man be grown.

The old, we know, must die away to Dust,
And a new Image rise amongst the juft;
When, at the End of temporary Scene,
Chrift shall appear, eternally to reign
In all his Glory, human and divine,
When **all the** born of God, **in** Him, shall **shine,**
Rais'd to **the** Life that was at first posseft,
And **bow** the Knee to JESUS, and be bleft.

Since **then** the **Cause of our eternal Life**
Is CHRIST in us, **what need of** any Strife
In his Religion? **Of *Lo Here! Lo** There!*
When to all Hearts **He is himself** so near?
With Pow'r to **save us from** the Caufe of **Ill,**
A worldly, felfish, **unbelieving** Will;
To blefs whatever tends to make the Mind
Meek, loving, humble, patient, and refign'd.

The

The Mind to *Chriſt* ſo far as God ſhall draw
By Nature, Scripture, Reaſon, Learning, Law,
Or aught beſide, ſo far their Uſe is right,
Proclaiming Him, and not themſelves the Light:
From firſt to laſt His Goſpel is the ſame;
And of all Worſhip, that deſerves a Name,
The Word of Life by Faith to apprehend
That was in the Beginning——is the End.

A Memorial Abstract

OF A

Sermon preached by the Rev. Mr. H——,

On Proverbs, C. 20, V. 27.

THE human Spirit, when it burns and ſhines,
   Lamp of JEHOVAH *Solomon* defines——
Now, as a Veſſel, to contain the Whole,
This Lamp denotes the Body, Oil the Soul;
(As *H——* obſerves) which, tho' itſelf be dark,
Is capable of Light's enkindling Spark;
But, as conſider'd in it's own dark Root,
Still wants the Unction, and the Light's Recruit.

Brighter than all, that now is look'd upon,
This Lamp of God, at it's Creation ſhon;

The

The Body, purer than the fineft Gold,
Had no Defect in its material Mold;
The Soul's enkindl'd Oil was heav'nly **bright,**
Till evil Mixture darken'd its good Light;
And hid the fupernatural Supply,
That fed the glorious Lamp **of the** *moft High.*

That fatal Poifon quench'd, in human **Frame,**
The Spirit flowing from the vital Flame:
Adam's free Will confenting to fuch Food,
Death, **as** its natural Effect, enfu'd:
True Life departing **left him naked, blind,**
And fpiritlefs, in Body, **Soul, and Mind;**
Dead to his *paradific* **Life, a Birth**
From *Sin* began his *mortal* **Life on** Earth.

His Faith, his fpiritual Difcernment gone,
He fell into a poring, reas'ning one;
Into a State of Ignorance he fell,
Which **brutal** Inftincts very oft **excel:**
What **his** *Self-feeking* Will *would* know *was* known,
The Light of this terreftrial **Orb** alone;
Dark, in Comparifon, **when this was** done,
As Moon, or **Starlight to** meridian Sun.

What Help when leffer Light fhould vanifh too,
And Death difcover a ftill *darker* View?
Had **not the** Christ **of God,** *fole* Help for Sin,
Rais'd up *Salvation* **as a** *Seed within?*

M m

That

That fprouting forth by *Penitence*, and *Faith*,
Could pierce thro' Death, and diffipate its Wrath;
Till God's true Image fhould again revive,
And rife, *thro' Him*, to its firft Life alive.

    This *Parent Saviour*, God's-anointed Son,
Begets the Life that *Adam* fhould have done;
Reforms the Lamp; renews the holy Fire,
And fends to Heav'n its flaming *Love-Defire*:
'Tis *He——the Life that was the Light of Men*——
Who fits them to be Lamps of God again;
Reftores the Veffel, Oil, and Light, and all
The Spirit-Life that vanifh'd at the *Fall*.

    Reafon has Nothing to proceed upon,
Without an *Unction* from this *Holy One*;
Without a Spirit, to difpel the Damp
Of *Nature*'s Darknefs, and light up the Lamp:
Nothing whatever, but the *Touch* divine,
Can make its higheft Faculties to fhine;
All juft has helplefs in their felfifh Ufe,
As Lamps their own enkindling to produce.

    All true Religion teaches then to trim
The Lamp, that muft receive its Light from *Him;*
From Him, the *quick'ning* Spirit, to obtain
The Life that muft for ever bleft remain:
The *Life* of *Chrift* arifing in the Soul,
This, This alone makes human Nature whole;
Makes ev'ry Gift of Grace to reunite,
And fhine *for ever* in JEHOVAH's Sight.

O N

ON THE

Union and Three-fold Diſtinction

OF

GOD, NATURE, and CREATURE,

PART FIRST.

ALL that comes under our Imagination
 Is either *God*, or *Nature*, or *Creation*:
God is the free eternal Light, or Love,
Before, beyond all Nature, and *above*:
The one unchangeable, unceaſing Will
To ev'ry Good, and to no Sort of Ill.

 Nature, *without* him, is th' *abyſſal* Dark,
Void of the Light's beatifying Spark;
Th' Attraction of Deſire, by Want repell'd,
Whence circling Rage proceeds, and Wrath unquell'd.
But, by the Light's all-joyous Pow'r, th' Abyſs
Becomes the Groundwork of a *threefold* Bliſs.

 Creation is the Gift of Light, and Life,
To Nature's Contrariety and Strife;
For without Nature, or deſirous Want,
There would be nothing to receive the Grant;

M m 2

Noe

Nor could a Creature, or created Scene
Exift, did no fuch *Medium* intervene.

Creature and *God* would be the fame; the Thought,
Which Books inform us that *Spinoza* taught,
Would then be true; and we be forc'd to call
Things good, or bad, the *Parts* of the great *All:*
In whatfoever State itfelf may be,
Nature is *his*, but Nature is not *He.*

Like as the Dark, behind the fhining Glafs,
By hindring Rays that of themfelves would pafs,
Affords that Glimpfe of Objects to the View,
Which the tranfparent Mirror could not do;
So does the Life of Nature, in its Place,
Reflect the Glories of the Life of Grace. .

Of ev'ry Creature's Happinefs, the Growth
Depends upon the *Union* of them both;
And all, that God proceeded to create,
Came forth, at firft, in this united State;
No evil Wrath, or Darknefs could begin
To fhow itfelf, but by a *Creature's* Sin.

And were not *Nature* feparate, alone,
Such a dark *Wrath*, it could not have been fhown:
Its hidden Properties are Ground as good
For Life's Support, as Bones to Flefh and Blood:

The

The falfe, unnatural, ungodly Will,
That lays them open, is fole Caufe of Ill.

When it is **caus'd**, *renouncing*, **to** be fure,
All fuch-like Wills, contributes **to** the Cure;
That Nature's *wrathful* Forms may not appear,
Nor what is made fubfervient domineer;
But God's *good* Will all *evil* ones fubdue,
And blefs all *Nature*, and all *Creature* too.

PART SECOND.

THIS univerfal Bleffing **to** infpire
   Was God's eternal Purpofe, or Defire;
Defire, **which never could** be unfulfill'd;
Love put it **forth, and** Heav'n was what it will'd;
And the Defire had, in itfelf, the Means,
From whence the Love cou'd raife the heav'nly Scenes.

Hence an *eternal Nature*, to proclaim
By outward, vifible, majeftic Frame,
The *hidden Deity*, the Pow'r **divine,**
By which th' **innumerable Beauties** fhine;
That by Succeffion, without End, recall
A God of Love, **a** prefent ALL in ALL.

From Love, thus manifefted in the *Birth*
Of *Nature,* and the Pow'rs of Heav'n and Earth,

The

The various *Births* of *Creatures*, at the Voice
Of *God*, came forth to fee, and to rejoice;
To live within his Kingdom, and partake
Of ev'ry Blifs, adapted to their Make.

For as, *before* a Creature came to fee,
No other *Life* but that of *God* could be;
No other place but *Heav'n*, no other State;
So, when it pleas'd th' Almighty to create,
From *him* muft come the Creature's Life *within*;
Its *outward* State from *Nature* muft begin.

Oh! what angelic Orders! what divine,
And heavenly Creatures anfwer'd the Defign
Of God's communicative Goodnefs, fhown
By giving Rife to *Offsprings* of his own!
With *Godlike* Spirits how was Nature fill'd,
And *beauteous* Forms, as its great *Author* will'd!

Thus in its full Perfection then it ftood,
Seeking, receiving, manifefting Good,
By Virtue of that *Union* which it had
With Him, who made no Creature to be bad;
But highly bleft; and with a potent Will
So to continue, and to know no Ill.

Nature's *united* Properties had none——
Whence then the Change that it has undergone?
But from the Creatures ftriving to afpire
Above the *Light*, which their own *dark* Defire

Quench'd

Quench'd in themfelves, and rais'd up all the Storms
Of Nature's wrathful, feparated Forms.

So *Lucifer* and his proud Legions fell,
And turn'd their *heav'nly* Manfion to an *Hell*;
To that dark, formlefs *Void*, wherein the Light
Entring again with Nature to unite,
The *new* Creation of a World began,
And God's *own Image* Lord of it——*A Man*.

ON THE
ORIGIN of EVIL.

I.

EVIL, if rightly underftood,
  Is but the Skeleton of Good,
Divefted of its Flefh and Blood.

II.

While it remains, without Divorce,
Within its hidden, fecret Source,
It is the Good's own Strength and Force.

III. As

III.

As Bone has the fupporting Share,
In human Form divinely fair,
Altho' an Evil when laid bare;

IV.

As Light and Air are fed by Fire,
A fhining Good, while all confpire,
But (feparate) dark, raging Ire;

V.

As Hope and Love arife from Faith,
Which then admits no Ill, nor hath;
But, if alone, it would be Wrath;

VI.

Or any Inftance thought upon,
In which the Evil can be none,
Till Unity of Good is gone;

VII.

So, by Abufe of Thought and Skill,
The greateft Good, to wit, *Free-will*,
Becomes the *Origin* of Ill.

VIII. Thus

VIII.

Thus when rebellious Angels fell,
The very Heav'n, where good ones dwell,
Became th' apostate Spirits Hell.

IX.

Seeking, against eternal Right,
A Force without a Love and Light,
They found, and felt its evil Might.

X.

Thus *Adam* biting at their Bait,
Of Good and Evil when he ate,
Di'd to his first thrice happy State.

XI.

Fell to the Evils of this Ball,
Which, in harmonious Union all,
Were *Paradise* before his Fall.

XII.

And when the Life of *Christ* in Men
Revives its *faded* Image, then,
Will all be *Paradise* again.

N n

A Friendly

A

Friendly Expoſtulation with a Clergyman,

CONCERNING

A PASSAGE in his SERMON, relating to the REDEMPTION of MANKIND.

’TWAS a good Sermon; but a cloſe Review
    Would bear one Paſſage to be alter’d too;
Becauſe it did not, in the leaſt, agree
With the plain Text (as it appear’d to me)
Nor with your Comment, on what God had done
To ſave Mankind, by his Redeeming Son.

    You did, if I remember right, admit
That *other* Means, if He had ſo thought fit,
Might have obtain’d the ſalutary Views,
As well as thoſe which he was pleas’d to chuſe;
That it was too preſumptuous to confine,
To thoſe alone, th’ Omnipotence divine;
As if a Wiſdom infinite could find
No other Method, how to ſave Mankind:
Tho’ *that*, indeed, which had been fix’d upon,
Was, in effect, become the only one.

    Now this, however well deſign’d, to raiſe
An awful Senſe, by its reſpectful Phraſe,

An

An Adoration of the boundless Pow'rs
Of the ALMIGHTY, when compar'd with ours;
To sink in humble Rev'rence, and profound,
All human Thoughts of fixing any Bound
To an unerring Wisdom, which extends
Beyond what finite Reason comprehends;
Yet, if examin'd by severer Test,
It is, at least, incautiously exprest;
And leaves the subtlest of the Gospel's Foes,
The *Deists*, this Objection to propose,
To which they have, and will have, a Recourse,
And still keep urging its unanswer'd Force.

" If there was no Necessity, they say,
" For saving Men in this mysterious Way,
" What Proof can the Divines pretend to bring,
" (While they confess the Nature of the Thing
" Does not forbid) that the celestial Scenes
" Will not be open'd by some other Means?
" What else but Book Authority, at best,
" Asserts this Way, exclusive of the rest,
" Of equal Force, if the Almighty's Will
" Had but appointed them to save from Ill?
" This Way, in which the Son of the most High
" Is, by his Father's Pleasure, doom'd to die,
" For Satisfaction of paternal Ire;
" Which (when they make Religion to require)
" Confounds all Sense of Justice, by a Scheme
" The most unworthy of the great Supreme:

" As

" As other Ways might have obtain'd the End,
" Nature, and Reafon, force us to attend
" To huge Abfurdities which follow this,
" And, fince it was not needful, to difmifs."

This is the *Bourdon* of deiftic Song,
Which rifing Volumes labour to prolong;
Take this away, the reft would all remain
As flat, and trifling, as it is profane;
But this remaining, hither they retreat,
And lie fecure from any full Defeat.

But when the *Need*, moft *abfolute*, is fhown
Of Man's Redemption, by the Means alone,
The *Birth*, and *Life*, and *Death*, and *Re-afcent*,
Thro' which the one *The-andric* Saviour went,
To quench the Wrath of Nature in the Race
Of Men (not God, in whom it has no Place)
Then Scripture, Senfe, and Reafon coincide,
And all confpire to follow the one Guide;
Of *Poffibilities* to wave the talk,
In which it is impoffible to walk;
And raife the Soul to feek, and find the Good,
By this one Method, which no other could.

Then true Religion, call it by the Name
Chriftian, or *natural*, is ftill the fame;
From CHRIST deriv'd, as Healer of the Soul,
Or *Nature*, made by his *Re-entrance* whole;

Who

Who is, in ev'ry Man, th' enlightning Ray,
The Faith, and Hope, of *Love*'s redeeming **Day;**
The *only* Name, **or** Pow'r, **that can affure**
Nature's Religion, that is, *Nature's* **Cure:**
But if Salvation might have been **beftow'd**
By *other* Means, than **what** the facred Code
Declares throughout, **the** *Deifts* will foon fay,
The Means, that *might* be poffible, ftill *may;*
And, led to think that Scripture is at Odds
With Nature, take **fome** *other* to be God's:
Thus may a *no Neceffity*, **allow'd,**
Tend to increafe the **unbelieving Croud.**

  As *Adam* **di'd, and in him all his** Race,
Not to the Life of Nature, but of Grace;
There could be no new Birth of it, or Growth,
But from a parent Union **of** them both;
Such as, in ev'ry poflible Refpect,
Jesus incarnate only could effect;
From *Him* alone, who *had* the Life, could Men
Have it *reftor'd, renew'd, reviv'd* again:
But——I am trefpaffing **too much, I fear,**
And preaching, when my Province is to hear——

  Millions of Ways could we fuppofe **befide,**
This, we are fure, which faving Love has tri'd,
Muft be the beft, muft be the ftraighteft Line
Of Action, when confider'd as divine;
This Way *alone* then muft as **fure** be gone,
As that a Line, if **ftraight, can** be but one.

On

On the same SUBJECT,

Written upon another Occasion.

MANKIND's Redemption, you are pleas'd to say,
  By JESUS CHRIST, was not the *only* Way
That could succeed; indefinitely *more*
Th' *Almighty*'s Wisdom had within its Store;
By any chosen one of which, no doubt,
The same Redemption had been brought about.

  For who shall dare, you argue, in this Case,
To limit the Omnipotence of Grace?
As if a finite Understanding knew
What the *Almighty* could, or could not do:
Tho', since He chose this Method, we must own,
That our Dependence is on This alone.

  Now, Sir, acknowledging his Pow'r immense,
Beyond the Reach of all created Sense;
Does it not seem to follow, thereupon,
That *his* true Way must be directly *One?*
To save the World he gave his *only Son,*
Therefore ——— by *Him alone* it could be done.

  Variety of Ways is the Effect
Of finite View, that sees not *the direct;*

But

But the *Almighty*, having all in View,
Muſt be ſuppos'd to ſee, and take it too;
To ſee at once, tho' *we* are in the Dark,
The one ſtraight Line to the intended Mark.

Saint *Paul*'s Aſſertion of——*no other Name
Given under Heav'n*——appears to be the ſame
With this——no other Name, or Pow'r, could ſave
But that of JESUS, which JEHOVAH gave:
More *Sons*, more *Saviours*, as conſiſtent ſeem
As more effective *Methods* to redeem.

I am the Way——ſaid CHRIST; there could not be,
By juſt Concluſion, any, then, but *He:*
I am the Truth——whence it appears anew,
That no Way elſe could poſſibly be *true :*
I am the Life——to which, as *Adam* di'd,
Nothing could bring Mankind again, beſide.

A N

Expoſtulation with a zealous Sectariſt,

Who inveighed in bitter Terms againſt the C L E R G Y and CHURCH INSTITUTIONS.

NO Sir; I cannot ſee to what good End
   Such bitter Words againſt the Clergy tend;
Pour'd from a Zeal ſo ſharp, ſo anallay'd,
That ſuffers no Exception to be made;

While

While the moſt mild Perſuaſions to repreſs
The bitter Zeal ſtill heighten its Exceſs.

Its own relentleſs Thought while it purſues,
What unreſtrain'd Expreſſions it can uſe!
Places of Worſhip, which the People call
Churches, are Synagogues of *Satan* all;
At all *liturgic* Pray'r and Praiſe it ſtorms,
As *Man's Inventions*, **Spirit-quenching Forms;**
And, from *baptiſmal* down to *burial* Rite,
Sets ev'ry Service in an odious Light:
All previous Order, with regard to Time,
Place, or Behaviour, paſſes for a Crime.

Of *Phariſaic* Pride it culls the Marks,
To repreſent the *Biſhop* and his *Clarks;*
Who are, if offer'd any gentler Plea,
The *Devil's Miniſters*, both He and They;
Blind Guides, *falſe Prophets*, and a lengthen'd Train
Of all hard Words that choſen Texts contain:
Theſe are the *Forms* which, when it would object
To thoſe in Uſe, it pleaſes to ſelect;
Repeated by its Devotees, at once,
As like to Rote as any Church Reſponſe:
Nor is a Treatment of this eager Kind
To this, or that Society confin'd,
Sect, or Profeſſion——no, no Matter which,
Leaders, or *led*, all *fall into the Ditch;*
None but its own ſevere Adepts can claim
Of Truth and Spirit-Worſhippers the Name.

It

In vain it feeks, by any facred Page,
To juftify this unexampled Rage:
Prophets of old, who fpake **againft th' Abufe**
Of outward Forms, were none of them fo loofe
As to condemn, abolifh, or forbid
The Things prefcrib'd, but what the People did;
Who minded nothing but the mere Outfide,
Neglecting wholly what it fignifi'd;
At this Neglect the Prophets all exclaim'd;
No pious Rites has any of them blam'd;
Their true Intent was only to reduce
All outward Practice to its inward Ufe.

The World's **Redeemer,** coming **to fulfil**
All paft Predictions **of** prophetic Quill,
Who more, amidft the *Jewifh* prieftly Pride,
Than He, with **all** *Mofaic* Rites compli'd?
Say that the *Chriftian* Priefts are, now, as bad
As thofe blind Leaders which the Jews then had,
Was *Zachariah*'s, *Simeon*'s, *Anna*'s Mind,
Any good Prieft, or Man, or Woman blind,
To offer Incenfe, **or to bear a** Part
In Temple Service, **with** an upright Heart?

Can then **the** Faults of *Clergymen,* or *Lay,*
Deftroy Heart-Worfhip at this prefent Day?
Will Pray'r, **in** vain by *Pharifees* prefer'd,
Not from repenting *Publicans* be heard?
Will the devout amongft the Chriftian Flock
Not be accepted, tho' the Prieft fhould mock?

O o

If they do right in their appointed Spheres,
His Want of Truth and Spirit is not *Theirs*.

    Our Lord's Apoſtles, with an inward View
To reconcile the *Gentile*, and the *Jew*,
To Faith in Him, made ev'ry outward Care
The moſt ſubſervient to that main Affair:
The greateſt Friend to Chriſtian Freedom, *Paul*,
Intent to ſave, was ev'ry Thing to All;
To keep, whatever Forms ſhould riſe, or ceaſe,
Union of Spirit in the Bond of Peace;
Th' Effects of haſty, raſh, condemning Zeal
He ſaw, and mourn'd, and labour'd to repeal.

    Succeeding Saints, when Prieſt, or Magiſtrate
Became tyrannical in Church, or State,
Reprov'd their evil Practices, but then
Rever'd the Office, tho' they blam'd the Men:
They gave no Inſtance of untemper'd Heat,
That roots up all before it, Tares or Wheat;
As if, by humanly invented Care
Of Cultivation, Wheat itſelf was Tare:
'Tis true, all Sects are grown corrupt enough,
But Zeal, ſo indiſcriminately rough,
May well give others Reaſon to ſuſpect
Some want of Knowledge in a Novel Sect,
(If ſuch there be) that ſeems to take a Pride
In *ſatanizing* all the World beſide;
Without the leaſt Authority, yet known,
Or Species of Example, but its own.

One

One Mifchief is, that its unguarded Terms
Hurt many fober Truths which it affirms;
Worfhip in *Truth* and *Spirit* fuffers too,
By being plac'd in fuch an hoftile View:
" *Oh! but all felf-will Worfhipping is wrong*"——
True; but to whom does that Defeft belong?
Is the Obedience to a Rule, or Guide,
For Order's Sake, fair Proof of fuch a Pride?
If it be none at all for Men to broach
Rude, harfh, and undiftinguifhing Reproach,
With Refolution to repeat it ftill,
Pray by what Marks are we to know *Self-Will?*

Thoughts on imputed Righteoufnefs,

OCCASIONED

By Reading the Rev. Mr. HERVEY's **DIALOGUES**,
between THERON and ASPASIO.

A FRAGMENT.

*I*MPUTED *Righteoufnefs!*——beloved Friend,
  To what Advantage can this Doftrine tend?
If, at the fame Time, a Believer's Breaft
Be not by *real* Righteoufnefs poffeft;
And if it be, why Volumes on it made
With fuch a Strefs upon *imputed* laid?

Amongft

Amongſt the Diſputants of later Days,
This, in its Turn, became a fav'rite Phraſe,
When, much divided in religious Schemes,
Contending Parties ran into Extremes;
And now it claims th' Attention of the Age,
In *Hervey's* elegant and lively Page:
This **his** *Aſpaſio* **labours to** impreſs,
With ev'ry Turn of Language and Addreſs;
With **all the Flow of** Eloquence, that ſhines
Thro' all his (full enough) embelliſh'd Lines.

Tho' now ſo much exerting to confirm
Its vaſt Importance, and revive the Term,
He was himſelf, he lets his *Theron* know,
Of diff'rent Sentiments not long ago;
And Friends of yours, it has been thought, I find,
Have brought *Aſpaſio* **to** his preſent Mind.
Now having read, **but unconvinc'd, I own,**
What various Reaſon for it he has ſhown,
Or rather **Rhetoric——if** it be true,
In any Senſe that **has** appear'd **to you,**
I reſt ſecure of giving no Offence,
By aſking—— how you underſtand the Senſe?
By urging, in a Manner frank and free,
What Reaſons, as I read, occur to me,
Why *Righteouſneſs,* **for** Man to reſt upon,
Muſt be a *real,* not *imputed,* one.

To ſhun much novel Sentiment, and nice,
I take the Thing from its apparent Riſe:

It

It should seem then, as if *imputed Sin*
Had made *imputed Righteousness* begin;
The one suppos'd, the other, to be sure,
Would follow after——like Disease and Cure:
Let us examine then imputed Guilt,
And see on what Foundation it is built.

As our first Parents lost an heav'nly State,
All their Descendents share their hapless Fate;
Forewarn'd of God, when tempted, not to eat
Of the forbidden Tree's pernicious Meat;
Because incorporating mortal Leaven
Would kill, of course, in them, the Life of Heav'n:
They disobey'd, did *Adam*, and his Wife,
And died of Course to their true heav'nly Life:
That Life, thus lost the Day they disobey'd,
Could not by them be possibly convey'd;
No other Life could Children have from them,
But what could rise from the parental Stem:
That Love of God, alone, which we adore,
The Life, so lost, could possibly restore:
Their Children could not, being born to Earth,
Be born to Heaven, but by an *heav'nly Birth*:
God found a Way, explain it how we will,
To save the human Race from endless Ill;
To save the very disobeying Pair;
And made their whole Posterity his Care.

Has this great Goodness any thing akin
To God's *imputing* our first Parent's Sin

To

To their unborn Posterity?——What Senfe
In fuch a ftrange, and fcripturelefs Pretence?
For the Men feel——fo far we are agreed,
The Confequences of a finful Deed;
Yet where afcrib'd, by any facred Pen,
But to the *Doers*, is the *Deed* to Men?
Where to be found, in all the Scripture thro',
This *Imputation*, thus advanc'd anew?

   Adam and *Eve*, by *Satan*'s Wiles decoy'd,
Did what the kind Commandment faid——*avoid*——
To them, with Juftice therefore, you impute
The Sin of eating the forbidden Fruit;
And ev'ry Imputation muft in Fact,
If juft, be built on fome preceding Act;
Without the previous Deed fuppos'd, the Word
Becomes unjuft, unnatural, abfurd.

   If, as you feem'd to think the other Day,
All *Adam*'s Race, in fome myfterious Way,
Sinn'd when he finn'd; confented to his Fall;
With Juftice then impute it to them all:
But ftill it follows, that they all contract
An Imputation founded upon Fact;
And *Righteoufnefs* of *Chrift*, in Chriftian Heirs,
Muft be as deeply, and as truly theirs,
An heav'nly Life in order to replace,
As was the Sin that made a guilty Race:
So that imputing either Good, or Ill,
Muft prefuppofe a correfpondent Will;

Or

Or elfe Imputers certainly muft make
'Thro' Ignorance, or other Caufe, Miftake.

Old *Eli* thus, not knowing what to think,
Imputed *Hannah*'s filent Pray'r to Drink;
Little fuppofing that it would prepare
A Succeffor to him, her filent Pray'r.
There may be other Meanings of the Phrafe,
To be accounted for in human Ways;
But *God*'s imputing to the future Child
The Sin, by which his Parents were beguil'd,
Seems to eftablifh an unrighteous Blame,
That brings no Honour to it's Maker's Name.

·God's Honour, Glory, Majefty, and Grace,
I grant, is your Intention in the Cafe;
But wifh revolv'd in your impartial Thought,
How far the Doctrine tends, when it is taught,
To fuch an honeft Purpofe; and how far
Juftice and Truth may feem to be at War,
If God impute to guiltlefs Children Crimes,
Committed only in their Parents Times.

Pious *Afpafio*, I imagine, too,
Had God's *refiftlefs Sov'reignty* in View;
The Charge of *Puritan*, or other Name,
He fcorn'd aright, and making Truth his Aim,
Found it, he thought, in eminent Divines;
Of whofe Opinion thefe are the Outlines:

They

They think, at leaft they feem to reprefent,
That God, in Honour, upon Sin's Event,
Could not forgive the Sinners that had ftray'd,
Without a proper *Satisfaction* made
To his *offended* Juftice; and becaufe,
Upon their Breach of the Almighty's Laws,
None elfe was adequate to what was done,
The *Vengeance* fell on his *beloved Son;*
Who gave himfelf to fuffer in *our Stead,*
And thus to Life again reftor'd the dead;
Becaufe, confiftently with Juftice, then
God could beftow his Mercy upon Men:
Man had contracted, in that fatal Day,
Debt fo immenfe, that Man could never pay;
He who was *God* as well as *Man,* he could;
And made the Satisfaction thro' his Blood;
Paid all the juft Demand——imputed thus
Our Sin to him, *his Righteoufnefs* to us——
This fets the Doctrine, if I take aright
Their Words and Meaning, in the plaineft Light.

Now fince accounting for the Truth amifs
May give Diftafte, in fuch an Age as this;
And be a Stumbling-block to them who might
Receive an Explanation, that was right;
Not as a captious Foe, but hearty Friend,
May one intreat fuch Teachers to attend,
And reconcile their Syftem, if they can,
To God's Proceeding with his Creature Man;

To

To that paternal, tender Love and Grace,
Which at Man's Fall immediately took Place;
That inward, holy Thing, inbreathed then,
Which would re-kindle Heav'n in him again:
Does *Wrath*, or *Vengeance*, or a *Want* appear
Of *Satisfaction*, or of *Payment* here,
In Man's Creator? For Mankind had he
A *purchas'd* Grace, which contradicts a *free?*
Is it not plain, that an *unalter'd Love*
Sent Help to poor fall'n Creatures from **above**,
Unbargain'd, unsollicited, **unmov'd**,
But by itself, **as its Exertion prov'd;**
No foreign Promise; no imputed Ease;
But Remedy as real as Disease;
That would, according to true Nature's Ground,
Bring on the Cure, and make the Patient found.

That *Christ*, that *God*'s **becoming Man** was it,
Your Friends, with highest Gratitude, admit;
Whose utmost Talents are employ'd to show
The Obligations that to **him we owe;**
To press the Object of **our Faith and Trust,**
Christ, ALL in ALL, the righteous, and the just;
The *true*, *redeeming Life*——essential this
To ev'ry Christian who aspires to Bliss;
Why not subjoin——I cite the Hero *Paul*,
And make Appeal **to Christians**——*in you all?*
Form'd in you, *dwelling in* you, **and within**
Regenerating Life, dethroning Sin;
Working, in more and more resigned Wills,
The gradual Conquest of all selfish Ills;

P p

'Till

'Till the true Christian to true Life revive,
Dead to the *World*, to *God*, thro' him, *alive*.

What num'rous Texts from *Paul*, from ev'ry Saint,
Might **furnish** out Citations, did we want?
And **could not** see, that Righteousness, or Sin,
Arise **not from** *without*, but from *within?*
That *Imputation*, where they **are not** found,
Can reach no **farther than an** empty Sound;
No farther than imputed Health **can reach**
The Cure of Sickness, tho' a Man **should preach**
With **all the** Eloquence of Zeal, and tell
How Health imputed makes a sick Man well:
Indeed, if Sickness be imputed too,
Imputed Remedy, no Doubt, may **do;**
Words may pour forth their entertaining Store,
But **Things are just**——as Things were just before.

In so important **a Concern, as that**
Which good *Aspasio's* **Care is pointed at,**
A small Mistake, which at the **Bottom** lies,
May sap the Building that shall thence arise:
Who would not wish that Architect, so skill'd,
On great Mistake might not persist to build;
But strictly search, and for sufficient While,
If the Foundation could support the Pile?

This *Imputation*, which he builds upon,
Has been the Source of more Mistakes than one:
Hence rose, to pass the intermediate Train
Of growing Errors, and observe the main,

'That

That worfe than *pagan* Principle of Fate,
Predeftination's partial Love and Hate;
By which, not ti'd, like fanci'd *Jove*, to look
In ftronger Deftiny's decreeing Book,
The *God* of *Chriftians* is fuppos'd to will
That *fome* fhould come to *Good*, and *fome* to *Ill;*
And for no Reafon, but to fhow, in fine,
Th' Extent of *Goodnefs*, and of *Wrath divine.*

Whofe Doctrine this? I quote no lefs a Man
Than the renowned *Calvin* for the Plan;
Who having labour'd, with Diftinctions vain,
Mere Imputation, only, to maintain,
Maintains, when fpeaking on another Head,
This horrid Thought, to which the former led;
" Predeftination here I call," (fays he
Defining) " God's eternal, fix'd Decree;
" Which, having fettl'd in his Will, he paft,
" What ev'ry Man fhould come to at the laft;
And left the Terms fhould be conceiv'd to bear
A Meaning lefs, than he propos'd, fevere,
" For all Mankind (he adds to Definition)
" Are not created on the fame Condition:
Pari Conditione——is the Phrafe;
If you can turn it any other Ways;
" But Life to fome, eternal, is reftrain'd,
" To fome, Damnation endlefs pre-ordain'd.

Calvin has pufh'd the Principle, I guefs,
To what your Friends would own to be Excefs;

And

And probably *Aspasio*, less inclin'd
To run directly into *Calvin*'s Mind,
Would give *imputing* a more mod'rate Sense,
That no *Damnation* might arise from thence :
But how will mollifying Terms confute
The fam'd Reformer's Notion of *impute?*
If it confer such *arbitrary* Good,
The dire Reverse is quickly understood;
So understood, that open Eyes may see
'Tis *Calvin*'s Fiction, and not *God*'s Decree :
Not his, whose forming Love, and ruling Aid,
Ceaseless extends to all that he hath made ;
Who gave the Gift which he was pleas'd to give,
That *none* might perish, but that *all* might live,
His *only Son*, in whom the Light, that guides
The born into the World to Life, resides :
A real Life, that by a real Birth
Raises a Life beyond the Life of Earth,
In all his Children——But no more to you,
Better than me, who know it to be true;
And if *Aspasio*'s really humbl'd Soul
Be by a touch of Garment Hem made whole,
He might, as I should apprehend, be sure
That *Imputation* could not cause the Cure :
When the poor Woman, in the Gospel, found
Touch of the *Saviour*'s Cloaths to make her sound,
We know the Virtue did from him proceed,
That, mix'd with Faith, restor'd her, as we read :
Gone out of him obliges to infer,
That 'twas by Faith *attracted into* her.

ON

O N   T H E

Nature of FREE GRACE,

A N D   T H E

Claim to Merit for the Performance of good WORKS.

GRACE to be sure is, in the laſt Degree,
  The *Gift* of God, divinely pure and free;
Not bought, or paid for, merited, or claim'd,
By any Works of ours that can be nam'd.

What Claim, or Merit, or withall to pay,
Could Creatures have before creating Day?
Gift of Exiſtence is the gracious one,
Which all the reſt muſt needs depend upon.

All boaſting then of Merit, all Pretence
Of Claim from God, in a deſerving Senſe,
Is in one Word excluded by St. *Paul*——
Whate'er thou haſt, thou haſt receiv'd it all.

But ſure the *Uſe* of any gracious Pow'rs,
Freely beſtow'd, may properly be ours;
Right Application being ours to chuſe,
Or, if we will be ſo abſurd, refuſe.

In this Reſpect what need to controvert
The ſober Senſe of *Merit,* or *Deſert?*

Works,

Works, it is faid, will have, and is it hard
To fay deferve, or merit their Reward?

Grace is the real faving Gift; but then,
Good Works are profitable unto Men;
God wants them not; but, if our Neighbours do,
Flowing from Grace, they prove it to be true.

When human Words afcribe to human Spirit
Worthy, Unworthy, Merit, or Demerit,
Why fhould Difputes forbid the Terms a place,
Which are not meant to derogate from Grace?

All comes from God, who gave us firft to live,
And all fucceeding Grace; 'tis ours to give
To *God alone* the *Glory*; and to *Man*,
Impow'r'd by Him, to do what *Good* we can.

A SOLILOQUY,

On reading a Difpute about FAITH and WORKS.

WHAT an exceffive Fondnefs for Debate
    Does this dividing *Faith* from *Works* create!
Some fay, Salvation is by Faith *alone*——
Or elfe, the Gofpel will be overthrown:
Others, for that fame Reafon, place the Whole
In *Works*, which bring Salvation to a Soul.

Gofpel

Gofpel of *Chrift*, confiftently appli'd,
Unites together what they both divide:
It is itfelf, indeed, the very Faith
That works by Love, and faves a Soul from Wrath:
A new Difpute fhould fome third Party pave,
Nor Faith, nor Works, but *Love* alone would fave.

The *Solifidian* takes a Text from *Paul*,
And Works are good for Nothing, Faith is all;
Doctrine, which his Antagonift difclaims,
And fhows how Works muft juftify, from *James*;
A Third, in either, foon might find a Place,
Where Love is plainly the exalted Grace.

There is no End of jarring Syftem found,
In thus contending not for Senfe, but Sound;
For Sound, by which th' *infeparable* Three
Are fo diftinguifh'd, as to difagree;
Altho' Salvation, in its real Spring,
Faith, *Work*, or *Love*, be one and the fame Thing.

One Pow'r of *God*, or Life of *Chrift* within,
Or *Holy Spirit* wafhing away Sin;
Not by Repentance *only*; or Belief
Only, that flights a penitential Grief,
And its meet Fruits, and juftifies alone
A full conceiv'd Affurance of its own;

Nor by Works *only*; nor, tho' *Paul* above
Both Faith and Works have lifted it, can Love

Have,

Have, or defire to have, th' exclufive Claim,
In Mens Salvation, to this *only* Fame;
By *All* together Souls are fav'd from Ill,
When e'er they yield an unrelifting Will.

God has a never-ceafing Will to fave,
And Men, by Grace, may favingly behave:
This would produce lefs Fondnefs for a Sect,
And more Concern about the main Effect;
Then Faith *alone* might fave them from the Fall,
As one good Word, in Ufe, that ftood for all.

By native Union, all the bleffed Pow'rs
Of Grace, that makes Salvation to be ours,
One in another, fpring up in the Breaft,
No Soul is fav'd by one without the reft:
Since then they *all* fubfift in any *one*,
Divifion ceafes,——and *Difpute* is gone.

THOUGHTS

ON

PREDESTINATION and REPROBATION.

A FRAGMENT.

FLATTER me not with your *Predeftination*,
　Nor fink my Spirits with your *Reprobation*:
From all your high Difputes I ftand aloof,
Your *Pre*'s and *Re*'s, your *Deftin*, and your *Proof*,

And

And formal, *Calvinistical* Pretence,
That contradicts all Gospel, and good Sense.

When God declares, so often, that he wills
All sort of Blessings, and no sort of Ills;
That his severest Purpose never meant
A *Sinner's Death*, but *that he should repent*:
For the *whole* World, when his beloved Son
Is said to do whatever he has done;
To become Man, to suffer, and to die,
That *all* might live, as well as you, and I;
Shall rigid *Calvin*, after this, or you,
Pretend to tell me that it is not true?
But that eternal, absolute Decree
Has damn'd beforehand either you, or me,
Or any Body else? That God design'd,
When he created, not to save *Mankind*,
But only *some*? The rest, this Man maintain'd,
Were to *decreed* Damnation pre-ordain'd:
No, Sir; not all your metaphysic Skill
Can prove the Doctrine, twist it as you will.

I cite the Man for Doctrine, so accurst,
In Book the *third*, and Chapter *twenty-first*,
Section the *fifth*——an horrid, impious Lore,
That one would hope was never taught before;
How it came after to prevail away,
Let them, who mince the damning Matter, say;
And others judge, if any *Christian* Fruit
Be like to spring from such a *pagan* Root.

Q q

Pagan

Pagan——said I——I muſt retract the Word,
For the poor Pagans were not ſo abſurd;
Their *Jupiter*, of Gods and Men the King,
Whenever he ordain'd an hurtful Thing,
Did it, becauſe he was oblig'd to look,
And act, as *Fate* had bid him, in a Book:
For Gods and Goddeſſes were ſubject, then,
To dire *Neceſſity*, as well as Men;
Compell'd to cruſh an Hero, or a Town,
As *Deſtiny* had ſet the Matter down.

But, in your Scheme, 'tis *God* that orders Ill,
With ſov'reign Pow'r, and with reſiſtleſs Will;
He, in whoſe bleſſed Name is underſtood
The one eternal Will to ev'ry Good,
Is repreſented, tho' unti'd by *Fate*,
With a Decree of damning to create
Such, as you term the *Veſſels* of his *Wrath*,
To *ſhow his Pow'r*, according to your Faith:
Juſt as if God, like ſome tyrannic Man,
Would plague the World, to ſhow them that he can:
While others, (they, for Inſtance, of your Sect)
Are *Mercy's Veſſels*, precious and elect;
Who think, God help them! to ſecure their Bliſs
By ſuch a partial, fond Conceit as this.

Talk not to me of *Popery* and *Rome*,
Nor yet foretel its *Babyloniſh* Doom;
Nor canonize *reforming* Saints of old,
Becauſe *they* held the Doctrine that *you* hold;

For

For if they did, altho' of *Saint-like* Stem,
In this plain Point we muſt *reform* from them:
While freed from *Rome*, we are not ti'd, I hope,
To what is wrong in a *Geneva* Pope;
Nor what is right ſhould Sirname ſuperſede
Of *Luther*, *Calvin*, *Bellarmine*, or *Bede*.
Rome has been guilty of Exceſs, 'tis true,
And ſo have ſome of the *Reformers* too;
If in their Zeal againſt the *Roman* Seat,
Plucking up Tares, they pluck'd up alſo Wheat;
Muſt we to Children, for what they have ſaid,
Give this *Predeſtination* Stone for Bread?

Sir, it is worſe, is your Predeſtination,
Ten thouſand Times than Tranſubſtantiation:
Hard is the Point, that Papiſts have compil'd,
With Senſe and Reaſon to be reconcil'd;
But yet it leaves to our Conception, ſtill,
Goodneſs in God, and Holineſs of Will;
A juſt, impartial Government of all;
A ſaving Love; a correſpondent Call
To ev'ry Man, and, in the fitteſt Hour
For him to hear, all offer'd Grace and Pow'r;
Which he may want, and have, if he will crave
From him, who willeth Nothing but to ſave.

Whereas, this *Reprobation* Doctrine, here,
Not only Senſe and Reaſon would caſhier,
But take, by its Pretext of ſov'reign Sway,
All Goodneſs from the Deity away;

Both

Both Heav'n and Hell confounding with its Cant,
Virtue and Vice, the Sinner and the Saint;
Leaving (by irrefiftible Decree,
And Purpofe abfolute, what Man fhall be,)
Nothing, in Sinners, to deteft fo much,
As God's Contrivance how to make them fuch.

That ever *Chriftians*, bleft with Revelation,
Should think of his *decreeing* Men's Damnation!
The GOD of LOVE! the FOUNTAIN of ALL GOOD!
*Who made, fays Paul, all Nations of one Blood
To dwell on Earth; appointing Time, and Place——*
And for what End this *pre-ordaining* Grace?
That they might *feek*, and *feel* after, and *find*
The Life in God, which God for Man defign'd.

We are his Offspring——for, in that Decree,
The *pagan* Poet and St. *Paul* agree:
We are his Offspring——Now, Sir, put the Cafe
Of fome great Man, and his defcending Race;
Conceive this common Parent of them all,
As willing fome to *ftand*, and fome to *fall:*
Mafter, fuppofe, of all their future Lot,
Decreeing fome to Happinefs, fome not;
In fome to bring his Kindnefs into View;
To fhew in others what his Wrath can do;
To lead the chofen Children by the Hand,
And leave the reft to fall——who *cannot* ftand.

I might proceed, but that the fmalleft Sketch
Shows an abfurd, and arbitrary Wretch,

Treating

Treating his Offspring fo, as to forbid
To think, that ever *God Almighty* did;
To think that Creatures, who are faid to be
His Offspring, fhould be hurt by his Decree;
Which had they always minded, *Good* alone,
And not a Spark of *Evil*, had been known:
For his Decree, Appointment, Order, Will,
Predeftinating Goodnefs, Pow'r, and Skill,
Is, of itfelf, the unbeginning Good,
The pouring forth of an un-ending Flood
Of ever-flowing Blifs, which only rolls
To fill his Veffels, his created Souls.

Happy Himfelf, the true divine Defire,
The Love that flames thro' that eternal Fire,
Which generates in him th' eternal Light,
Source of all Bleffing to created Sight,
Longs with an holy Earneftnefs to fpread
The boundlefs Glories of its Fountain Head;
To raife the Poffibilities of Life,
Which reft, in *him*, into a joyful Strife;
Into a feeling Senfe of *him*, from whom
The various Gifts of various Bleffings come.

To *blefs* is his immutable Decree,
Such as could never have begun to be:
Decree (if you will ufe the word decreed)
Did from his *Love* eternally proceed,
To manifeft the hidden Pow'rs, that reign
Through outward Nature's univerfal Scene;

To

To raife up Creatures from its vaft Abyfs,
Form'd to enjoy communicated Blifs;
Form'd, in their fev'ral Orders, to extend
Of God's great Goodnefs Wonders without End.

Who does not fee that *Ill*, of any Kind,
Could *never* come from an *all-perfect* Mind?
That its Perception never could begin,
But from a Creature's voluntary Sin,
Made in its Maker's Image, and impreft
With a free Pow'r of being ever bleft;
From ev'ry Evil, in itfelf, fo free,
That none could rife but by its *own* Decree?
By a Volition, oppofite to all
That God could will, did Evil firft befall,
And ftill befalls; for all the Source of Ill
Is Oppofition to his bleffed Will;
And Union with it plainly underftood
To be the Source of ev'ry real Good.

To certain Truths, which you can fcarce deny,
You bring St. *Paul*'s Expreffions in Reply;
Some few obfcurer Sayings prone to chufe,
Where he was talking to the *Roman Jews*;
You never heed the num'rous Texts, and plain,
That will not fuit with your *decreeing* Strain,
Confirming God's unalter'd Will to blefs,
In Words as clear as Language can exprefs:
Who willeth all Men to be fav'd——is one
Too plain for Comment to be made upon:

So

So that, if *some* be not the fame as *all*,
You muft directly contradict St. *Paul*,
Whene'er you pufh to its direct Extreme,
Your wild, abfurd *Predeftination* Scheme.

   Paul's open, generous, enlight'ned Soul,
Preach'd to Mankind a *Saviour* of the *Whole*,
Not *Part* of human Race; the blinded *Jew*
Might boaft himfelf in this conceited View;
Boaft of his Father *Abraham*, and vent
The carnal Claims of Family Defcent:
But the whole Family of Heav'n and **Earth**,
Paul knew, if bleft, muft have *another* Birth;
That *Jew* and *Gentile* was, in ev'ry Place,
Alike the Object of a faving Grace:
Paul never tied Salvation to a Sect;
All who love God, with him, are God's *Elect*.

   This plain, good Maxim he himfelf premis'd
To thofe fam'd Chapters, which were fo difguis'd
By ftudied Comments of a later Day;
When Words were preft to ferve a partial **Fray**;
And Scripture turn'd into a Magazine
Of Arms, for fober, or for frantic Spleen.

   All who love God——how certain is the Key!
Whate'er difputed Paffages convey;
In *Paul*'s Epiftles if fome Things are read,
Hard to be underftood, as *Peter* faid,

Muft

Muſt this be urg'd to prove in Men's Condition
Their *Pre-election*, and their *Præterition*,
Or *Predamnation?* for that monſtrous Word,
Of all abſurd Decree the moſt abſurd,
Is into formal Definition wrought
By your Divines——unſtartl'd at the Thought
Of ſov'reign Power decreeing to become
The Author of Salvation but to *ſome;*
To ſome, reſembling others, they admit,
Who are rejected——why? *He ſo thought fit:*
Hath not the Potter Pow'r to make his Clay
Juſt what he pleaſes?——well, and tell me pray,
What Kind of Potter muſt we think a Man,
Who does not make the beſt of it he can?
Who, making *ſome* fine Veſſels of his Clay,
To ſhow his Pow'r, throws all *the reſt* away,
Which, in itſelf, was equally as fine?
What an Idea this of Pow'r divine!
Happy for us, if under God's Commands
We were as Clay is in the Potter's Hands;
Pliant, and yielding readily to take
The proper Form, which he is pleas'd to make!
Happy for us that he has Pow'r! becauſe
An equal *Goodneſs* executes its Laws;
Rejecting none, but ſuch as *will* behave
So, as that no Omnipotence can ſave.

Who can conceive the *infinitely Good*
To ſhow leſs Kindneſs than he really could?

To

To pre-concert Damnation, and confine,
Himfelf, his own Beneficence divine?
An *Impotency* this, in evil Hour,
Afcrib'd to God's beatifying Pow'r,
By bitter Logic, and the four Miftake,
Which overweening Zeal is apt to make;
Defcribing Sov'reignty as incompleat,
That does not fhow itfelf lefs *good* than *great:*
Tho' true in earthly Monarchs it may be,
That *Majefty* and *Love* can fcarce agree,
In his Almighty Will, who rules above,
The Pow'r is *Grace*, the Majefty is *Love:*
What beft defcribes the Giver of all Blifs,
Glorious in all his Attributes, is this;
The fov'reign Lord all Creatures bow before,
But they, who *love* him moft, the moft *adore.*

   From this one Worfhip if a Creature's Heart,
Fixt on aught elfe, determines to depart,
There needs no *pre-determining* the Cafe;
Idolatry enfues, and Fall from Grace;
Without, and *contrary* to God's Intent,
Its own Self-ruin is the fure Event:
The Love forfaken, which alone could blefs,
It needs muft feel Wrath, Anger, and Diftrefs;
The *Senfibilities* that muft arife,
If *Nature* wants what *facred Love* fupplies.

(Calera defant)

The

The POTTER and his CLAY,

An Hymn afcribed to Dr. WATTS.

The HYMN.

I.

BEHOLD the Potter and the Clay,
    He forms his Veffels as he pleafe;
Such is our God, and fuch are we,
The Subjects of his high Decrees.

II.

Does not the Workman's Pow'r extend
O'er all the Mafs——which Part to chufe,
    And mould it for a nobler End,
And which to leave for viler Ufe?

III.

May not the fov'reign Lord on high
Difpenfe his Favours as he will?
    Chufe fome to Life, while others die,
And yet be juft and gracious ftill?

IV.

What if, to make his Terror known,
He lets his Patience long endure,
    Suff'ring vile Rebels to go on,
And feal their own Deftruction fure?

V. What

T H E
C O N T R A S T.

I.

BEHOLD the Potter and the Clay,
  He forms his Veffels to his Mind;
   So did creating *Love* difplay
Itfelf in forming human Kind.

II.

  Th' Almighty Workman's Pow'r, and Skill
Could have no *vile* but *noble* Ends;
   His one immutable *good Will*
To *all*, that he hath made, extends.

III.

  This gracious fov'reign Lord on high,
By his eternal Word and Voice,
   Chofe *all* to live, and *none* to die,
Nor will he *ever* change his Choice.

IV.

  Not by *his* Will, but by their *own*,
Vile Rebels break his righteous Laws;
   And make the Terror to be known,
Of which they are *themfelves* the Caufe.

V. His

V.

What if he means to fhew his Grace,
And his electing Love employs,
  To mark out fome of mortal Race,
And form them fit for heav'nly Joys.

VI.

Shall Man reply againft the Lord?
And call his Maker's Ways unjuft,
  The Thunder of whofe dreadful Word
Can crufh a thoufand Worlds to duft?

VII.

But, O my Soul! if Truth fo bright
Should dazzle and confound thy Sight,
  Yet ftill is written Will obey,
And wait the great decifive Day.

VIII.

Then fhall he make his Juftice known,
And the whole World before his Throne,
  With Joy, or Terror, fhall confefs
The Glory of his Righteoufnefs.

V.

His *all-electing* Love employs
All means the human Race to bless,
   That Mortals may his heav'nly Joys,
By *re-electing* him, possess.

VI.

Shall Man reply that God *decreed*
Fall'n *Adam*'s Race *not* to be blest?
   That for a *few* his Son should bleed,
And *Satan* should have *all the rest?*

VII.

Do thou poor sinful Soul of mine,
By Faith and Penitence, embrace
   Of doubtless, *boundless Love* divine,
The *free*, the *universal* Grace.

VIII.

Let God, within thy pliant Soul,
Renew the Image of his Son,
   The Likeness *marr'd* will then be *whole*,
And show what he, *in Christ*, has done.

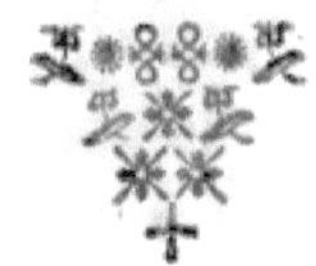

An AR-

An ARGUMENT,

FOR

DAVID's Belief of a Future State,

INFERRED FROM

BATHSHEBA's laſt Words to him, upon his Death-Bed.

IF *David* knew not of a future Life,
  How underſtood he *Bathſheba* his Wife?
Who, when he lay upon his Death-bed, came
To plead for *Solomon's* ſucceeding Claim;
And, having proſper'd in her own Endeavour,
Said——*Let my Lord, King David, live for ever.*

  What real Wiſh was *Bathſheba's* Intent,
If Life hereafter was not what ſhe meant?
Say that——*for ever*——to a King in Health,
Meant a long Life, Proſperity, and Wealth;
To one, that lay a dying, you muſt own,
'Twould be a mere Burleſque upon his Throne.

  If ſhe had pray'd for *David's* mild Releaſe,
Or——Let my Lord, the King, depart in Peace——
(Tho', even then, 'twere difficult to ſtint
Her utmoſt Thought to ſo minute a Hint)

The

The fhort-liv'd Comment might have fome Pretence,
But——*Live for ever*——has no Sort of Senfe,

    Unlefs we grant her Meaning to extend
To *future Life*, that never has an End:
Piety will, and Reafon muft, confefs,
That her Intention could be nothing lefs:
King *Live for ever*——and——*God fave the King*——
Old, or new Phrafe, *Salvation* is the Thing.

    No poor Salvation to be quickly paft,
And with a deadly *Exit* at the laft;
To which, when *David* was fo near, what Share
Could he enjoy of *Live for ever's* Pray'r?
Had he not known what *Bathfheba* defign'd,
A Life to come, of everlafting Kind.

    Tho' num'rous Proofs might, readily, be brought
That this was always holy *David*'s Thought;
Yet fince by learned, and long-winded Ways,
Men feek to break the Force of ancient Phrafe,
I fingle out this plain, familiar one——
Now give as plain an Anfwer thereupon.

O N

FALL of MAN:

OCCASIONED BY THE

Following Reprefentation of that Event.

———" *Neither can it feem ftrange, that God fhould lay*
" *Strefs on fuch outward Actions, in their own Nature nei-*
" *ther good nor evil, when we confider, that in all his Dif-*
" *penfations to Mankind he has done the fame. What was it*
" *he made the Teft of Adam's Obedience in Paradife, but the*
" *eating of a Fruit? An Action in itfelf perfectly indifferent,*
" *and from which, if God had not forbidden it, it would have*
" *been Superftition to have abftained.*" P 28 of a Perfua-
five to Conformity, addreffed to the Quakers by John
Rogers, D. D.

OF Man's Obedience, while in *Eden* bleft,
   What a mere Trifle is here made the Teft!
An outward Action, in itfelf, defin'd
To be of *perfectly indiff'rent* Kind;
Which, but for God's forbidding Threat fevere,
It had been *Superftition* to forbear.

  A ftrange Account; that neither does, nor can,
Make any Part of true Religion's Plan;

But

But muſt expoſe it to the Ridicule
Of Scoffers, judging by this crooked Rule:
Its Friends, defending Truth, as they ſuppoſe,
Lay themſelves open to acuter **Foes**.

To ſay that Action, neither good nor bad,
From which no Harm in Nature could be had,
Was chang'd, by poſitive, commanding Will,
Or Threat forbidding, to a deadly Ill,
Charges, by Conſequence the moſt direct,
On God himſelf that Ill, and **its Effect**.

Language had ſurely come to a poor Paſs,
Before an Author, of diſtinguiſh'd Claſs
For ſhining Talents, could endure to make,
In ſuch a Matter, ſuch a groſs Miſtake;
Cou'd thus derive Death's Origin, and Root,
From *Adam*'s eating of an *harmleſs* Fruit.

From Adam's eating?——Did not God forbid
*The Taſte of it to Adam?——*yes, he did——
And was it harmleſs, muſt we underſtand,
To diſobey **God'**s *poſitive Command?——*
No, by **no Means**; but then the *Harm*, we ſee,
Came not from God's *Command*, but from **the** *Tree*.

If He command, the Action muſt be good;
If He forbid, ſome Ill is underſtood:
The Tree, the Fruit, had dreadful Ills conceal'd,
Not *made* **by** his Forbidding, but *reveal'd;*

S f

That

That our firſt Parents, by a true Belief,
Might know enough to ſhun the fatal Grief.

The dire Experience of a World of Woe,
Forbidding Mercy will'd them not to **know**;
Told them what Ill was in the *falſe Deſire*,
Which their free Wills were tempted to admire;
That, of ſuch Fruit, the Eating was —— *To die* ——
Its *harmleſs* Nature was the *Tempter*'s Lie.

To urge it *now*, and ro impute the Harm
Of Death, and Evil, to the kind Alarm
Of God's Command, ſo juſtly underſtood
To will his Creatures Nothing elſe but Good,
Is, for a *Babel Fiction*, to reſign
Right Reason, Scripture, and the Love divine.

⬦⬦⬦⬦⬦⬦⬦⬦⬦⬦⬦⬦⬦⬦⬦⬦⬦⬦⬦⬦⬦⬦⬦⬦⬦⬦⬦

A LETTER to a FRIEND,

UPON THE

Meaning of St. PAUL's Expreſſion of " *ſpeaking with
Tongues*" 1 Corinth. 14.

IF you remember, Rev'rend Sir, the Talk
That paſt betwixt us in the Garden Walk,
The *Gift* of *Tongues* was mention'd; when I thought
That Notion wrong, which learned Men had taught,
And that this Gift was not at all concern'd
With that of ſpeaking Languages unlearn'd.

St.

St. *Paul*, I faid, in his *Corinthian* Charge,
Had treated on the Subject more at large;
From whofe Account one plainly might deduce
The genuine Gift, its Nature, and its Ufe;
And make appear, from Paffages enoo,
The vulgar Notion not to be the true:
But that to fpeak in Tongues, or fpeak in Tongue,
Was meant of Hymns which the *Corinthians* fung:
This is the Gift which the Apoftle paints,
And lays its Practice under due Reftraints.

You know the Chapter——Firft then let **us fee**
How Tongues do there with Languages agree;
Then how with Hymns; and let which better fuits
Th' Apoftle's Context regulate Difputes.

Firft; **he** *that fpeaketh in a Tongue* (*unknown*,
Tranflators add, for Reafons of their own)
Speaketh to God, and fpeaketh *not to Men*——
Peculiar Tokens of an Hymn——again,
For *no Man underftandeth him*——from hence
'Tis plain, that Languages was not **the Senfe:**
Would he rife up, who had them at Command,
To fpeak in one, that none could underftand?
What can be more unlikely to fuppofe?
Yet thus the learned Commentators glofe;
As their Miftake about the Gift imply'd
The Chriftians guilty of this aukward Pride:
Such Fact they make no Scruple to advance,
As would appear abfurd in a Romance:

S f 2

One

One in his softer, one his harsher Terms,
The same miraculous Disgrace affirms:
All, from the Difficulty, try some Shape,
Whilst there is no escaping, to escape.

Whereas, to Hymns all Phrases correspond;
Of them *Corinthian* Converts were too fond;
And *Paul*, who will'd them really to rejoice,
But more with Heart affected, than with Voice,
Authority, with Reason mix'd, employs,
Not to repress, but regulate their Joys:
The Benefit of Hymns he understood;
But, most intent upon the Church's Good,
The Gift *prophetic* more expedient found,
(That is, to preach the Gospel, or expound)
Than to sing Hymns——*the Prophet speaks, says Paul,
To Men; instructs, exhorts, and comforts all.*

Speaking in Tongue, or Hymning, to proceed,
May edify the Singer's Self indeed;
But *Prophecy the Church;* a private Soul
Should always yield the Pref'rence to the Whole:
Consistent all, if Hymning he explains;
If Languages unknown, what Sense remains?
Would *Paul* affirm, that speaking might do good,
In foreign Languages, not understood,
To a Man's Self? Would he so gently treat
Such a suppos'd enormous Self-conceit?
Would he vouchsafe to pay, the Chapter thro',
Respect to Tongues, if taken in this View?

Would

Would he allow, nay chuse it? —— for that next
Is ſaid of Tongues in the ſucceeding Text.

I will you all to ſpeak with Tongues——to ſing
Makes this a plain, intelligible Thing;
The **other** Meaning, which they ſpread about,
No Commentators have, or can make out:
That **he** ſhould will them all to ſing was juſt,
And properly to uſe the Gift, or Truſt;
For his Intention was not to reduce
Singing itſelf, but its improper **Uſe**:
It was the **good** Apoſtle's great **Concern**,
To preach the **Goſpel** ſo that moſt might learn:
This was the Gift, in which he rather will'd
Such as had been converted to be ſkill'd.
Speaking in Tongue was good; but this, he knew,
Was the more uſeful Talent of the two:
Greater its Owner, but with an *Except*,
That ſhows the Juſtice for an Hymner kept;
The Matter ſung, who, if he could expreſs
To edify the Hearers, was not leſs;
Interpretation render'd them alike;
But does not this abſurd Suppoſal ſtrike,
That in plain Speaking, on ſome **Chriſtian Head**,
One ſhould interpret what himſelf had ſaid?
Firſt uſe a Language to the Church unknown,
Then, in another, for his Fault atone?
What Reaſon, poſſible, can be aſſign'd,
Why the known Tongue ſhould be at firſt declin'd?

This

This Difficulty, and fo all the reft,
The Nature of an Hymn explains the beft.

Now fhould I come amongft you, fays the Saint,
Speaking with Tongues (fhould only come to chant)
What fhall it profit you, except I preach?
Some Revelation, Knowledge, Doctrine teach?
And here the vulgar Meaning of the Word,
For Apoftolic Ufe, is too abfurd;
He fcarce would *if* the fpeaking in a Tongue,
Unknown to Chriftians, whom he came among;
Nor **would** a Queftion find with him a Place,
About their Profit, in fo grofs a Cafe:
He, plainly, hints a Coming, not defign'd
To pleafe their Ear, but to inftruct their Mind:
The real Profit which he pointed at;
And Hymns themfelves were ufelefs without that.

That fuch a Speaking, as is mentioned here,
Was mufical, is evidently clear
From the Allufion, which he then propounds,
To *Pipe*, and *Harp*, and inftrumental Sounds;
Which none can urge, with Reafon, to belong
So properly to Language, as to Song;
Tho' it may ferve for both, in fome refpect,
Yet here one fees to which it muft direct:
If Pipe, or Harp, be indiftinctly heard,
No Tune, or Meaning can be thence infer'd;
If an uncertain Sound the Trumpet yield,
How fhall a Man make ready for the Field?

Thus

Thus of dead Inſtruments; of them that live,
So ye, th' Apoſtle adds, except ye give
Words, by the Tongue, that Men can apprehend,
Ye ſpeak, but, as to Hearers, to no End;
And (what with hymning Poſture ſeems to ſquare)
Will be like Men who ſpeak into the Air.

So ye, to ſhew how Tune and Song agree,
Except ye utter with the Tongue, ſays he,
Words that are eaſy to be underſtood
(Which in a foreign Tongue they never could)
How ſhall the Thing be known to any one
That ye have ſpoken (that is, ſung) *upon?*
And, what with hymning Poſture ſeems to ſquare,
He adds, *for ye ſhall ſpeak into the Air.*

Except ye utter with the Tongue——unknown——
Tranſlators here thought fit to let alone;
Unknown, and eaſy too to underſtand,
That could not be——*unknown* they muſt diſband.
It was enough to ſhew them their Miſtake,
To ſee what Incoherence it would make;
Yet they not minding, juſt as they think fit,
Sometimes inſert it, and ſometimes omit:
But if the Epithet, at firſt, be right,
Why is it kept ſo often out of Sight?
Do not Omiſſions carry, all along,
Tacit Confeſſion of it's being wrong?
Tacit Confeſſion, which is open Proof
How little can be ſaid in its Behoof.

They

They who shall speak in Tongue, and they who hear,
Unless the Meaning of the Voice be clear,
(The Sense not being within mutual Reach,)
Will be, says Paul, *Barbarians each to each,*
Or Foreigners——and therefore, is his Drift,
With all your Fondness for the speaking Gift,
Have the whole Church's Benefit in View;
Let him, who speaks in Tongue, interpret too.

    Can such Concession, such Allowance made,
Suit with that insupportable Parade,
And Show of Gift, which Commentators vent,
Giving a Meaning that could scarce be meant?
While Zeal for Hymns, a natural Effect
In Novices, tho' wanting to be check'd,
Accounts for checking, for allowing Phrase,
For ev'ry Motive that St. Paul displays;
His placid Reas'ning, and his mild Rebuke;
For which no Insolence of Gift could look:
No Insolence, I say, of such a Kind
As Commentators, rashly, have assign'd
To the first Christians; which the latter now,
Suppose it offer'd, never would allow.

    For if I pray in Tongue, St. Paul pursues,
My Spirit prayeth; but *no Fruit accrues*
To them, who do not understand my Pray'rs——
And what the Remedy which he prepares?
Why, it is this——*I will so* (sing or) *pray,*
That all may understand what I shall say:

Plain

Plain the two Phrafes in the Verfe proclaim,
That praying here, and finging is the fame;
That fome Corinthians fo difplay'd their Art,
That none but they themfelves could bear a Part:
Hence to interpret Hymns his Words ordain,
Or elfe to fing intelligibly plain;

Praying, or praifing——for, fays he again,
How fhall unlearned Perfons fay Amen
To thy Thankfgiving, if, when thou fhalt blefs,
They underftand not what thy Words exprefs?
Thou verily haft given Thanks, and well;
But this, unedifi'd, they cannot tell;
The common Benefit is ftill his Aim,
True, real Glory of the Chriftian Name.

In Languages unknown, was Pray'r and Praife
Perform'd by Chriftians, in th' Apoftles Days?
Was that a Time, or was the Church a Place,
For gifted Oftentation to difgrace?

(*Cætera defunt.*)

T t

Familiar Epistles to a Friend,

Upon a SERMON entitled,

The Office and Operations of the Holy Spirit.

By the Rev. Mr. WARBURTON.

LETTER I.

A Strange Difcourfe, in all impartial Views,
   This that you lent me, Doctor, to perufe:
Had you not afk'd——a Subject of this Sort
Might, of itfelf, a few Remarks extort,
To fhow how much a very learned Man
Has been miftaken in his preaching Plan.

Preaching (a Talent of the Gofpel Kind,
By——*preaching Peace through* JESUS CHRIST——defin'd)
Should, one would think, in order to encreafe
The Gofpel Good, confine itfelf to Peace;
Exert it's milder Influence, and draw
The lift'ning Crowds to Love's uniting Law:
For fhould the greateft Orator extend
The Pow'rs of Sound to any other End;
Regard to healing Sentiments poftpone,
And battle all that differ from his own;
'Tho' he could boaft of Conqueft, yet how far
From *Peace*, through *Jefus*, through *himfelf* is *War!*

How

How widely wanders, from the true Defign
Of preaching *Chrift*, the bellicofe Divine!

If amongft them, who all profefs Belief
In the fame Gofpel, fuch a warlike Chief
Should, in the Pulpit, labour to erect
His glaring Trophies, over ev'ry Sect
That does not juft fall in with his Conceit,
And raife new Flourifh upon each Defeat;
As if, by dint of his haranguing Strain,
So many Foes had happily been flain;
Tho' it were fure that what he faid was right,
Is he more likely, think you, to invite,
To win th' erroneous over to his Mind,
By Eloquence of fuch an hoftile Kind,
Or to difgrace, by Arts fo ftrongly weak,
The very Truths that he may chance to fpeak?

Like Thoughts to thefe would, naturally, rife
Out of your own occafional Surprize,
When, purchafing the Book, you dipt into't,
And faw the Preacher's Manner of Difpute;
How Man by Man, and Sect by Sect difplay'd,
He pafs'd along from Preaching to Parade;
Confuting all that came within his Way,
Tho' too far off to hear what he fhould fay:
Reafon, methinks, why Candour would not chufe,
Where no Defence could follow, to accufe;
Where gen'rous Triumph no Attacks can yield
To the unqueftion'd Mafter of the Field:

T t 2

Where

Where Names, tho' injur'd without Reason why,
Abfent, or prefent, can make no Reply
To the moft falfe, or difingenuous Hint,
Till Time, perchance, produces it in Print:
When, we may take for granted, it is clad
In it's beft Fafhion, tho' it be but bad.

This one Difcourfe is printed, we are told,
The Main of fev'ral Sermons to unfold:
For one grand Subject all of them were meant——
The *Holy Spirit*, whom the Father fent;
Th' indwelling Comforter, th' inftructing Guide;
Who was, *Chrift* faid, for ever to abide
With, and *in* his Difciples here below,
And teach them all that they fhould want to know.

A glorious Theme! a comfortable one!
For Preachers to exert themfelves upon;
Firft taught themfelves, and fitted to impart
God's Truth, and Comfort, to an honeft Heart:
Some fuch, at leaft, imagine to have been
Amongft the Flock that came to *Lincoln*'s *Inn*;
With a fincere Defire to hear, and learn
That, which became a *Chriftian*'s chief Concern:
Pleas'd with the Preacher's Text, with Hopes that he
Might prove an Inftrument, in fome Degree,
Of their Perception of an holy Aid,
Fruit of that Promife which the Saviour made:
Might help them, more and more, to underftand
How near true Help and Comfort is at Hand;

How

How foon the Spirit moves upon the Mind,
When it is rightly humbled and refign'd:
With what a Love to ev'ry Fellow-foul
One Member of the Church regards the Whole;
Looks upon all Mankind as Friends, or fhares
To heartieft Enemies his heartier Pray'rs.

I might go on; but you, I know, will grant,
Such is the Temper that we really want:
And fuch, if Preachers ever preach indeed,
If Paftors of a Flock will really feed,
They will endeavour folely **to excite,**
And **move divided** *Chriftians* **to unite;**
If not in outward Forms, that but fupply
A loftier *Babel* without inward Tye,
Yet in a common Friendlinefs of Will,
That wifhes well to ev'ry Creature ftill;
That makes the Centre **of** Religion's Plan
A god-like Love embracing ev'ry Man.

LETTER II.

NO Office feems more facred, and auguft,
   Than **that of** Preachers who *fulfill* their *Truft*;
Working **with God,** and helping Men **to** find
The Prince of Life, the Saviour **of** Mankind:
Who came himfelf a Preacher, from on high,
Of Peace to all; the diftant, and the nigh.

So

So said the Saint; whose preaching was the same,
To *Jew*, to *Greek*——Salvation thro' his Name——
Who taught, thro' him, to preach immortal Life,
Avoiding Questions that engender Strife;
Patient, and meek, and gentle unto all,
Instructing ev'n Opposers without Gall;
If peradventure God might give them Grace
The Truth, when kindly offer'd, to embrace,

If these Conditions Preaching may demand,
What must we think of the Discourse in Hand?
Which, when we read, is apter to suggest
A diff'rent Temper in the Preacher's Breast;
A Text perverted from its native Scope;
A Disappointment of all *hearing* Hope.
Here is a long Dispute, in his first Head,
About what *Doctor Middleton* had said;
That " when the Gift of Tongues was first bestow'd,
" 'Twas but an instantaneous Sign, that show'd
" The Gospel's chosen Minister; and then,
" That Purpose signifi'd, it ceas'd again:
" So was its Type, the fiery Tongue, a Flash
" Of Light'ning quickly vanish'd"——and such Trash——
To which a Minister, who knew the Press,
Ill chose the Time, when preaching, to digress;
To take a Text affording, thro' the Whole,
Such grounds of Comfort to a christian Soul,
And then neglect; to preach a poor Debate,
That could but shine at pamphleteering Rate;

That

'That, from the Pulpit, muft difguft the Pew
Of fager Bench, and fober Students too.

   You may, hereafter, if you chufe it, fee
How they miftook, both *Middleton* and *he*,
'The Gift of Tongues; how little, quite throughout,
'They knew, tho' learned, what they were about:
In prefent Lines, I fhall but juft relate
One Inftance of the, no uncommon, Fate
Of learned Men, who, in deep Points exact,
Forget, fometimes, the moft apparent Fact.

   Th' Apoftles, gifted by the Holy Ghoft,
Began to fpeak with Tongues, at Pentecoft;
" But did not——fo the Preacher fays——begin
To fpeak, before the Multitude came in."
He urges roundly how, in this Refpect,
" The learned *Middleton* did not reflect,
" That in a private Room they all were fet,
" And Tongues not fpoken, till the People met.

   Now if you read the Pentecoftal Facts,
As you will find them written in the *Acts*,
From *his* Reflection tho' the Point lay hid,
The Text affirms, exprefsly, that they *did*.
No Learning wanted to determine this;
'Tis what a reading Child could never mifs:
This very Gift, it is exceeding clear,
Was that which brought the Multitude to hear:
Speaking with Tongues foregoing Words proclaim;
The next——*when this was nois'd abroad*——they came.

Scarce

Scarce to be thought that, studying the Case,
With formal Purpose to explain a Place,
A Man so learned, and acute, could make,
Could preach, could publish, such a flat Mistake:
But 'tis the Fate of great, and eager Wits,
To trust their Memory too much, by Fits.

To prove that *Middleton*'s Dispute was wrong
Takes up the Pages, for a Sermon long :
Soon after this you'll see another start,
To fill his first Division's second Part:
For having touch'd upon the Names of all
The Gifts enumerated by Saint *Paul*,
Then, in what Sense the Scripture was inspir'd,
Higher, or lower, comes to be enquir'd:
The high he calls *organical;* the low
Partial; and *true;* as he proceeds to show.

This is the Summary of what is said,
Touching the Holy Ghost, in his first Head;
As *Guide to Truth,* and aiding to excite,
To clear, to give the *Understanding* Light.
What makes it *Sermon* is the *Text* prefixt,
Tho' scarce a Word of it is intermixt;
Consistently enough, for it has none
Which suit the Topics that he dwells upon:
Topics, without a Dignity to grace
Text, Office, Audience, Person, Time, or Place.

But, were this all, and did not what he spake
Lead, by Degrees, to serious Mistake,

Taking

Taking a Text, for Form Sake, to prepare
The Church to hear some *Shop-renown'd* Affair,
(Too oft the Turn of the polite Divine)
Would hardly merit your Regard, or mine;
But, Sir, it is not only misappli'd,
This glorious Text, but in effect deni'd;
Or misconceiv'd; and therefore cutting short,
At present, Errors of less fatal Sort,
Let us pursue this Subject, in the next,
And from the *Sermon* vindicate the *Text*.

<hr>

LETTER III.

YOU wonder'd much, why any Man of Parts
  Would use, in Preaching, low, invective Arts;
By which the vain Disputings, that infest
The christian World, have seldom been suppress;
But often heighten'd, and that use destroy'd,
For which fine Talents ought to be employ'd.

If one can judge from reading this *Divine*,
Whose Parts, and Talents, would be really fine,
If juster Notions of the *heav'nly* Grace
Taught but the *earthly* not to quit their Place,
If one can judge, I say, from stated Laws,
In his Discourses, what should be the Cause
Of such Perversion of a lively Wit,
In erudite Possessors, this is it.

U u

They

They think that, *now*, Religion's sole Defence
Is Learning, History, and critic Sense;
That with Apostles, as a needful Guide,
The *Holy Spirit* did indeed abide;
But, having dictated to them a Rule
Of Faith, and Manners, for the *Christian* School,
Immediate Revelation ceas'd, and Men
Must now be taught by apostolic Pen:
Canon of Scripture is compleat; and they
May read, and know, what Doctrine to obey:
To look for *Inspiration* is absurd;
The Spirit's Aid is in the *written Word:*
They who pretend to his immediate Call,
From Pope to Quaker, are *Fanatics* all.

Thus, having prov'd, at large, to Christians met,
What no one Christian ever *doubted* yet,
That the New Testament was really writ
By Inspiration, which they all *admit,*
He then subjoins that——" this inspir'd Record
" Fulfill'd the Promise of our blessed Lord;"
(Fulfill'd it " *eminently,*" is the Phrase)
" For tho' the Faithful, in succeeding Days,
" Occasionally find, in ev'ry Place,
" The Spirit's *ordinary* Help, and Grace,
" His Light supreme, his constant, fixt Abode,
" Is in the Scriptures of this sacred Code.

This was the Sense, not easy to explore,
When, reck'ning up the Spirit's Fruits before,
                              " Scripture,"

" Scripture," faid he (which this Account explains)
" Does not *record* them only, but *contains;*
" CONTAINS," in Capitals——as if he took
The Scripture to be fomething *more* than *Book;*
Something *alive*, wherein the Spirit dwelt,
That did not only *tell* his Fruits, but *felt.*
" **The fure** Depofit of the Spirit's Fruits
" **In** holy Scripture," (he elfewhere computes)
" Fulfill'd the Saviour's Promife, in a Senfe
" Very fublime"——So it fhould feem, from **hence,**
That *eminently*, and *fublimely*, thus
The Holy Spirit fhould abide *with Us.*

If I miftake him, or mif-reprefent,
You'll fhew me where, for 'tis not with Intent:
I want, if poffible, to underftand
A Sentence coming from fo fam'd a Hand:
Tho' plain the Words, 'tis difficult **to** folve
What chriftian Senfe he meant them to involve:
In ev'ry Way that Words, and Senfe agree,
'Tis perfect *Bibliolatry* **to** me:
No *Image Worfhip* can be more abfurd,
Than idolizing thus the written Word;
Which, they who wrote intended to excite
Attention to our Lord's predicted Light;
To that fame Spirit, leading human Thought,
By which themfelves, and all the good were taught;
Preaching that Word, which a diviner Art,
Which God himfelf had *written* on the *Heart.*

How

How can the beſt of Books (for 'tis confeſſ
That, of all Books, the Bible is the beſt)
Do any more than give us an Account
Of what was ſaid, for Inſtance, on the Mount?
Of what was done, for Inſtance, on the Croſs,
In order to retrieve the human Loſs?
What more than tell us of the Spirit's Aid,
Far as his Fruits by Words can be diſplay'd?
But Words are only the *recording* Part,
The *Things* contain'd muſt needs be in the *Heart;*
Spirit of God no more in *Books* demands
To dwell, Himſelf, than *Temples made with Hands.*

Fruits of the Spirit, **as** St. *Paul* defin'd,
Are Love, Joy, Peace——the Bleſſings of the *Mind;*
The *Proofs* of *his abiding*——who can brook
A meek, a gentle, good, long-ſuff'ring Book?
Or let true Faith, and Temperance, be ſunk
To Faith in Writings, that are never drunk?
In fine, whatever Pen, and Ink, preſents,
Can but contain *hiſtorical* Contents;
Nor can the Fruits of Spirit be in *Print,*
In any Senſe, but as *recorded* in't.

Plain as this is, and ſtrange, as you may think,
The learned Worſhip paid to Pen and Ink,
It is the main Hypotheſis, you'll find,
On which are built Diſcourſes of this Kind;

Which

Which yet can give us, for a Scripture Clue,
What contradicts its very Letter too:
As this has done——be shown as we go on——
By these important Verses of St. *John*.

L E T T E R   IV.

THE Gospel's simpler Language being writ,
   Not for the Sake of Learning, or of Wit,
But to instruct the pious, and the meek;
When its Intent mere Critics come to seek,
We find, on plain intelligible Text,
The *variorum* Comments most perplext.

   Such is the Text before us; and so plain
The Saviour's Promise, which the Words contain,
That Men, for modern Erudition's Sake,
Must read, and *study* to *acquire* Mistake;
Must first observe the Notions that prevail,
Amongst the famous in their Church's Pale;
Firm in the Prejudice, that all is right
Which Books, or Persons, most in Vogue, recite;
Then seek, to find, how Scripture coincides
With each Decision of their knowing Guides.

   Without some such Preparatives as these,
How could the forc'd Interpretation please,

That

That makes a sacred Promise, to bestow
Perpetual Aid, exhausted long ago?
In one short Age?——for God's abiding Guide
Withdrew, it seems, when the Apostles di'd;
And left poor Millions, ever since, to seek
How dissonant Divines had constru'd Greek.

   In graver Writers one has often read
What in Excuse of Bookworship is said;
" It is not *Ink*, and *Letter*, that we own
" To be divine, but *Scripture Sense* alone;
" We have the *Rule* which the Apostles made,
" And no Occasion for *immediate* Aid."——
Suppose, for once, the gross Delusion true;
What must a plain, and honest Christian do?
The Spirit's Aid how far must he extend,
To bring his Saviour's Promise to an End?
This he perceives Discourse to dwell upon;
And yet——*for ever to abide*——has none.
He, for the Sake of Safety, would be glad
To have that Spirit which Apostles had;
Not one of them has writ, but says, *he may:*
That 'tis the Bliss for which he ought to pray:
That God will grant it him, his Saviour said,
Sooner than Parents give their Children Bread.
If *reading* Scripture can improve a Soul,
This is the Sum, and Substance of the whole;
And gives it Value of such high Degree:
For tho' as sacred as a *Book* can be,

'Tis

'Tis only fo, becaufe it beft revives
Thought of that Good which animated *Lives;*
Becaufe its Authors were infpir'd to write,
And faw **the** Truth in 'it's own heav'nly Light;
Becaufe it fends us **to** that *promis'd* Source
Of Light, and Truth, which govern'd their Difcourfe,
The *Holy Spirit's* ever prefent Aid,
With us, and *in us*——fo the Saviour pray'd——
That, when he left the World, the *Holy Ghoft*
Might dwell with Chriftians, as an *inward Hoft;*
That Teaching, Truth, and Comfort in the Breaft,
Might be fecur'd **by** this abiding **Gueft.**

" *Yes; with Apoftles*"——funk, by fuch a Thought,
Th' ineftimable Treafure down to Nought;
An Hiftory of Sunfhine may, as foon,
Make a blind Man to fee the fhining Noon,
As Writings *only,* without inward Light,
Can bring the World's Redemption into Sight:
Jefus——the *Chrift*——the very **Book has fhown,**
Without the Holy Spirit none **can** own:
In *Words* they may, but, what is plainly meant,
They cannot give a real, *Heart Confent.*
What Friend to Scripture, then Sir, can difplace
This inward Witnefs of redeeming Grace?
And reft the *Gofpel* on fuch outward View,
As any *Turk* may reft his *Coran* too?
Nay, he can own a written Word, or Work
That *Chriftians* **do, and yet** continue *Turk.*

Why

Why do the Chriſtian Diſputants ſo fill
The World with Books, of a polemic Skill,
When 'tis the ſacred, and acknowledg'd *one*
That all their jarring Syſtems build upon?
But that the *Spirit* does not rule their Wit,
By which at firſt the *ſacred one* was writ:
Of whoſe Support great Scholars ſtand in need,
As much as they who never learnt to read:
Unhappy they! but for that living Guide,
Whom God himſelf has promis'd to provide!
A Guide, to quote the bleſſed Text again,
For ever to abide with Chriſtian Men.

Fond of its Books, poor Learning is afraid;
And higher Guidance labours to evade:
Books have the Spirit in *ſupreme* Diſplay!
Men but in lower, *ordinary* Way!
This ſtrange Account of Men and Books is true,
It ſeems, *according to the Promiſe* too!

Such wild Conceits all Men have too much Wit
Or learned, or unlearned, to admit;
But when ſome *Intereſt*, or *Cuſtom* rules,
And chains obſequious Wills to diff'rent Schools,
The wiſeſt, then Sir, will relinquiſh Thought,
And ſpeak, like Parrots, *juſt* as they are *taught*.
What this ſhould be, what ſpends in vain the Fire
Of briſker Tempers——let us next enquire.

LETTER

LETTER V.

WHEN Chriſtians firſt receiv'd the joyful News——
    Meſſiah come——unmixt with worldly Views;
When the whole Church with heav'nly Grace was bleſt,
And (from the Spirit Comforter) poſſeſt
One Heart, one Mind, one View to common Good;
Then was the real Goſpel underſtood.

   Then was the Time——to cite what you will find
The Preacher noting——" when the World combin'd
" Its Pow'rs againſt it, but could *not* deſtroy;
" When holy Martyrs, with enraptur'd Joy,
" Encounter'd Death; enabled to ſuſtain
" Its utmoſt Terror, and its utmoſt Pain:
" At ſuch a Juncture, Heav'n's uncommon Aid
" Shon forth, to help Humanity diſplay'd.

   " But now"——his Reaſon for abated Grace,
Diff'rence of primitive and preſent Caſe——
" Now——Eaſe, and Honour" (mind the Maxim Friend)
" On the Profeſſion of the Faith attend:
" At firſt, eſtabliſh'd by diviner Means,
" On human Teſtimony, now, it leans;
" Supports itſelf, as other Facts muſt do,
" That reſt on human Teſtimony too;
" Sufficient Strength is the Conviction there,
" To make the preſent Chriſtian perſevere.

X x

Here

Here lies the Secret——that may foon unfold
Why modern Chriftians fall fo fhort of old;
Why they appear to have fuch diff'rent Looks,
The Men of *Spirit*, and the Men of *Books:*
When Racks and Gibbets, Torment and Diftrefs
Attended them who ventur'd to confefs,
They had, indeed, a fixt, and firm Belief,
To die **for one** who fuffer'd like a Thief;
Stretch'd on the Wheel, or-burning in the Flame,
To preach a crucifi'd Redeemer's Name;
Courage like this compendious Proof fuppli'd
Of Heav'ns true Kingdom, into which they di'd:
Thus was the Wifdom of the World ftruck dumb,
And all the Pow'rs of Darknefs overcome;
Gofpel prevail'd, by its internal Light,
And gave the Subject for the Pen to write.

    But when the World, with a more fatal Plan,
To flatter, what it could not force, began;
When *Eafe,* and ***Honour,* as the** Preacher faith,
Attended the Profeffion of the Faith;
Then wrought its Mifchief, in the too fecure,
The fecret Poifon, flower, but more fure:
Commodious Maxims then began to fpread,
And fet up Learning in the Spirit's Stead:
The Life diminifh'd, as the Books encreas'd,
'Till Men **found out** that Miracles were ceas'd;
That, with refpect to **Succours** more fublime,
The Gofpel Promife **was but for a** Time;

That

That Inſpiration, amongſt Men of Senſe,
Was all a mere fanatical Pretence:
And diverſe like Diſcoveries, that grant
To *Eaſe*, and *Honour*, juſt what Faith they want.

'Faith to profeſs that wond'rous Things of old
Did really happen, as the Books have told;
But, with a Caution, never to allow
The Poſſibility of happ'ning now:
For, as the World went on, it might affect
An honourable Eaſe, in ſome reſpect,
To own celeſtial Comfort ſtill inſpir'd,
And ſuff'ring Courage, as at firſt, requir'd;
Quite proper then; but equally unfit,
When once the ſacred Canon had been writ:
For upon that (is gravely here aver'd)
Part of the *Spirit's* Office was transferr'd;
Books once compos'd, th' illuminating Part
He ceas'd himſelf; and left to human Art
To find, within his *ſcriptural* Abode,
Th' enlight'ning Grace that Preſence once beſtow'd.

Theſe Suppoſitions, if a Man ſuppoſe,
You ſee th' immediate Conſequence that flows;
That Men, and Churches afterwards attack'd,
Are pre-demoliſh'd, by aſſerted Fact;
Which, once advanc'd, may, with the greateſt Eaſe,
Condemn whatever Chriſtians he ſhall pleaſe:
Owing to his Forbearance, in ſome Shape,
If aught th' extenſive Havock ſhall eſcape.

X x 2

With

With fuch a Fund of Learning, and a Skill
To make it ferve what Argument he will;
With choice of Words, for any chofen Theme,
With an Alertnefs rulingly fupreme ;
What, **Sir**, can fingle Perfons, or a Sect,
When he is pleas'd to preach at 'em, expect?

    Juft **what they meet with, in the** prefent Cafe ——
All the dogmatic **Cenfure,** and Difgrace,
That a commanding Genius can **exert,**
When it becomes religioufly alert ;
With narrow Proofs, and Confequences wide,
Sets all Opponents of its Rote afide ;
The PAPISTS firft, and then th' inferior Fry
FANATICS; vanquifh'd with a ——*who but I?*
Thefe are the modifh **Epithets** that ftrike
At true Religion, **and at** falfe alike ;
Of thefe Reproaches Infidels are full ;
Their **Ufe** in others verging down to dull :
How one, who is no Infidel, applies
The hackney'd Terms——may next falute your Eyes.

L E T T E R VI.

BY Reformation from the *Church* of *Rome*
   We mean, from Faults and Errors, I prefume ;
Againft her Truths to profecute a War
Is proteftant Averfion pufh'd too **far :**

I_N

In them, should *Ease*, and *Honour not* attend
The fair Profession, one should be her Friend.

She thinks that *Christ* has given to his Bride,
His holy Church, an ever present Guide;
By whose divine Affistance she has thought,
That Miracles sometimes were really wrought;
That, by the Virtue which his Gifts infpire,
Great Saints and Martyrs have adorn'd her Quire.
Now say the worft, that ever can be faid,
Of that Corruption which might overfpread
This Church in gen'ral——caft at her the Stone,
They who poffefs Perfection in their own;
Yet, were inftructive Volumes to enlarge
On bright Exceptions to the gen'ral Charge,
They that love Truth, wherever it is found,
Would joy to fee it, ev'n in *romish* Ground;
Where, if Corruption grew to fuch a Size,
The more illuftrious muft Examples rife
Of Life, and Manners——thefe, you will agree,
Are true Reformers, wherefoe'er they be.

Of all the Churches, juftly loth to claim
Exclufive Title to a facred Name,
What one, I afk, has ever yet deni'd
The Infpiration of the promis'd Guide?
Our own——to which the Deff'rence that is due
Forbids no juft Refpect for others too——
Believes, afferts, that what Reform fhe made
Was not without the *Holy Spirit's* Aid:

If

If to expect his Gifs, however great,
Be popish, and fanatical. Deceit,
She, in her Offices of ev'ry Kind,
Has also been fanatically blind.
What Form, of her compofing, can we trace
Without a Pray'r for his unftinted Grace?
Taught, by the facred Volumes, to infer
A Saviour's Promife reaching down to **her,**
Greatly fhe values **the recording** Books;
But, **for fulfilling, in herfelf fhe looks.**

    That fhe may always think aright, and act,
By God's good Spirit, is her pray'd for Fact;
Without his Grace confeffing, as fhe ought,
Her Inability of Act, or Thought:
Nor does fhe fear fanatical Pretence,
When afking Aid in a fublimer Senfe;
Where fhe records, amongft the martyr'd Hoft,
A Stephen — filled with the Holy Ghoft ——
She prays for that fame Plenitude of **Aid,**
By which the Martyr for his Murd'rers pray'd;
That fhe, like him, in what fhe undergoes,
May love, and blefs her perfecuting Foes.

    Did **but one Spark of** fo fupreme a Grace
Burn in the Breaft, when Preaching is the Cafe,
How would a Prieft, unperfecuted, dare
To treat, when mounted on **a facred Chair,**
A Church of *Chrift*, or any fingle Soul,
By Will enlifted on the *Chriftian* Roll,

With

With such a prompt, and contumelious Ire,
As Love, nor Blessing ever could inspire?

Altho' untouch'd with the celestial Flame,
How could an *English* Priest mistake his Aim?
So far forget the Maxims that appear,
Throughout his Church's Liturgy, so clear?
Wherein the Spirit's ever constant Aid,
Without a feign'd Distinction, is display'd;
Without a rash attempting to explain,
By Limitations foolish and profane,
When, and to Whom, to what Degree, and End,
God's Graces, Gifts, and Pow'rs were to extend;
So far withdrawn —— that Christians must allow
Of nothing *extra-ordinary*, now :
The vain Distinction, which the World has found,
To fix an unintelligible Bound
To Gospel Promise; equally sublime,
Nor limited by any other Time
Than that, when Want of Faith, when earthly Will,
Shall hinder Heav'ns Intentions to fulfill.

If, not confining any promis'd Pow'rs,
The *Romish* Church be faulty, what is ours?
Does our own Church, in her ordaining Day,
Does any consecrating Bishop say,
When on the future Priest his Hand is laid,
Receive the Spirit's *ordinary Aid?*
Do awful Words——*Receive the Holy Ghost* ——
Imply that He abides in *Books* the most?

Books——

Books——which the Spirit who firſt rul'd the Hand,
They ſay themſelves, muſt teach to underſtand.

   His Inſpiration, without Limits too,
All Churches own, whatever Preachers **do**:
Not even Miracles, tho' ſet aſide
In private Books, has any Church deni'd:
How weak the Proofs, which this Diſcourſe has brought,
To juſtify the faſhionable Thought,
That Goſpel Promiſes, of any Kind,
By Spirit, **or** by Scripture, are **confin'd**
To apoſtolic, or to later Times,
May be the Subject of ſucceeding Rhimes.

Miscellaneous Pieces.

CONSISTING OF

Thoughts on various Subjects, Fragments, Epigrams, &c.

WITH peaceful Mind thy Race of Duty run;
    God Nothing does, or suffers to be done,
But what thou wouldst Thyself, if thou couldst see
Through all Events of Things, as well as He.

NATURAL Knowledge is a Moonshine Light,
    And dreaming Sages still keep sleeping by't;
But heav'nly Wisdom, like the rising Sun,
Awakens Nature, and good Works are done.

LET thy Repentance be without Delay——
    If thou defer it to another Day,
Thou must repent for a Day more of Sin,
While a Day less remains to do it in.

TO be religious something it will cost;
    Some Riches, Honours, Pleasures will be lost;
But if thou countest the Sum total o'er,
Not to be so will cost a great deal more.

HE,

HE, that does Good with an unwilling Mind,
    Does **that to** which he is not well inclin'd:
'Twill be Reward sufficient for the Fact,
If God shall pardon his obedient Act.

IF outward Comforts, without real Thought
    Of any inward Holiness, are sought,
God disappoints us oft, and *kindly* too ——
To make us holy is his constant **View.**

THINK, and be *careful* what thou art within;
    For there is Sin in the Desire of Sin:
Think, and be *thankful*, in a diff''rent Case;
For there is Grace in the Desire of Grace.

PRAY'R does not ask, **or want** the Skill and Art
    Of forming Words, but a devoted Heart:
If thou art really in a Mind to pray,
God knows thy Heart, and all that it would say.

CONTENT is better, **all** the Wise will grant,
    Than any earthly Good that thou canst want;
And Discontent, with which the Foolish fill
Their Minds, is worse than any earthly Ill.

TWO

TWO Heav'ns a right contented Man furround,
  One here, and one hereafter to be found:
One, in his *own* meek Bofom, here on Earth,
And one, in *Abraham's*, at his future Birth.

NO Faith towards God can e'er fubfift with Wrath
  Tow'rds Man, nor Charity with want of Faith;
From the fame Root hath each of them it's Growth;
You have not either, if you have not both.

FAITH is the burning Ardor of Defire;
  Hope is the Light arifing from it's Fire;
Love is the Spirit that, proceeding thence,
Compleats all Virtue in a Chriftian Senfe.

NOR Steel, nor Flint alone produces Fire;
  No Spark arifes till they both confpire:
Nor Faith alone, nor Work without is right;
Salvation rifes, when they both unite.

ZEAL without Meeknefs, like a Ship at Sea,
  To rifing Storms may foon become a Prey;
And Meeknefs without Zeal is like the fame,
When a dead Calm ftops every failing Aim.

IF

IF Gold be offer'd Thee, Thou doſt not ſay,
  To-morrow I will take it, not To-day:
Salvation offer'd, why art Thou ſo cool,
To let Thyſelf become To-morrow's Fool?

AN heated Fancy, or Imagination,
  May **be** miſtaken for an Inſpiration——
True; but is this Concluſion fair to make,
That Inſpiration muſt be all Miſtake?
A Pebble Stone is not a **Diamond**——true;
But muſt a Diamond be a Pebble too?

HYPOCRITES in Religion form a Plan
  That makes them hateful both to God and Man;
By ſeeming **Zeal they loſe** the World's Eſteem,
And God's, becauſe they are **not** what they ſeem.

AN *humble* Man, tho' all the **World** aſſault
  To pull him down, yet God will ſtill exalt;
Nor can a *proud*, by all the World's Renown,
Be lifted **up**, for God will pull him down.

HE is no Fool, who charitably gives
  What he can only look at whilſt he lives;
Sure as he is to find, when hence he goes,
A Recompence which he can never loſe.

IF

IF giving to **poor** People be to lend
  Thy Money to the Lord, who is their Friend,
The higheſt Int'reſt upon Int'reſt ſure
Is **to let out** thy Money to the Poor.

WHEN Grief **or Joy** ſhall preſs upon thee hard,
  Be then eſpecially upon thy Guard;
Then is moſt Danger of not acting right:
A calmer State will give a ſurer Light.

IF we mind nothing but **the** Body's Pride,
  We loſe the Body and the Soul beſide;
If we have nothing **but** the Earth in View, .
We loſe the Earth, and heav'nly Riches too.

HE is a Sinner, you are pleas'd to ſay,
  Then love him for the Sake of Chriſt, I pray,
If on his gracious Words you place your Truſt,
——" I came to call the Sinners, not the Juſt"——
Second his Call; which if you will not do,
You'll be the greater Sinner of the two.

PRAY'R **and** Thankſgiving is the vital Breath,
  That keeps the Spirit of a Man from Death;
For Pray'r attracts into the living Soul
The Life, that fills the univerſal Whole;

And

And giving Thanks is breathing forth again
The Praise of him, who is the Life of Men.

TO own a God, who does not speak to Men,
   Is first to own and then disown again;
Of all Idolatry the total Sum
Is having Gods that are both deaf and dumb.

LOVE does the Good which God commands to do;
   Fear shuns the Ill which he prohibits too:
They both describe, tho' by a diff'rent Name,
A Disposition of the Mind the same.

WHAT is more tender than a Mother's Love
   To the sweet Infant fondling in her Arms?
What Arguments need her Compassion move
To hear it's Cries, and help it in it's Harms?
Now, if the tend'rest Mother were possest
Of all the Love, within her single Breast,
Of all the Mothers, since the World began,
'Tis nothing to the Love of God to Man.

WHY should I be so eager to espy
   The Mote that swims upon my Brother's Eye?
And still forget, as if I had not known,
The dark'ning Beam that overspreads my own?

O! let

O! let me play the Hypocrite no more!
But ftrive to cure my own obftructed Sight!
Then fhall I fee, much clearer than before,
To fet my undifcerning Brother right.

On the Epicurean, Stoic, and Chris-tian Philosophy.

THREE diff'rent Schemes Philofophers affign;
   A Chance, a Fate, a Providence divine:
Which to embrace of thefe three fev'ral Views,
Methinks, it is not difficult to chufe.

   For firft; what Wifdom, or what Senfe, to cry
Things happen as they do——we know not why?
Or how are we advanc'd one Jot, to know,
When Things once are——that they muft needs be fo?

   To fee fuch Order, and yet own no Laws;
Feel fuch Effects, and yet confefs no Caufe;
What can be more extravagant and odd?
He only reafons, who believes a God.

Atheism the only Ground of Discontent.

IF Reafon does each private Perfon bind,
   To feek the public Welfare of Mankind;
If this be Juftice, and the facred Law,
That guards the Good, and keeps the Bad in Awe;

If

If this great Law but op'rates, to fulfill
One vaſt Almighty Being's righteous Will;
And if he only, as we all maintain,
Does all Things rule, and all Events ordain;
Then Reaſon binds each private Man t'aſſent,
That none but Atheiſts can be diſcontent.

GOD the only true TEACHER.

THE Lord is my Light; by his Teaching **I learn,**
   With a right Underſtanding his Works to **diſcern:**
While I dwell in his Preſence 'tis then that I live,
And enjoy **a Content** which he only **can** give:
In all other Things **I have** labour'd to find
That Truth which might fill an intelligent Mind;
But I labour'd in vain, for it is He alone
That can give me Inſtruction, and make himſelf known.

An EPIGRAM, on the Bleſſedneſs of DIVINE LOVE.

FAITH, **Hope,** and Love, were queſtion'd what **they**
     thought
Of future Glory, which Religion taught:
Now Faith *believ'd* it, firmly, to be true;
And Hope *expected* ſo to find it too;
Love anſwer'd, ſmiling with a conſcious Glow,
Believe? Expect? I *know* it to be ſo.

A Contraſt

A Contrast between two eminent Divines.

TWO diff'rent Painters, Artifts in **their Way,**
   Have drawn Religion in her full Difplay;
To both fhe fat——One gaz'd at her all o'er;
The other fix'd upon her Features more:
Hervey has figur'd her with ev'ry Grace
That Drefs could give —— but *Law* has hit her Face.

On Preaching—An Epigram.

THE fpecious Sermons of a learned Man
   Are little elfe **but** *Flafhes in the Pan;*
The mere Haranguing upon (what they call)
Morality is *Powder* without *Ball;*
But He, who preaches with a Chriftian Grace,
Fires at our Vices, and the *Shot* takes Place.

F I N I S.

www.ingramcontent.com/pod-product-compliance
Lightning Source LLC
Chambersburg PA
CBHW051117120726
47905CB00005B/1315